The Inventor's Clone

by

Blythe Ayne

The Inventor's Clone

by

Blythe Ayne

The Inventor's Clone
Blythe Ayne

Emerson & Tilman, Publishers
129 Pendleton Way #55
Washougal, WA 98671

Book and cover design by Blythe Ayne
Interior graphics – original drawings © Blythe Ayne
or pastiches of public domain images

The Inventor's Clone

www.BlytheAyne.com

Paperback ISBN: 978-1-947151-19-2

[1. FICTION/Magical Realism
2. FICTION/Science Fiction/Steampunk
3. FICTION/Fantasy/Urban] I. Title.
BIC: FM

First Edition

DEDICATION

To all Those Who Believe

Love is All We Need

Chapter 1

The more everyone conspired to keep Heart from viewing the carnage and destruction of Pink during the Bot Invasion, the more intent she became to witness it. She knew they were trying to minimize her pain in losing Xavier.

But nothing could.

She finally managed to steal away from everyone—Jackson, her father and HelperFriend. She even slipped away from Violet and Equuleus, who had gone into stasis in response to Heart's continual sleeping, sleeping, sleeping as she'd never done in her life. Only in sleep could she be with Xavier—this was her private secret, which she told no one.

As she crept down the castle's winding stairs, the light from Pink's new little moon, silver and dusky, filtered through the dome skylight, bathing all it fell upon—the stairs, the railing, the art upon the walls, the dark energy chandelier, the floor with the inset marble image of Earth, everything—in a delicate, fairy-like, bas-relief.

At the front entrance, the environmental locks shunted. Heart stepped through the baffle out into the still of the synthetic moon's evening. Braced for the possibility that her flowers had been destroyed during the Bot Invasion, she released a deep sigh to see the two greenhouses still intact, and through the translucent green of the structures, her sweet flowers shone.

She considered stepping inside with the flowers, ignoring all the tragedy and pain that swirled around and around on the little moon, when she heard a wrenching, high-pitched, wail, an agonized keening. Heart shrank back into the shadows of the front entryway, hoping the traumatizing sound would cease.

But it didn't. She knew she had to step into the moment. She crept toward the poignant sound—not quite as loud as she first thought, as it was much closer. Moving along the edge of the castle, she came upon Lady Gervi's peculiar little mechanical dog, Yippee, making the impossibly woeful sound.

"*Yippee*," she said softly, kneeling down on the ground, "what is it?"

The little dog moved toward Heart haltingly, torn between fear and trust. He looked up at her in pain, whining, whimpering and crying, unbearably piteous.

Heart picked him up, holding him close. "It's all right now, Yippee, the bots have been destroyed, we're safe now. You needn't be afraid."

At first he relaxed into her embrace, seeming to understand her words, but then he became agitated. He leaped out of her arms and shook his little head, looking up at her. He grabbed her pant leg in his metal teeth, pulling at her, insisting she follow him.

"Okay, Yippee, all right. I understand I'll follow you. Let go and I'll come along."

He released her, and, continuing along the base of the castle, he looked back, again and again, to assure himself that she followed him. As they turned the corner of the castle, Heart stopped in shock.

The destruction of the hillside dome, home of all the mechanical, clockworks, and hybrid beings on Pink, took her breath away. She couldn't recognize anything. There was no dome—twisted metal stretched as far as she could see.

"Oh, no!" Heart whispered, wishing she'd not come out here alone, disoriented by the shock of the magnitude of the destruction.

Yippee began to whine louder, demanding Heart's attention. Confused, she looked down at him. "Yes, Yippee, I see ... I see ... horrible. It's ... *horrible.*"

Yippee grabbed onto her pant leg again and tugged at her. She reached over to try to pick him up, but he jumped away from her, moving his head back and forth, and finally, Heart understood that he meant for her to continue following him.

She didn't want to see more if that's what Yippee had in his little metal mind. What stretched before her was more than she could now take in. But, in the wake of his insistence, she followed him. He led her into a narrow cranny of the castle. Giant stones had toppled from the castle parapet, high above, and now lay in a pile of rubble before them.

Yippee clambered up the stones, most of which were larger than he, continuing to whine, and looking back at Heart. He suddenly disappeared into a cavern of the precarious ruins.

"*Yippee, no!*" Heart cried. But the little dog only howled more pitifully from the depths he'd jumped into. Setting thoughts of her own safety aside, Heart climbed up the pile of stones, hoping to reach down and pull Yippee out, against his will, if she must.

As she perched upon stones that rocked dangerously, she slowly kneeled down and reached into the cavernous space. As she peered, she began to make out something besides Yippee in the darkness below. It looked like black gears.

Lady Gervi!—trapped under these tons of stone. "All right, Yippee, all right, I see her. Come to me now, and we'll go get help. Come on, I can't leave you here, these stones could shift more at any moment." She reached her arms down to him, relieved when he jumped softly into her embrace.

Maneuvering with all her strength and agility, she lifted him out and crept cautiously back down the pile. Even so, the stones shifted, and with every movement, Yippee whined.

Not until this moment had Heart noticed no one was around. She'd been so preoccupied with her passing thoughts—about Xavier, about her flowers, her concern about Yippee, and then reeling from the shock of the damage, she hadn't noticed *no one was around*. No matter how many residents of Pink may have been harmed in the conflict, the rest of them ought to be scurrying about, energetically clearing up the rubble, and working on rebuilding.

She hurried to her father's modest room at the back of the castle, surprisingly intact, at the edge of the destruction. Still carrying Yippee, she passed through the double baffle of his doors, coming upon a bustling frenzy of mechanical, clockwork, and hybrid gear-bio beings, along with HelperFriend and Jackson.

Her father stood before everyone, gesturing in front of a large 3-D monitor displaying image after image of Pink's destruction from every angle, followed by overlays of how it was before the Bot Invasion.

Everyone stood in poised anticipation, the energy knife-edged, everyone anxious to rebuild their home, while learning what must be done, and how. No one—not even Jackson nor Helper-Friend, the gear man, noticed her enter the room. But Yippee would not be ignored.

He let out a growl ten times his size.

Father Inventor stopped talking and gesturing. Every mechanical, clockwork, hybrid and bio eye turned to Heart and Yippee.

"Father!" Heart exclaimed, "Lady Gervi is under a gigantic pile of stones. I don't know if she ...." Heart stopped, not entirely certain if Yippee could understand her or not. "We must get her out immediately!"

"Of course!" Her father gestured to the crowd, "HelperFriend, go with Heart and help direct the rescue of Lady Gervi, while Jackson and I get into protective gear."

"Yes, sir!" HelperFriend saluted her father, which Heart found extremely strange. She would have made fun of him under less terrible conditions.

Heart, with HelperFriend by her side, led the group to the pile of stones, hugging the whimpering little dog. They stood before the sight, daunted. How could they possibly move the rubble without stones dropping down upon Lady Gervi?

"You three, get the power lights," HelperFriend commanded, gesturing. He turned to Heart. "Where did you see Lady Gervi?"

Heart went to the pile and pointed to the specific stone she'd leaned over. "From that stone, there. But, even as I crawled back down with Yippee, the stones shifted."

"Hmmm ... yes," HelperFriend said. Heart watched as he studied the pile of stones, his gear eyes performing calculations. "Yes, all right." He turned and gestured to two mechanical women standing by him. "You two get a rope, go up to that castle window and let the rope down."

They scurried off to do as they were bid.

Then HelperFriend addressed Yippee in Heart's arms. "They're going to let down a rope, I'll put a loop in it. Do you think, Yippee, you can wrap the rope around the stones securely, so they can be moved in order to make the hole bigger?"

Heart was a bit stunned as Yippee nodded vigorously and growled with a sound much like, "yesyesyesyesyes." His little gear eyes whirled in edgy anticipation.

"Very good." HelperFriend patted Yippee.

Moments later, intensely bright lights lit up the scene, while a rope dropped from the castle window above. Heart set Yippee on the pile of stones, and with surprising dexterity, he ran up the pile and wrangled the rope around the stone Heart had leaned against, the two women cautiously, slowly, hoisted it, and moved it over to the side where HelperFriend could reach it.

He removed it, and the process was repeated three or four more times when finally Jackson and her father, suited up against the environment, joined them.

"HelperFriend appears to have everything under control here," her father observed, clearly relieved with the progress.

"Oh, Father, he's amazing," Heart said. "He's calculating the risk of stones shifting with every move, and look at that little dog! Goodness, he's brilliant—and intrepid!"

Her father nodded in agreement.

Everyone not actively engaged in the rescue watched the event with rapt attention. In short order, the pile of stones had been brought down to where HelperFriend took it upon himself to climb into the hole that had been exposed.

Everyone held their breath, hoping no stone would shift, hoping Lady Gervi would be brought out of the rubble intact—or enough intact to be repaired and reanimated.

Yippee stood at attention at the base of the pile of rubble, not even whimpering, poised, holding the equivalent of his little mechanical breath.

Heart could hear Helper Friend say something from within the stone vault, but she couldn't determine if he talked with Lady Gervi, or himself.

Then, suddenly, Lady Gervi seemed to levitate as HelperFriend held her aloft above the stone pile.

Yippee went into a paroxysm of yelps, leaping about at the sight of his beloved mistress.

HelperFriend's voice came from inside the stone pile, "If someone would come to my left side and take Lady Gervi. The stones are fairly solidly intertwined there."

Heart noticed that Wonderman One and Wonderman Two had joined the crowd.

"Wonderman One and Wonderman Two are here, HelperFriend," she called.

"Excellent! They can reach across and take her."

Without comment, the two Wondermen did as they were bid. The invisible HelperFriend reached Lady Gervi over in their direction, while the Wondermen extended their long arms and prodigious height. With the ends of their supernaturally strong fingers, they brought the unconscious Lady Gervi into the midst of the crowd, little Yippee almost turning himself inside out for joy.

Heart exchanged a look of consternation with her Father. Lady Gervi did not seem to have the least bit of animation in her, and one of her beautiful gear legs was horribly mangled.

Heart turned her face away from the dreadful sight, unable to forestall the memory of Xavier's torn body.

Her father came up to her and put his arm around her. She leaned into him, wordlessly, as they shared their unspoken empathy—the loss of their beloved Xavier.

"Take her into my room," Heart's father said. Heart stooped to pick up Yippee, then followed the Wondermen inside, along with her father, Jackson, and HelperFriend.

After the door baffles shunted closed, Jackson and her father stepped out of their protective gear, while Wonderman One and Wonderman Two gently laid Lady Gervi on Father Inventor's cot and began their reanimation procedure.

Yippee quivered in Heart's arms, and she held him closer, trying to comfort him, but at a loss, in the midst of her own apprehension and pain.

At that moment, Equuleus came charging through the door at the other end of the room, from the interior of the castle, gears whirring, his wings stretched to the limits of the ceiling, Violet clinging to his back, her little lavender rabbit ears bouncing.

"It's all right, Equuleus," Heart reassured.

"*You were gone!*" Violet squeaked, alarm in her voice. "How did you leave the room without us knowing?"

"You went into stasis since I've been sleeping so much. But ...." Heart's attention came back to the activities of the Wondermen, "I needed to see things for myself."

Violet took in Yippee, quivering in Heart's arms.

"Yippee," Violet said, "What's the matter with you? Are you injured?"

Yippee started a series of growls and yips.

"Oh, my little friend, I'm *so sorry!*"

Yippee pointed his nose where Lady Gervi lay, largely blocked by the massive bodies of the Wondermen.

"Oh!" Violet exclaimed. "Oh, dear!"

Yippee's peculiar monologue continued, Violet nodding. "Oh, Heart! You saved Lady Gervi!"

"I found her because Yippee led me to her."

"Yes, Heart, he just said that."

"Well, *I* can't understand him!"

"Really? How is that? He's perfectly articulate."

"Stand clear!" Wonderman One ordered.

Everyone moved back a step, while Wonderman One and Wonderman Two removed their healing vials from their chests, and then made a circuit with Lady Gervi between them. Then they sparked their reanimating charge, the only sound that of the electrical energy passing in the circuit between the clockwork beings, and Yippee's soft whimpering.

With their gigantic backs to the room, all that could be seen were blue and red pulsing lights, coalescing, gradually into a homogenous purple.

"Oh, my!" they heard Lady Gervi's cultured tone a few interminable moments later, soft and weak, but unmistakable. "I seem to have come upon a misfortune!"

"Yes," Wonderman Two agreed. "Please relax while we complete the reanimation, Lady Gervi."

"Of course," she said, compliant. But she suddenly became extremely agitated. "*Yippee!* Yippee was with me when the stones fell. You must go find him!"

Yippee yipped noisily, growling, chirping and yelping in Heart's arms, clearly letting his mistress know he was fine.

"Oh, Heart! Thank you, my dear. Oh, goodness, Heart saved me, I can't ... I don't ... *goodness!* How will I ever thank you? *Quite extraordinary!*"

"Not extraordinary, Lady Gervi," Heart replied, wishing she could be at Lady Gervi's side to reassure her, while Yippee seemed about to blow a cog from excitement. "I'm very happy Yippee took me to you!"

"Must be still!" Wonderman One said quite sternly. "Hush everyone. We must have silence to listen to Lady Gervi's clockworks."

The room fell as silent as a vacuum. Even Yippee became passive as a stuffed toy.

After a few more resounding clicks and clangs, Wonderman Two announced, "Success. Lady Gervi is fully reanimated. We go now."

Without ceremony, they replaced their healing vials back in their chests and moved from the room, each taking a turn in the door baffle as they were too large to pass through together. They were showered with a barrage of gratitude from everyone in the room, the most piercing being Yippee's own joyous howl. Heart rushed up to Lady Gervi's side and put Yippee by her where she lay on the cot.

He began a deluge of chatter, and she nodded at him, looking up at everyone around her, smiling sweetly. "Yes, Yippee, I do understand. Please, let us save some of the details for later. But, again, Heart, thank you! I dread to think what would have happened if you'd not come along when you did."

"Me too, dear Lady. I'm so glad I was able to be helpful."

As Heart spoke, Lady Gervi moved about, clearly intending to stand up.

"Oh, Lady," Heart gasped, seeing Lady Gervi did not yet realize her left leg had been destroyed. She watched as Lady Gervi looked down to see the mangle of gears that had previously been her beautiful limb.

"Oh, dear," she said softly.

Heart knelt down on the floor by her and took her hand. "It'll be all right, dear Lady. We'll make it right, won't we Father?"

She looked up at her father who had moved to stand by Lady Gervi.

"Ahm ....." he said, hesitating.

"Not likely," Lady Gervi answered Heart. "Not likely, dear Heart. With all the destruction brought about by the bots, combined with the contingent of residents who moved to Yellow, taking with them a considerable amount of components from here to build a supporting system there, there are few gear components left here. And what remains ... will have to be put to the highest use of reconstruction.

"No, not likely I'll be reconstructed," Lady Gervi concluded, while Yippee whimpered softly but piteously.

"Oh, Father, this can't be true!" Heart stood and faced him, agitated.

"Lady Gervi has stated the situation most accurately, I am profoundly sorry to say," her father said, a deep, sad, furrow in his brow. "For the time being, in any case. Eventually, when things are put back in order, we can probably cast a few gears out of the damaged and distempered metals from the dome with strength too compromised to be used again in a building, but will suffice for a clockworks being."

"Thank you, dearest Father Inventor, for your kind words," Lady Gervi said modestly. "But we both know that there are no doubt many clockwork beings yet to be exposed under the rubble, who are in worse condition than I am, and who will need gears more urgently than my mere leg."

"That's ridiculous!" Heart interjected. "You need to be able to get around. It's not just a case of vanity. *You must be able to move about!*"

"It will be up to her, Heart, if she'll want to accept a compromise, have her damaged leg removed, and replaced with a bit of tubing, or whatever we can improvise."

"Oh!" Heart breathed softly, looking into Lady Gervi's twirling gear eyes, as she pictured her handsome self, reduced to a sad, cobbled together wreck.

What made Lady Gervi, *Lady Gervi*, Heart thought, was the sensual, fascinating movement of her gears beneath the gear-tight black covering. Her tall, regal-yet-modest presence was intrinsic to the morale of the population of Pink.

They had built one another from scraps of broken and abandoned clockworks and mechanical beings. They had created Lady Gervi, each contributing their vision of beauty and magnificence, as a reflection of themselves. She needed to be whole!

"I will, like everyone else," she said bravely, "make the best of it, with gratitude that I'm still here. If I can move about, then I will be content to contribute to the reconstruction of my beloved Pink."

"*Hear, hear!*" Violet called, jumping down from Equuleus and hopping up beside Yippee, giving him a big, Violet hug.

"Hear, hear," everyone else, but Heart, echoed.

"Well said," Heart's father agreed. "Always a lady, my dear friend, and now you show exemplary bravery and dedication to all of Pink's population. We have much work to do to bring our home back to habitable condition. Your example will encourage everyone to continue the hard work and sacrifice required in the process of recovery."

Heart heard her father's words—they rang kind and true enough. But she couldn't keep from thinking about the first time she'd seen Lady Gervi, when she met her at the farewell party for Xavier, before his return to Earth.

Lady Gervi had immediately made a profound impression on Heart. Taller than everyone except the Wondermen, she'd sailed among the crowd, gracious and graceful, while at the same time, intriguingly sultry. In Heart's sheltered life, she had never encountered anyone with such a natural way with guileless bodily self-appreciation.

"I think," Father's voice, addressing Helper-Friend broke in on Heart's reverie, "we will have the Lady stay with us in the castle."

"Excellent, yes," HelperFriend agreed. "Which room?"

"I'll leave it up to you, HelperFriend. You and Lady Gervi. Whatever accommodations are most suitable for everyone is fine with me. Will you carry her, HelperFriend?"

"I shall, indeed."

"Wait!" Heart interjected, exchanging a look with Equuleus, in which she communicated her intention. Equuleus nodded. "Why not have Equuleus carry her? Does that suit you, Lady Gervi?"

"Oh, my! No, I would not want to impose. That's too much, really, Heart. I'm not worthy ...."

"Goodness, I won't hear it! Equuleus would be honored if you'd allow him to take you to a room of your liking."

Equuleus whinnied his agreement. He then moved alongside the cot, and HelperFriend lifted her onto his back, then out they trouped—Lady Gervi on Equuleus, Yippee, and Violet leaping alongside, followed by HelperFriend and Heart.

Heart looked over her shoulder at her father and Jackson. She knew her father had things to attend to and was clearly anxious to get at them.

"You coming?" she said to Jackson.

He glanced at her father, and he nodded.

"Sure," he said, joining them.

But something in the look exchanged between her father and Jackson arrested her attention. What loomed in the unspoken dialogue between them?

Was there not enough going on without yet something *else* to deal with?

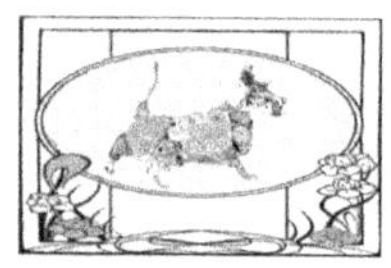

Chapter 2

There were three adjacent, beautiful, guest rooms on the ground floor, in the peaceful back of the castle, with a view of Pink's pale lavender and pink terrain, previously quite boring. But since Xavier launched the exquisite and dainty silver-white moon, it added much to the view. As it made its circuit across Pink's sky, it shed its mystical, silvery, faint sun-reflecting daylight upon Pink, that gave shape to the passing of time.

When they arrived at the three rooms, HelperFriend began a discussion with Lady Gervi about which room she might prefer. He solicitously opened each of the three doors, to interiors that were both sumptuous and spartan. The three rooms were, in every regard, identical. With one exception.

"I don't know," Lady Gervi said, while the gears of HelperFriend's eyes spun in anticipation of fulfilling his directive to make her feel at home. "They seem quite similar to me. I'm sure it doesn't matter."

"But you must choose," HelperFriend insisted, unable to attend to the business at hand without specific directive that put into motion his ever-painfully-logical mind.

Even Yippee ran from doorway to doorway, confused by the identical rooms.

"It's all right, HelperFriend. Let me make a suggestion, if I may," Heart said.

"Please do," Lady Gervi nodded.

"If it is at all of interest to you, Pink's new little moon will be most visible from this room on the left," Heart gestured. "Perhaps you and Yippee will enjoy watching the moon cross Pink's sky, and the charming shifting shadows the beautiful light makes."

Everyone—Lady Gervi, HelperFriend, Violet, Yippee, Equuleus, and even Jackson—listened with rapt attention, watching Heart's hands dance, as if to create the moonlight on the spot.

"*Yessss*," Lady Gervi sighed softly, "That sounds quite lovely."

"*Excellent!* Challenge resolved. Equuleus, please take Lady Gervi into her room, and HelperFriend, would you kindly scurry about getting some bedding and whatever else you might come upon that you think will make this room cozy? A lamp perhaps, maybe a few books. Do you enjoy reading, Lady Gervi?"

"Well, I believe I know how to read, though I've never had occasion to do so. It sounds most intriguing."

Not to have ever read a book! Heart thought in awe. She would now change Lady Gervi's life for all time. "Some books, HelperFriend, from Father's library," Heart directed.

"From your father's library?" HelperFriend asked in a raised, surprised voice.

"Yes. He won't mind. Books are meant to be read."

"All right. I will do as you bid. But, Heart, you'll tell him it was your idea, will you not?"

"Of course, dear HelperFriend."

"I'll be right back." HelperFriend clicked and clanked down the hall.

"Let's move this chaise lounge over near the window," Heart said to Jackson.

"Just tell me where you want it," Jackson lifted the heavy, antique, chaise over his head.

"All righty," Heart laughed. He appeared to be showing off just a little. Incongruous for Jackson!

Heart moved to the window and contemplated where the moon would soon appear. "Right here, Jackson. This would be good."

He set the chaise where Heart pointed. She sat, leaning back in it, looking at the sky. Then she jumped up and scooted the chaise lounge a small increment.

Yet three more such rearrangements, and she finally decided *this* position would afford the most comfortable and lengthy view of the moon's moon. There was even a little sliver of a view of Yellow, the neighboring moon, with Yellow's moon also occasionally visible when on the near side.

Lady Gervi, still on Equuleus, watched Heart attentively.

HelperFriend came through the door—or attempted to, his arms loaded with more paraphernalia than would reasonably fit in the *room*—let alone through the door.

Heart laughed, hurrying to unload him and bring some of the goods inside. "Did you leave anything in the rest of the castle?"

HelperFriend's eyes twirled and whirled, as if anxious. "I did, Heart. I did. I left most things in the rest of the castle. Do you want me to bring everything in the castle into this room, Heart? I must tell you now, it will not fit."

"Whoa," Jackson commented, "is he serious?"

"Frighteningly, so, yes," Heart answered, grinning, while Equuleus, witness to many occasions of HelperFriend's literal perceptions, snorted.

"No, HelperFriend," Heart said. "I'm speaking figuratively. As you have so many things, I'm teasing you, implying that it *looks* like you brought everything. But not literally."

"Figuratively. Yes, yes, teasing, a joke. A joke on HelperFriend ... ha-ha." He continued to struggle to get through the doorway, still too loaded down to enter.

"Put something down in the hall, HelperFriend, so you can get through the door."

"Yes. Of course. I know that. I'm distracted by too many things to attend to at once."

And, indeed, Heart saw, he may soon have a clockworks meltdown.

"There's you, Heart," HelperFriend continued, "sleeping all the time—not usual. There's Lady Gervi here, just look at her and say no more. Sorry, Lady, don't mean to offend. There's the dome, gone now. The Folks don't have a home. There's Jackson, here ...."

"What's wrong with Jackson?" Heart asked.

"He keeps starting to step outside without putting on proper gear. I've had to remind him ...."

"True," Jackson agreed. "Entirely too true. Sorry, HelperFriend. I shall try to be more attentive. It's just—I'm usually more outside than in, and ...."

Heart took his gaze. "And this business of staying inside is making you stir crazy."

"No, Heart. Not stir crazy ... maybe I'm a bit like our HelperFriend. I'm distracted by all I need to do. I keep forgetting that outside on Pink is ... well, it's not outside on Earth."

"No. For a fully bio, it's decidedly not," she agreed.

"I am, though," Jackson continued, *"curious* about what might happen to me if I went out without being suited up. Maybe it wouldn't bother me."

Heart silently shared with HelperFriend and Equuleus the memory of the terrible sight of Violet's violent reaction when Heart brought her inside the castle, as Violet's makeup was only suitable for outdoors. There prevailed a tacit understanding between them that a similar reaction might happen to Jackson if he went out, fully bio and not able to tolerate Pink's environment.

As Violet remained completely unaware that Father Inventor had revived her from death, they remained silent with the secret they kept.

Jackson raised an eyebrow. "What's not being said?"

"Ahm ... what's not being said needs to remain unsaid. But you can fill in the silence with our warning—*do not go out on Pink without proper covering,*" HelperFriend uttered in a no-nonsense voice.

"Right." Jackson saluted Helper Friend with a bit of a smirk.

"No Jest, Jackson," Heart added, furrowing her brow at him.

Jackson nodded at her. "Right, again."

Heart refused to release his gaze. "Yes, yes, yes," he said impatiently. "No going outside, or I'll die."

"There you have it," Heart nodded curtly.

"Well, I certainly didn't die," Violet squeaked. "But they *did* stick me in that glass thingy and I couldn't even stand up! It was just awful."

Jackson looked at Heart, and she saw he suddenly understood what she was *not* saying.

He went to the doorway and continued to unload HelperFriend. "Never mind all that. Our attention is upon the lovely Lady Gervi now, is it not?"

"It is," Heart agreed, picking and choosing from the plethora of items HelperFriend had brought.

She placed two charming matched floor lamps, one by the chaise lounge, the other across from it, while HelperFriend made the bed and arranged soft goods in a little closet.

"Now then, Lady Gervi, would you care to rest here on the chaise lounge?" Heart asked.

"I would! I would very much like that!"

Jackson carried her to the chaise lounge, and Equuleus stepped out of the room, watching the activities somewhat disinterestedly, while Violet and Yippee succeeded in being underfoot.

HelperFriend had brought two softly knitted throws, one predominately red, the other, predominately green. Heart held them up. "Would you like one of these?"

"Oh, yes please, the red one."

Heart arranged the throw over the reclining Lady Gervi, smiling down at her. Lady Gervi studied the result. "Well, now, that's fine. You wouldn't even think such a horrible sight lay underneath."

"*Oh!*" Heart gasped.

Lady Gervi took Heart's hand in her own beautifully-shaped gear-spinning hands. "Thank you, Heart. Thank you. You saved me, and you saved my little Yippee. I will tell you, he would have destroyed himself, if … if the worst had happened to me. I shall never forget your bravery and kindness."

Heart knelt down by her. "I'm so relieved that I *did find you!* But, in the end, Yippee remains the hero."

Yippee had come over to sit by them. He looked from Heart to Lady Gervi with true, devoted love shining from his whimsical little gear dog features. Heart picked him up and put him in Lady Gervi's arms, then stood, turning and taking in every detail of the room.

"One last thing, HelperFriend. Let's have that little table over here, within Lady Gervi's reach, and let's put a few of the wonderful books you brought, on the table."

HelperFriend placed the small bedside table where Heart directed, while Jackson picked through and chose half-a-dozen books. Heart looked at his choices, and chuckled, "very good, both of you." The stack of physical books included some of Heart's own favorites. One about horses, two about dogs, and another about Father Inventor's so, so very long ago first, beautiful clockwork inventions.

Oh, those beautiful inventions! Heart recalled fondly the ones she'd become acquainted with during her stay in The Museum of Scientific Improbabilities and Unpredictable Oddities.

But the most famous and beloved of all of Father Inventor's clockwork inventions stood at the moment, rather bored, in the hall. The magnificent first and only flying clockworks horse, Equuleus, wherein Heart's own heart was housed.

"I hope you'll enjoy these physical books, dear Lady. Of course, you can read millions of books on the 3-D. But, I do love the *experience* of holding a book, listening to the pages rustle, feeling the heft of the book in your hands, the pleasure of turning the pages as the story grows upon you.

"Hmmm, I guess that's about enough waxing poetic on books for the moment." Heart chuckled. "We will leave you to relax, and see you at dinner time." She moved to the door, Jackson and HelperFriend with her. She looked back and saw Violet looking up at Yippee.

"Are you staying, Violet?"

"If Lady Gervi doesn't mind, I will stay for a while."

"I'd love it if you stayed!" Lady Gervi exclaimed.

Heart, smiling at the sweet picture despite the underlying reason for it, closed the door noiselessly. Before them in the hall was a muddle of all the things HelperFriend had brought that they had not put in the room.

"Excuse me while I put all these things back where I found them. See you at dinner," HelperFriend said energetically.

"I'd offer to help, but I've never even seen most of these things. I have no idea where they go."

"Not to worry Heart, not to worry! I'll have it all sorted out quickly." HelperFriend lifted everything up in one scoop and headed off toward the mammoth kitchen with its seeming acres of cupboard-and-closet-lined walls—where, no doubt, he'd ferreted out most of the items. Jackson and Heart, with Equuleus behind, headed in the opposite direction.

"What a noisy silence from you, Jackson!" Heart exclaimed. "It's reached a pitch I can no longer ignore."

"Seriously?"

"Oh yes," Equuleus agreed. "Seriously."

"I wasn't talking to you," Jackson glanced back at the winged horse.

"Jackson, when you talk to me, you are, indeed, talking to Equuleus. I would have thought you knew that." Heart looked at Jackson and saw, much to her amazement, he'd been shamed.

"You're right, Heart. I apologize, Equuleus. I imagine that there might be times when, if I want to reach you, Heart, it would be to my advantage to talk first with Equuleus."

"It's entirely possible," she agreed. "But, now, back to the subject—whatever it is—at hand."

Still, Jackson hesitated.

"*What is it?* I've never seen you like this. You can handle anything. Jackson?"

"I can handle any *doing* sort of thing. *Talking* things are ... in a different category."

"*Sheesh*, Jackson." Heart shook her head in near disgust. "Don't send a boy to do a man's job ...."

"Right." He squared his shoulders as if bracing for a fight. "Right. Then, I have to ask you two questions. You will not like either one of them."

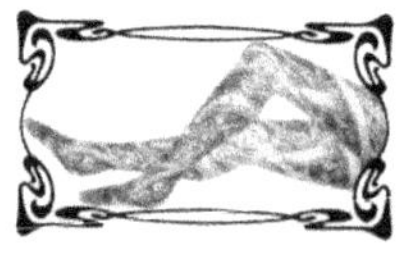

Chapter 3

nxiety washed over Heart. She just couldn't face something so big that Jackson feared to bring it up, on the heels of everything else claiming her energy. "All right. I ... I'm braced, I guess. Let's have one of the questions."

They'd come around to the front domed entry, where Heart's favorite light on all of Pink filtered down upon them.

"Let's sit," Jackson moved over to sit on the stairs, his lanky yet muscular body tense. Heart had only seen him like this when he was about to spring into life-saving action.

Heart sat on the step beside him, leaning up against the stair spindles, while Equuleus nervously strode about, his hooves clicking on the marble floor.

"Equuleus, please!" Heart and Jackson said in unison, then they both broke into a nervous giggle. Equuleus stopped at the foot of the stairs, not moving, except for an intermittent nervous swish of his tail.

"I," Jackson started, "well, not only me—your father and the residents of Pink—want to, that is, they have the idea to lay Xavier to rest in Pink's moon. Inside of Pink's moon. But—we fear, and everyone is concerned, that this will cause you—it'll be too ...."

"Oh, Jackson ... no, that won't be too hard on me, I mean, it's all, all difficult. But, no, I think that's lovely—and loving. And appropriate. He'd be so honored. To be near his beloved Pink forever. It's perfect. It's a subject I haven't even thought about in the least. Though if I had, I would have thought he'd be returned to Earth, to The Periphery, to The Mystic's cottage. But, if she is all right with this idea ... is she all right with it?"

"Exceedingly. I contacted her as soon as I could when we got communications back up after the invasion. She said almost word for word what you've just said."

"Why was it so difficult to ask me that question, Jackson?"

"Like I said, we all thought it would be too hard on you to know he was there. Here, above us, around us. All the time ...."

"No. Not too difficult." Heart fell silent. She would not now—and perhaps never—tell him the secret she kept, close. "Let us not hesitate any longer,

Jackson. Let us give him the respect he is due, with ritual and love."

Jackson nodded, looking down, deep in thought.

"You are not relieved," Heart observed. "You've been struggling for some while over posing this question—and why you're asking me rather than my father I don't understand. But you've been struggling, afraid to ask me. Now that you have, and with a positive outcome, you're not relieved."

"I'm hugely relieved."

"And how well you express it!" Heart observed wryly.

"Right."

"Next question," Heart prodded.

"All right. The first question was from everyone, but this one is from me alone. It will not be popular with your father, or anyone else, for that matter." He paused.

"And?..." Heart said.

Equuleus murmured a whinny.

"Forge ahead, Jackson."

He breathed deeply and let the breath out slowly. "I think you'll jump at this opportunity, but you'll be concerned about your father's opinion. I want to ask that, for the moment, you set his considerations aside, and only think of yourself."

"Much easier said than done," Heart noted, "I'll give it a try, but I can't even do that if you don't tell me what it is."

"I ...." Jackson started haltingly, "need you to come back to Earth with me."

"*WHAT?!*" Heart leapt up from the step, then went down the three steps to stand by Equuleus on the marble floor. "Has clarity escaped your mind? With all that has to be done here? With the fact that if I'm that far from Equuleus my bios will die? With—and you're right about this one—my father needing me. You casually suggest I return to Earth with you?"

Heart strode around the rotunda, agitated, Equuleus following her, his feet making a steady rhythm, click-a-clok, click-a-clok.

She finally came back to face Jackson, who had not moved a muscle.

"Really, Jackson, what are you thinking? What are you suggesting? And *why?*"

"Please, please sit, Heart. Please hear me out. *This is extremely important,*" Jackson said in a voice both commanding and begging, that Heart had never heard from him. It arrested her attention.

"Just a moment." She went into the neighboring room and brought back a chair, then set it to face Jackson. "I want to see you face-to-face when you try to make a case for me to abandon Pink, at the very moment I'm most needed.

"Why would you want me to go to Earth when it's so many kinds of dangerous for me? What is your plan to keep me alive, since, as we learned, I cannot be that far from Equuleus for an extended period of time?

"Will your plan for me to be on Earth take less than a day? No. It cannot."

"Right, Heart. I've thought about everything, and, though my plan is imperfect, it's developing. It will become even more defined when you and your father contribute to it.

"It all ties into Xavier, Heart."

Heart leaned forward. "I'm listening."

"After you and Xavier left Earth, and before the Bot Invasion ...."

"A short period of time," Heart observed.

"A very short period of time, indeed," Jackson agreed. "In that short period of time, I studied the places Xavier had placed the magnetic dark energy resonators for the shield. I thought they were essentially random, placed so the shield could raise and be effective, nothing more. But then I noticed something peculiar. I noticed a very clear, *not random* placing of each resonator."

"I don't think so, Jackson." Heart countered. "He placed the one near The Darling Undesirables Residence of Long Prairie, because I was going there. Then we told him to place the others in a hurry, as we feared we were being followed, given Keeper A's strange behavior.

"So, no, I don't see that he had some sort of strong, pre-thought, predetermined placing of the magnetic dark energy resonators."

Jackson nodded in agreement. "That's what I thought, too. Until I started getting a signal, specifically directed at my vehicle. Then, Peter noted the same thing, which he sent me in a coded message. *Then* I picked this signal up in the *Heart!* The same message."

Heart recoiled reflexively at mention of Xavier's spacecraft, the *Heart!*

Jackson reached his hand toward her, then dropped it, as if helpless. "I'm sorry, Heart. I know this is hard on you. It's hard on me too. But—we have to honor what he meant to tell us. And, what could that be? Something of profound importance. Where or how he got his information, I don't know. We may never know.

"However, there's no accident. He gave us some clues of supreme importance. We must unravel the mystery."

"Why do you need *me?* Xavier didn't tell me any secrets. I don't know anything that you don't know, and better. Plus, you're much more capable of making something of it."

"Not true, Heart. The four points where Xavier posted the magnetic dark energy resonators sent signals attuned to only the three locations I told you. No one else would give this weak little signal the least attention. The two crossed lines that intersect from the energy of the magnetic dark energy resonators, with a stunningly accurate variation in the signals of each of the resonators, has produced a precise point.

"And that point ... *that point, Heart,* is in the center of The Darling Undesirables Residence of

Long Prairie." Jackson paused to let the fact sink in. "You know that place better than anyone in *The Cause of All Beings.* You know it just about better than anyone, anywhere. Except, of course, Keeper A."

Heart's mind reeled at the onslaught of information Jackson threw at her. "It must have made you nearly crazy, keeping this secret since you've arrived on Pink, Jackson," she finally observed.

"No. Not nearly crazy, but anxious, yes. Though we appear to be safe for the moment—that is to say, the shield is holding—experiments continue apace on Earth. Every day it becomes more apparent that it's of paramount importance to discover where Father Inventor's downloaded clone brain is, and neutralize it."

"Neutralize it," Heart repeated.

"Take it out. It's your father's cloned brain that continues to make life for all beings at risk. To put it mildly. I don't even want to tell you what movements are going on, but they are not pretty. And they're augmenting. Only you could prowl around The Darling Undesirables Residence at Long Prairie and know where to go from point A to point B. And, of course, your ability to shapeshift ...."

"Does come in handy at times. But, still Jackson! You'll have to find someone else. I'll do what I can—but from here. I can't leave Equuleus, as you well know. I certainly cannot leave my father now, nor can I leave Pink in the condition it's in. We need to rebuild."

"Only to, perhaps," Jackson said quietly, "have the whole of all your Father's synthetic moons destroyed. To have all Darling Undesirables destroyed. To have all clockwork and mechanical and hybrid beings destroyed?"

"Are you not exaggerating, Jackson?"

"Am I one for hyperbole?"

"No," she answered simply, "You are not." She looked over at Equuleus.

"Yes. Equuleus," Jackson said. "My plan, of course, includes Equuleus."

"Setting Equuleus aside for the moment, I must ask, Jackson, are you truly willing to endanger me? I shudder at the thought of being at The Darling Undesirables Residence of Long Prairie again. The one thing that gave me the greatest relief about rescuing Eye and Butterfly was the belief I would never, ever again have to set foot anywhere near there if I didn't want to. *And why would I want to?*"

"To save others."

Heart sighed deeply. "Simple enough, yes. But, given my loathing of the place, someone less emotionally involved would be better suited for your proposed mission. I'll give what I can. But I ... I can't go to Earth now."

Jackson held Heart's gaze, neither usual nor easy for him. *"You are the only one, Heart.* You are the best suited for this mission. You are the worst suited. You are the most medium suited. I say again, *there is no one else."*

Heart couldn't ignore Jackson cavalierly risking her, and on the heels of losing his cousin and best friend, Xavier. It felt strangely wrong.

She glanced at Equuleus, then back down to her agitated but folded hands in her lap. She wanted to be sure she had Equuleus's attention, while not drawing Jackson's attention. "Do you sense what's crossing my mind?" she thought to Equuleus.

"I do," Equuleus immediately answered. "How can Jackson so readily ask you to do a dangerous mission, when he seems otherwise—in his own stilted way—to care about you. Plus he's just lost Xavier ...."

"For the second time ...."

"For the second time. Now he has a plan to put you in the midst of possibly truly serious danger."

"Precisely."

"You're daring to wonder if he's a double agent."

"Yes."

"I ... I don't think so, Heart. I agree his request is shocking. But it's Jackson nature not to waver from his goal, no matter what lies between here and there. I can understand his thought that you are nearly indestructible and you know the facility like no one else on the outside. Like no one in *The Cause of All Beings*.

"I'm quite certain, this is not an easy conclusion for him. You know him. He's pragmatic. Once something makes sense to him, he only knows to move forward."

"All right, enough psychic chit-chat between you two," Jackson said, squaring his shoulders and sitting ramrod straight, clearly exasperated. "I can't sit here all day while you jabber away with one another. There's work to do.

"Look, Heart, this has not been an easy conclusion for me. I've just lost Xavier—*for the second time*," He emphasized. "I would not put you in harm's way for all the stars in the Universe. But you are the only one. You've not run from your calling before, Heart, I don't know why you're balking now ...."

"Mostly because I don't see *your* proposal for *my* life as my calling ...."

"Fair enough. Fair enough, Heart. But—if it's the most important pending event, and you're the only individual, both capable and equipped to function effectively in the situation, how can you *not* see it as your calling?"

Jackson's logic stopped Heart's thinking in its tracks. Why, in fact, did she not think of Jackson's proposal as her calling? She'd taken many dangerous actions, without a second thought. Without hesitation.

What was different now?

Aha, she hit upon it! "Because, Jackson, it's not my idea. Every time I've walked right into danger, it's been because it was my idea. I left The Darling Undesirables Residence of Long Prairie because it was my idea. I returned to Earth because it was my idea. I went to The Darling Undesirables Residence of Long Prairie when I came back to Earth with Xavier because it was my idea, to set up a rescue for Eye, and, as it turned out, Butterfly."

Jackson nodded while Heart talked, but a strange, nearly alien little grin spread across his features as she rambled on.

"What is that grin? Goodness, Jackson, don't smile like that, it's not a good look on you!"

Jackson uttered a slight chuckle.

"Equuleus, I've somehow broken Jackson," Heart exclaimed, not entirely certain she was teasing.

"You're rarely wrong, Heart," Jackson said. "But when you are, you do a grand job of it."

"Really? How am I wrong?"

"Everything you've done is not always your idea. It was *NOT* your idea to come to Pink. Martha and Peter and Key Man and I—we had to doggedly convert you to the idea. And it was *NOT* your idea to save Lady Gervi. Yippee had to practically drag you in his little metal teeth."

"Yes, but ... well, I ... that's because ... *hmmm* ...." Heart bunched up her face in vexation. "I think he's got me, Equuleus. Well played, Jackson. I had no idea you paid that much attention to me."

"I've memorized your every move, Heart. Your every move I've witnessed, your every move I've ever heard about, your every move I've seen on any 3-D. I know what makes your hybrid bio, mechanical, dark matter, dark energy brilliant self tick.

"I tell you again, there's no one equipped to take on this mission but you. I'll be there, willing to sacrifice myself at a moment's notice if that's what it calls for. There are others standing by who will do the same.

"But you, Heart, you, *once again!* are the only one who can fulfill this mission."

HelperFriend came rushing out of the hall from Father Inventor's room, and stopped short at the sight of them. "What ... this is strange, why, why are you sitting on the stairs? I've never seen ... strange behavior. What does it mean?"

Heart chuckled. "Come join us HelperFriend. Come sit on the stairs and see how cozy it is."

HelperFriend took a few hesitant steps toward them. "Ahm," he said, clearly confused.

"Conflicting orders, HelperFriend?"

HelperFriend sighed, relieved. "Yes! Yes, conflicting orders. Shall I fulfill your father's order to find you and bring you to him? Or shall I fulfill your order to," HelperFriend repeated in Heart's voice, "Come sit on the stairs and see how cozy it is."

Heart laughed. "Oh, it's unnerving when you do that! Well, dear friend, how urgent did my father's voice sound when he asked you to find us?"

HelperFriend then repeated his request: "Where is Heart? HelperFriend, will you kindly find her and ask her to come to my room."

"Hmmm, what say you, Jackson, does my father sound urgent or sociable?"

"Both."

"I agree. Come, HelperFriend. Sit with us for a few moments, and then off we'll go to help Father."

Hesitantly and somewhat awkwardly, the gear man made his way to stand on the stair above Jackson. "Now?"

"Now, *sit*, HelperFriend. Just—*sit!*"

"All right." HelperFriend sat. "Oh! I didn't know one could sit on the stairs. I believed they were specifically meant for walking up or for walking down. Perhaps to stand and pause for a moment, as I've seen you do Heart, to look at the light coming through the dome as it comes down upon you. Though that might be unique to you, Heart, I don't know. I've never seen Jackson nor Father Inventor do it. But to sit. Now that's an entirely different usage."

HelperFriend looked over his shoulder at the stairs above him. "Quite practical, too, as many individuals could reasonably sit on the stairs. Why have chairs?"

"Well, if the stairs were filled with individuals sitting on them rather than chairs, such as we're sitting on right now, how would others be able to use the stairs to go up or down?"

"Oh, yes, yes. I see your point, Heart. I didn't think it completely through. Well, this is quite nice, I must say. What is the topic of discussion? I seem to have happened on a serious conversation."

"As it happens, you did, HelperFriend, but now, I believe, we must fulfill your first directive, which is to go see what my father needs."

Heart and Jackson stood, Heart pulled the chair back into the adjacent room, while Jackson and Equuleus started down the hall.

When Heart came out of the room, HelperFriend remained on the stairs.

"Well, come along!" she said.

"I'm so confused, Heart. I thought we were going to engage in conversation. I thought that's why you invited me to sit on the stairs!"

"Another time for the conversation, Helper-Friend. It's enough for you to have expanded your awareness to imagine the stairs might be sat upon as well as gone up and down, don't you think?"

HelperFriend slowly stood. "Not sure, Heart. Not sure."

She watched as the gears in his head churned furiously, intrigued by his learning process. He took gigantic events and treated them as quite ordinary, while the most mundane of things, in her view, were major contemplations of learning.

"Get it sorted out?" she asked as his gears appeared to settle into calmer clicking.

"Not quite, to be truthful. But I'm getting there. I look forward to the time when we might have a conversation on the stairs. I believe that will permit closure on this bit of learning."

"Sorry to disrupt how your mind works, my dear friend. But I do feel we need to get to my father now."

"You're right, Heart. Absolutely. I feel him wondering where you are, and he has more than plenty to occupy him at present. So my peculiarities of learning must pause." He came, rather stiff-legged, down the stairs. "And now I use the stairs for descent."

"Beautifully done, I must say!" Heart smiled.

HelperFriend relaxed. "Oh! Thank you, Heart."

They hurried down the hall after Equuleus and Jackson, already in Father Inventor's room.

*   *

As Heart and HelperFriend entered her father's room, they were faced with him, Equuleus, and Jackson, all watching the door in silence, as if it was a pot refusing to boil.

"Sorry," Heart apologized. "Small learning curve glitch with HelperFriend. It's getting sorted out."

HelperFriend nodded vigorously. "Did you know, Father Inventor, stairs could be used to be sat upon? Quite extraordinary, this concept. Huge. When you consider how many individuals can be sat upon stairs, barring the need of anyone to actually use the stairs for ascent or decent, quite a meaningful seating facility. I don't know why no one has thought of it before. Only our Heart can come up with such magnificent brilliance."

"Ah, no, HelperFriend," Heart protested. "I did not originate this idea. You might peruse your data banks with the query, 'sitting on stairs' to see how this concept has been employed virtually since the invention of stairs."

41 - Blythe Ayne

"Oh!" HelperFriend's gears again whirred and whirled energetically. "Oh yes, I see what you say. Goodness, I'm uniquely naive!"

"On occasion," Heart's Father agreed.

"But it only endears you to us, and reminds us of our own learning paths." Heart patted Helper-Friend's arm. "But now to the business at hand. You asked HelperFriend to bring me to you, Father. Is there something specific?"

"Yes, Heart." Her father looked at Jackson. "Were you able to...?"

"Oh, is this about the way in which everyone wants to honor Xavier?"

"Yes."

"I'm very much in favor of the loving care of everyone. As I told Jackson, I can't imagine any-thing Xavier would have wanted more than to eter-nally oversee Pink, his beloved home."

Heart's sadness welled up in her again. She won-dered if the mysterious process of crying, which she'd almost never done before in her life, was about to begin again. She certainly hoped it would not.

Her father put his arm around her. "It's all right, my girl, if emotion overcomes you. It's quite natural."

"Not for me. This strange experience of crying simply takes my mind off of what needs to be done." She sighed deeply several times and the unnerving emotion dissipated enough for her to focus on the present moment. "What are the plans?"

"We thought that simple would be best. Jack-son and perhaps HelperFriend will fly up to Pink's moon. And then, everyone thought it would be the best part of a simple ceremony if you, Heart, pushed the button to slide one of the sections of the moon open, and said a few words.

"Jackson and HelperFriend will simply release Xavier in the moon, where he will remain suspended. Then you'll push the button to close the moon and Jackson and HelperFriend will return to Pink, during which time anyone who wants to share memories or thoughts of Xavier may do so."

Heart nodded. "Yes. That's perfect. I only wish The Mystic and others from The Periphery could be here."

We're intending to beam the event to them. Now that the shield is up, for the time being, it's safe to communicate with Earth. Of course, we won't transmit images of the population, keeping that fact secret, but the ceremony at the moon, we'll share with a small handful of people in The Periphery."

"*Oh!*" Heart exclaimed, with a bit of shock, thinking about Eye being in attendance on the receiving end of the transmission. He'd not be able to see the proceedings, but he'd see them in his own special way, and he would hear her. Again, she became awash with nearly overwhelming emotion.

Equuleus whinnied.

"Eye," Jackson said simply.

Heart nodded.

"Yes, Heart," her father agreed, "Eye will hear you, and see you in his mind. Ah, it is sweet!"

"Yes. Sweet. And difficult." Heart took a deep breath, and let it out slowly. "All right, then, let's figure out the details of the ceremony."

Left unspoken remained the subject of Jackson's second question.

*   *

While they made plans, HelperFriend slipped from the room. Heart thought he might be preparing something special for their dinner guests, Lady Gervi and Yippee. She'd already noticed that HelperFriend created spectacular treats for the clockworks population on Pink, as he, himself, was one.

When HelperFriend's voice came over the audio system suggesting they come to dinner, Heart and her father, followed by Equuleus and Jackson, walked down the hall to the dining room.

There they saw a sumptuous dinner spread out on the long dining table, the soft light of the wall sconces beaming a golden glow commingling with the orange glow of the fire in the fireplace, altogether warm and inviting.

But no HelperFriend.

They stood in the doorway for a moment, hesitating.

"I imagine," Heart suggested, breaking the silence, "HelperFriend is attending to Lady Gervi. Perhaps she prefers to dine in her room."

"There's a place for her," Jackson pointed out.

"Oh, yes," Heart nodded.

Just then they heard Yippee coming down the hall, so Equuleus settled in his place by the hearth, while Heart, Jackson, and her father remained standing to greet Lady Gervi, carried by HelperFriend.

But much to their surprise, she came flying into the room seated in a chair upon which wheels had been affixed. Yippee and Violet hopped and leapt joyfully at her side. HelperFriend finally entered the room, with a mixed look of doubt and pleasure on his features.

"Look what HelperFriend made me!" Lady Gervi declared. "Is it not wonderful? A chair with wheels. So logical! So thoughtful! Dear Helper-Friend!" She reached her hand out to him and he took it, shyly.

"Oh, HelperFriend," Heart exclaimed.

HelperFriend jumped, looking at Heart cautiously. "Yes?"

"That's superlative. You're amazing!"

"So, it's all right?"

"Better than all right, isn't it Father?"

"Quite surprising initiative for a clockworks man, HelperFriend. Yes, indeed. Quite a bit better than all right. Very good! But, I don't recognize the wheels, where did they come from?"

HelperFriend busied himself with situating Lady Gervi at the table, then pulling out Heart's chair for Heart to be seated. "I realize every scrap of metal is precious for the reconstruction. So I carefully scanned my inventory and found these four gears on a little device we've never used.

"Because I saw they were too distempered for construction, but fine for this use, I went to find that device in the rubble while you planned Xavier's ceremony. After I found them I sanded off all the gear teeth, which turned them quite effectively into wheels. Then I affixed the wheels to a chair ...."

"Brilliant, HelperFriend! Your initiative is inspiring."

"Ah ... awww ...." HelperFriend appeared unable to utter a word, but his eye gears spun happily.

"When did you have time to create this beautiful meal?" Heart asked.

"In between."

"In between what?"

"In between making Lady Gervi's chair."

Heart and her father laughed, and Jackson even managed a chuckle.

"Are you laughing at me?"

"No, dearest, we are *delighted* with your many talents." Heart held up her cup of tea. "Three cheers for our clever HelperFriend!"

Everyone with hands held up a glass and cheered, while Equuleus, Yippee, and Violet added their cheers to the chorus.

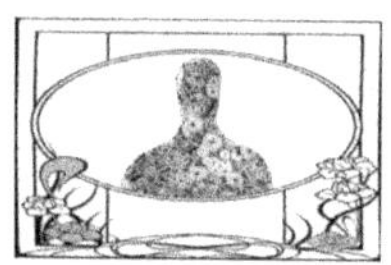

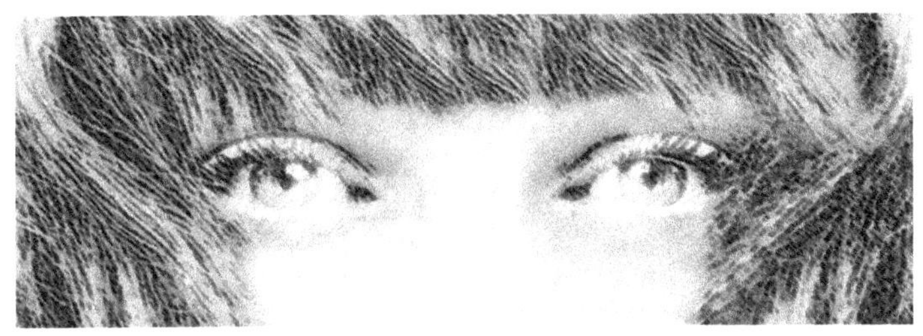

Chapter 4

Two circuits of Pink's new moon later, the entire population gathered outside the shattered dome. Even badly broken mechanicals and clockwork beings were present to honor their beloved Xavier.

Heart was encouraged to see that already the worst of the blackened, twisted metal of the dome had been removed, and shiny lengths of curved tubing stretched out on the ground, as every able-bodied and every injured individual began to peg the infrastructure together.

Heart realized that the hover rafts, directed by industrious residents, had been bringing great volumes of building materials from the storage hill where HelperFriend had taken her and Equuleus to gather the components for the greenhouses. That seemed like ages ago!

The thought reminded her that she'd neglected her flowers in the confusion and the planning, and the preoccupied thinking she'd been doing since the "stair-talk" about returning to Earth with Jackson.

"Oh, Equuleus! Why didn't I think of this before? Would it not be perfect to send a large bouquet of my flowers with Xavier?"

Equuleus nuzzled her shoulder. "Yes, perfect, Heart."

Her father and Jackson were still inside, so she slipped away to gather a bouquet of flowers to send with Xavier. "Stay here, Equuleus. Let me know if I need to return."

He nodded as Heart hurried to the front of the castle, happy in this sad moment to spend time with her flowers.

Stepping through the baffle of the closer greenhouse, the loamy aroma of earth, commingled with the sweetness of the flowers' various scents, rose up around her. She gasped in delight to see her wonderful flowers fully grown and in excellent health. *They were shockingly beautiful.*

The bulb flowers and the seed flowers growing stem to stem, blossom to blossom, short and tall, vibrant and pastel—they all grew together, although they still formed a clearly discernible plaid pattern.

Contemplative, Heart meandered among the flowers, taking in their aroma and their radiant, tender faces.

She sat among them, remembering the last time she'd done this. Only a few of Pink's short days ago, she'd sat here with Xavier, and he talked of love and flowers. He'd taught her more about herself in a dusky evening on Pink than she'd learned in all her previous life.

He taught her about love, about the honesty and clarity of naming it when it came. He taught her about not running away from love, even if it hurt, even if it was not returned. Even when it seemed like the greatest mystery of the Universe, and would never unfold.

"Just at that moment," Xavier had said, "when you completely give up on love, because it seems like it is a big lie, an illusion of society, a fantasy of untruth—just at that moment, some form of love rises up, like these flowers—rises up through the seeming dirt.

"But that which seems like dirt is the catalyst, is your very own catalyst, the seed of love that lies dormant in your substrata. From the place where you feel empty, loveless, unloved and unlovable, that's where the mysterious materials of the something-from-nothing grow. That's where love waits upon your awakening."

"Years ago, when I saw you on that 3-D, and you told the newshound you loved stars more than anything, something shifted in me. I knew who you were like I knew myself. Anyway, what I've learned is that love is not one 'thing.' It's not a 'thing' at all. It's an essence, it's the Thread of Life, pure and simple."

She'd listened to all his words, a contented disciple. She understood what he said. It had happened to her when she was a little girl at The Darling Undesirables Residence at Long Prairie. She felt confused by all the deformities around her, alienated, no one to talk to, the keepers patronizing and pitying.

Then they brought Eye to the newly vacated room next to hers. Keeper E asked her to take Eye by the hand to the dining hall for meals.

Keeper E, who'd been replaced at least twice since then—had condescendingly shown Heart how to hold Eye's hand and demonstrated walking to the dining hall, repeating himself several times.

Heart had nodded, saying nothing, wanting to shout, "I get it! I'm not an idiot!" Finally, Keeper E left. Heart stood facing Eye, with no idea what he comprehended. The first words she heard from his little 6-year-old mouth were, *"What an imbecile!"*

They'd burst into gales of laughter, leaning together, hugging. Awash with delight and relief that—*finally!*—she would no longer be entirely alone!

In that moment Heart had discovered her own, shielded garden of love between herself and Eye. After that, every sort of loving flower flourished in her previously unrealized garden.

Returning to the present moment, the sobering, present moment, with Eye far, far away on Earth, safe behind the wall of The Periphery, and Xavier gone from the three dimensions altogether, alone in the moment, yet not alone, she asked, "What flowers, Xavier, would you like to take with you?"

As she moved among the flowers, she held her hand over them. She sensed a hesitation and a warmth over particular ones, which she picked. Finally, when there were no more pulses of warmth, she looked down at the bouquet cradled in her arm. She saw a collection of modest, sweet flowers—multicolored primroses, deep blue bachelor buttons, happy-faced purple and orange pansies, pure white daisies, fragrant paperwhites, deep pink columbine, and a couple stalks of blue lupine, with snapdragon vines winding about them all.

"Yes, Xavier, lovely, these adorable, modest flowers. I'm going to add, as my own signature, Xavier, some bleeding heart."

She felt Xavier protest—he didn't want her bleeding for him.

"But this is a part of love, Xavier, my losing you immediately upon discovering the love I have for you—so different from the love I have for Eye, my brother-love. My love for you, mysterious and profound and generous and selfish. Yes, Xavier this Darling Undesirable, whose heart is housed in another creature, will add ...."

She saw the shadow of Equuleus fly over the greenhouse, "Come!" he called to her.

Heart picked two stalks of bleeding heart. "I will add bleeding hearts to the flowers, dear Xavier." Before passing through the rear double door baffle

protecting the flowers from the inhospitable environment of Pink, she smiled at all their glowing
faces. "Thank you for sharing."

She stepped through the baffle and expected to
see the flowers in her arms directly begin to wilt,
but, instead, in a trice, they crystallized into beautiful forms, each instantly mummified in pristine
beauty.

Equuleus had landed and greeted her at the
door. He took in her state of reverie, and kept silent.
As they walked back to the dome, Heart spied a
bit of twisted, blackened wire, which she wrapped
around the stems of the flowers, as symbolic of the
event in which Xavier gave up his life for all he
loved.

*   *

When they came around the corner of the castle,
everyone had silently gathered, waiting for her. She
looked across the population of Pink, "The Folks,"
as her father had christened them. Many intact,
while nearly as many were broken in an unfathomable array of brokenness.

She exchanged a look with Equuleus where
she felt her heart turn in pain. "We must make this
right," she whispered. Equuleus inclined his head
in agreement.

She scanned the gathering, looking for Jackson,
HelperFriend and her father. Seeing none of them,

she decided they must still be inside. As she moved to her father's room, the three of them stepped out, HelperFriend first, then Jackson and her father, suited up against the environment.

She approached Jackson with her bouquet. "Will you take these with you, to leave with Xavier?"

"Oh!" Both her father and Jackson exclaimed, seeing their light-radiance crystallized forms.

"So beautiful," her father said. "I had no idea this is what the flowers would do in Pink's environment."

"Perhaps Xavier has something to do with it," Heart answered simply.

"Perhaps."

Heart saw Jackson take in the unsightly bit of wire wrapped around the stems. "In remembrance of the occasion when he gave us everything he had."

Jackson nodded, and wordlessly took the flowers from her. Then, with HelperFriend at his side, he went to the interior of the ruined dome.

Heart moved back to Equuleus, at a bit of distance from everyone. Yes, she had Equuleus, but she suddenly felt shockingly lonely. No Eye, no Swen, no Xavier, no Jackson, no Father, no Violet at her side.

But, at that moment, Violet burst from the ranks of the crowd and hopped up to her, looking up at Heart. Heart picked her up and hugged her close. "Thank you," she whispered.

From Violet's beautiful lavender eyes, sparkling violet tears fell upon Heart's wrist. Heart watched in fascination as her wrist turned lavender. She felt a different sort of sadness from her own course through her. *Ah!* This feeling, this strange but understood feeling, coursed through the entire population of mechanical and clockwork and hybrid beings.

A profound silence enveloped them. No one moved. No one spoke. The tableau of lavender dusk shifted as the light of Pink's moon, cresting the horizon, fell upon them. From within the dome came the unfathomably mysterious sound of HelperFriend's mystical, alien, moving music, echoing through the shattered dome, pouring out onto the open terrain.

Then, slowly, the *Heart!* hovered into view, close to the surface of Pink.

The *Heart!* Heart gasped. The last time she'd seen it, it had been ruined by the Bot Invasion. The last time she'd been in the *Heart!* was when she crawled through the shattered viewport to rescue Xavier.

She could have done with never seeing the *Heart!* again, but here it shone before her, rebuilt in all its glory, just as Xavier had originally constructed it. She knew now that Jackson, with the help of Pink's brilliant residents, had brought the *Heart!* back to its state of perfection.

Jackson sat at the controls with HelperFriend seated beside him, producing his *Song for Xavier*, full of pathos and strains of bravery, humor, laughter, cheer.

A perfect portrait of Xavier, somehow, in audio form. Xavier's mischievous grin, his twinkling green eyes, his dancing freckles came clearly into Heart's mind. His guileless expression of love—not just for her, but for every precious moment of life itself—was heard in HelperFriend's song.

As the *Heart!* slowly moved out onto the plain, Heart, holding Violet, and with Equuleus by her side, moved to her father.

"When you push this button," he said, handing her a small device, "it will slide open a section of the moon."

Heart nodded. She didn't want to push the button. She didn't want to release Xavier. But she would do as her father bid.

She put Violet on Equuleus's back and took the device from her father.

"And then say a few words."

"Oh, Father, I feel like it's so presumptuous of me. You, and all the residents of Pink have shared your lives with Xavier. And I ... I ...."

"Whatever you say, Heart, will resonate with everyone. Simply say what comes from your soul. It will be healing for everyone, including yourself."

The spacecraft's engines leapt into life, and the *Heart!* lifted away from Pink. With lightning speed, it rose into the air and jetted toward Pink's silvery moon.

HelperFriend's music continued as though he were still on the surface of Pink. All eyes raised and followed the trajectory of the *Heart!*

Jackson circumvented Pink's moon once, then hovered on the near side, anticipating the opening of the moon. Heart and her father exchanged a look, and she pressed the button. Slowly a section of the moon slid open. Then the back hatch of the *Heart!* opened and Jackson emerged, carrying his beloved cousin with his arms full of crystallized flowers. Even from this distance, they glinted with their sparkling, crystallized forms.

Heart's breath left her, and she trembled. Her father put his bulky, suited arm around her, steadied her. Then a strength came upon her. She sensed Xavier supporting her, just as he had done before.

"We honor one among us who insisted he was no better than anyone," Heart heard herself say. "Xavier, ever modest, ever brave, ever loving, ever shy, ever mischievous, ever brilliant—gave each of us a perfect template to imitate. We can do nothing more to honor him than to live as he lived, believe as he believed. He believed in love before, after, and through everything. We can champion the causes for right as he championed the rights of everyone.

"We can enjoy life as he enjoyed life—to know beauty, to understand beauty as he understood beauty. To give ourselves to being and ever becoming the best, the highest, the kindest, as ever we can.

"Remember how he loved candy? Just to stand before it and simply adore its charm. May we ever be charmed by simplicity.

"We thank you, dear Xavier, for saving us, for loving us, for entertaining us, and, now, too, forever and forever, watching over us. In whatever ways Pink may change and its population may shift and grow, you will always be caring for us, in Pink's day and through Pink's night.

"We love you, Xavier. Sweet dreams."

At her last words, Jackson emerged from the interior of the moon, having, Heart knew, spent a few moments talking with his cousin. Probably making some droll comment about Heart's long-winded discourse below, which could be heard over HelperFriend's music, now softened to a quiet lullaby while she spoke.

When she stopped speaking, she heard crying and sighing throughout the assemblage.

Jackson floated back through the hatch into the *Heart!,* which then made a leisurely trip back to the surface of Pink.

"Beautiful, my precious daughter," her father said. "Simply beautiful. No one, *no one* could have said it better." Tears streamed unashamedly down his face. "I'm so proud of you."

"The only person to be proud of at this moment is Xavier. He saved us."

"Yes. He did," he agreed. But he could not hide the unspoken disquiet in his tone.

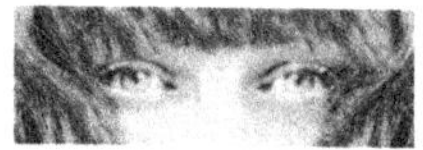

Chapter 5

After Jackson and HelperFriend stowed the *Heart!* in the dome where Heart did not have to look at it, her father invited them all to come inside.

"I thought you might like to see this, Heart and Jackson. I knew it'd be a bit hard on you Heart, so I didn't show you right away." He turned on a 3-D, and into the space between them leapt the sight of The Mystic's cottage. Outside her cottage, a bevy of people stood, watching a 3-D above them. Heart heard her own voice, as she made her statement of love and respect for Xavier.

There stood The Mystic, Zack, Amdrona, several people she did not know, and Swen's fully bio-dog cousin, she believed, at attention between Butterfly, and, of course, Eye.

At her first words, Eye gasped audibly, and Butterfly reached out to take his hand. As Heart heard her own voice, she saw Butterfly write what she saw of the *Heart!*'s journey to Pink's moon.

Oh, how Heart loved these people! How happy-sad it made her to see Eye, healthy and strong. Even becoming muscular and, strangely, "man-like." Her own little Eye. Growing up without her. She never would have imagined this future for them while they lived captive in The Darling Undesirables Residence of Long Prairie.

Heart looked at Jackson. He wore a stoic expression that revealed a need to endure yet more emotion. Even if the emotion was sweet. His look could be summed up in the phrase, "and this too."

"It's good that they were able to witness this ceremony," he finally said.

"Yes, Jackson," Heart agreed. "Very good, very painful for me, too, to see them, and be so far away. You, of course, will soon be returning to them."

Jackson gave her a hard look, yet more unspoken language, as if to say, "have you forgotten our conversation?"

Heart shook her head. "Not right now, Jackson. Besides, Equuleus needs to be present and he's outside."

"He's right there," Jackson pointed out the window, where Equuleus stood, watching the exchange between them, Violet on his back.

"I don't want Violet in on it. She'll run amok."

"True," Jackson agreed.

Heart's father looked from one to the other of them. "Why does this peculiar exchange make me extremely uncomfortable?"

"Just a moment." Jackson stepped outside, and while Heart and her father watched, removed Violet from Equuleus's back. setting her on the ground. She complained vociferously to no avail, of course, and then Jackson ushered Equuleus inside.

"Now, Heart, we must have this discussion."

"Sooner or later, yes. It may as well be now," she reluctantly agreed. "But, at the outset, I have to say, Father, that, unlike before, I am not favorable to this plan of Jackson's. I want to stay here, and be with you, and protect you, and help rebuild Pink."

"Of course," he agreed. "That's the only way I want it, too. Although it's awful for you to have to deal with the sad work that's at hand, it's what we must do. But before long, my dear, everything will be back to normal."

"Have you forgotten the single biggest problem we're facing?" Jackson asked.

"No," he replied quickly. "I have not, but it's ... we have to deal with the immediate situation, which is to bring Pink as close to its state before the Bot Invasion as we can. For morale. And to honor Xavier, which is important to everyone here, including me."

"With utmost respect, Father Inventor, I need to ask if you've studied Xavier's placement of the magnetic dark energy resonators on Earth when he set up the shield?"

Heart watched as her father hesitated, furrowing his brow. She'd never seen him disconcerted—which disconcerted her in turn. "I have not. Are you saying Xavier had specific intention with the placements beyond successfully mounting the shield to protect Yellow and Pink?"

"I am."

"Which is what?"

Jackson moved to the wall of 3-D projection and computing devices. "May I show you something?"

"Of course."

Jackson entered a code. Up came the image that he'd shown Heart. "Here are the locations of the four magnetic dark energy resonators."

Heart's father nodded. "I'm familiar with their placement."

"When I first looked at this," Jackson said, "I thought, now this is strange because one would think they'd either be equidistant from one another, or in some reasonable pattern. But they're not. They look randomly placed."

"I tried to argue," Heart interjected, "that it's because I insisted that one of them end up close to The Darling Undesirables Residence at Long Prairie, as that's where I needed to go."

"Yes," Jackson agreed. "Heart did try to make that argument. But it's irrelevant. The magnetic dark energy resonators could have been placed anywhere.

What's intriguing is the obvious thought Xavier put into the programming after the magnetic dark energy resonators were placed.

"When you engage their individual signals, they are wildly varying, which, again, seemed to make no sense. Except, I know Xavier. And, boyish as he may have seemed, he did nothing haphazard or random.

"I knew he had intention. Had things not been ... the way they were, we'd probably know why the resonators were seemingly illogical, random, signals. But if you ...."

"If you see where the signals intersect ...." Heart's father said with lightning insight.

"Precisely," Jackson agreed, turning on the two intersecting lines. "If you turn on the lines that intersect, you see they cross squarely over The Darling Undesirables Residence of Long Prairie."

Father Inventor reached into the 3-D, enlarging it. "Even more precisely," he observed, "it's squarely on the garden house in Keeper A's garden." He turned to Heart. "So you want to go to Earth, and again endanger yourself, to see what Xavier may— or may not!—have been trying to discover."

"No, Father. I do *not* want to go, which I told Jackson. I want to stay here. I want to be near you, to keep you protected. I want to help rebuild Pink. Although there are people and creatures on Earth I love, and would adore being near them, I do *NOT* feel this is a good time to leave Pink. But ... Jackson is insistent that I'm the only person—the *only being of any sort*—and I quote, who is an acceptable choice to go on this mission."

"Jackson," Heart's father said sternly, "have you qualms endangering Heart?"

"I do. But, even so, I am more concerned with the endangerment of all the beings the Purists are intent upon destroying. I'm intent upon finding your downloaded clone brain, Father Inventor. The Purists' movement continues. Their plans grow apace. How long will it be before your cloned brain figures out how to bring down the shield, neutralize it, or counter its energy in some way?

"The clone is focused on opposing everything you do, have done, and stand for. Pitted against you, to imagine what you might contrive in the future. Working, even as we hesitate here, to overtake and destroy all the Darling Undesirable facilities, wherever they may be. I ... I don't think we dare hesitate.

"Only Heart knows The Darling Undesirables Residence at Long Prairie like the back of her hand."

"I don't know Keeper A's garden at all," Heart protested. "She never let any of us in it. Not even Keepers, except perhaps one or two, that I ever saw."

"You still know the grounds better than anyone in *The Cause of All Beings*. And you are the only being I personally know, besides Amdrona, who can shapeshift. You are the only person who has an idea where all the 3-D cameras are located at The

Darling Undesirables Residence. And—if you come to believe, as I do, that Xavier intended to tell us something he did not have a chance to ...."

"He could have told me."

"When, exactly, Heart? When you were dying on the flight back to Pink? When you were recovering and surrounded by others? When, Heart? Only now, after he's departed, can he share with us his somewhat cryptic, but I'm certain, all-important message."

The room fell silent with the truth of Jackson's comment.

"Why did we nearly lose her, Jackson?" Heart's father asked. "Because she cannot be separated that long and that far from Equuleus. Have you forgotten that?"

"I have not, nor could I. HelperFriend and I will build an accommodation for Equuleus on the *Heart!*"

"On the *Heart!*" Heart fairly squeaked. "Even if ... *even if* this idea comes to fruition, I don't want to ride on the *Heart!* I don't want to go near the *Heart!*" Heart involuntarily shuddered.

"You won't be riding on the *Heart!*" Jackson said.

"Really? How am I to get to Earth, then?"

"You'll be flying the *Heart!* I'll have to fly my own spacecraft. Eventually, you and Equuleus will need to return to Pink, I'l need to stay on Earth." At this, Jackson paused, looking down, he sighed deeply. Gathering himself, he returned his attention to the 3-D hovering in the air between them, writing their future with its simple diagram.

"I'll be flying the *Heart!*—solo?" Heart asked, trying to believe what she heard.

"That's as it must be."

Heart, overwhelmed, fell silent, remembering how she'd wheedled Xavier to let her fly the *Heart!* and he'd said the time was not right. Apparently, the time had become right.

Life was nothing if not ironic, she mused.

"So far, that's not much of a plan," Heart's father observed.

"No, it's not," Jackson agreed. "I've been contriving it by myself. I need you, I need Peter, I need Zack. I need the other great minds waiting to be put into motion. All the great minds in *The Cause of All Beings*, gathered to staunch, once and for all, the wickedness of The Purists."

"Here, here," Equuleus said in subdued tones.

Everyone turned to him. "You are in favor of this fool's mission?" Heart asked, stunned. Every now and then, her own heart appeared to betray her.

"I am."

"Say more," Heart demanded.

"Our purpose, Heart, is to make the world a better place for all beings. You are a hybrid, I am clockworks, we are freaks, sorry Father, no insult intended ...."

Father Inventor inclined his head in acquiescence to Equuleus's comment. "We are anomalies of consciousness that The Purists will forever attempt to eliminate. We will never live a free life, you will never know the flowering of your deepest desires, Heart, until the mindset of the Purists has changed. We must attempt to get at the root of it, to begin to change it.

"At present, our Father's clone is the single biggest challenge in the path of that goal. You know, and I know, Heart, that Xavier did nothing by accident. A child with arrested-development, a devoted friend, but do not forget, a brilliant strategist. There is, no doubt, something of vital importance likely to be discovered in Keeper A's garden."

Stunned and wordless, Heart looked from Jackson, looking down, nodding thoughtfully, to her father, upon whose features settled an utterly unfathomable look of perplexity.

"What are you thinking, Father?"

"A variety of things so complex and numerous, they defy vocalizing."

With that cryptic answer, Heart turned her attention to Equuleus. "And—you're willing to be somehow tied down in the *Heart!*, with me, not a pilot, hating to be in the *Heart!*, at the helm?"

"Where you go, I go. In addition, I have complete faith in Jackson's ability to teach, and your ability to learn. You readily took my instruction when I taught you how to ride me, and I'm sure you'll do the same with the *Heart!*"

"Well," Heart interjected, "with one exception."

"Yes. One dramatic exception. Do not jump out of the *Heart!* while it's still in flight," Equuleus said.

"Oh, so funny," Heart noted with honeyed sarcasm.

Chapter 6

Heart and her father, both now precariously recruited to Jackson's underdeveloped plan, shamed into it by the clockworks horse, began to build upon it.

Still hating the idea of having anything at all to do with the *Heart!*, much less actually learning to pilot it, Heart did her best to set aside her pain to imagine becoming as lean and mean a soldier as Jackson. Or, at least, her best imitation. Again she recalled when she'd begged Xavier to teach her how to fly the *Heart!*

Now, strangely, the day had arrived.

After some time, HelperFriend came cautiously into Father Inventor's room. "Sorry to bother ... sorry!" he apologized. "I know you're engrossed in extremely important business, but, I must remind you that you've gone a considerable length of time without pause or repast. And, although that's fine for Heart and Equuleus, it's not fine for fully bios, Jackson, and even less fine for Father Inventor, pushing two-hundred-and-fifty years and needing to eat!"

"Do not hold my age up to me," Heart's father protested. "I'm fine."

"Let's not push it then," Heart said. "I'm feeling a bit bored anyway. I'd like to spend some time assimilating this gigantic task we're making for ourselves."

"Good idea," Jackson agreed. He began to climb into protective gear. "Before eating, I've really got to move about."

"Me too," Heart agreed. "See you at dinner, Father."

He nodded and waved them outside, while he and HelperFriend moved to the interior of the castle, no doubt the kitchen, where, Heart knew, her father enjoyed chatting with HelperFriend, while HelperFriend worked his culinary magic for bios and non-bios alike.

Outside, though it was the darkest it ever became on Pink, even though never a true darkness, great activity flurried about. Powerful lights shone upon the new infrastructure being put in place for the dome. Fascinated, Heart watched intently as numerous hands of every description worked in perfect concert to raise the open grid work.

"Didn't you want to move about?" Jackson asked, clearly antsy.

"Yes. But this ... this is monumental." She continued her mesmerized gaze.

"Right. Well, I'm off. You can give me a full report at dinner."

Heart nodded, and off Jackson ran. "I wonder where Lady Gervi is," she said to Equuleus. "I haven't seen her all day. I feel a bit guilty not checking in on her."

As if summoned, Lady Gervi and Yippee came to stand beside her.

"Stunning sight, no?"Lady Gervi asked.

Startled, Heart turned to her. "I was just thinking about you!"

"And I, you," Lady Gervi said. Yippee jumped up and down and yipped with glee.

Heart tore her eyes from the incredible sight to reach down and pet Yippee. She jumped back in shock. "You're standing! Oh, Lady Gervi! Your leg, I mean, *oh!*" A giant wheel took the place of Lady Gervi's destroyed leg, It was attached to the end of a pole, attached to her body, her shattered leg having been amputated. Or however, Heart thought, clockworks referred to having a body part removed.

"Yes. Isn't it wonderful? HelperFriend is well-named! A helper and a friend. He's so thoughtful to come up with this invention. I can really get around on this giant wheel. In fact, when I learn to balance on it, Yippee can pull me around!"

At a complete loss for words, and still in shock at the appearance of the beautiful lady with this freakish contrivance, Heart could only think to say, "He's a very little dog!"

Lady Gervi's gear-face smile faded. "He's a machine, he's quite strong!"

"Yes. Of course. I didn't think it through. I see you'll enjoy the experience."

"Well, one must make the best of one's situation. I'm so much better off than many members of my family." She gestured at the hustle and bustle before them, where even badly damaged mechanical and clockwork beings worked unflaggingly.

Heart nodded. "But, dear lady, are you ... do you ... is this the result you prefer for yourself?"

The majestic lady looked down at her little dog, who stared intently up at her in return. "Of course I would prefer my leg, intact. I don't as much care about being able to move about rapidly, as I care to move about *grandly*."

Heart nodded, "That's precisely what I would have anticipated you to say, Lady Gervi." A plan began to form at that moment that would make her trip to Earth—if she must go in the midst of all that was happening here—more enjoyable. "Are you joining us for dinner?"

"No, Heart, thank you kindly for your invitation. But I feel I must join the work. Able-bodied as I am, thanks to you, dear Heart and HelperFriend, I can do much to move the work forward. Also, I'll be staying in the dome from now on, though the sweet room will always stay in my memory as a wonderful dream."

"Oh!" Heart said, disappointed. She liked thinking that Lady Gervi, though clockworks and so different from herself in every regard, but still, feminine, lived in the castle. Heart hadn't realized how specific and warm this feeling, until now, when Lady Gervi said she would no longer be there. "The room is always yours, any time you feel like staying the night. I'll have HelperFriend leave it as we arranged it."

Lady Gervi gave Heart a huge hug, startling her nearly as much as she'd been startled by the sight of the lady's wheel-replaced leg. "You're so precious, Heart. Truly. I will tell you, though, as a secret between us—if any of those folks heard me say this, they'd think I had really crossed a line. I *sooooo* loved reading! It came easily. I guess I have something in my components that knows how to read. I honestly wasn't sure I could.

"I love those old physical books, the rustle-y pages and, well everything about it. All the information, and the stories, the wonderful made-up stories. Ummm ... that part I will miss. I read every book HelperFriend brought to me."

"Every one? Goodness, he brought about thirty books I think."

"Oh, yes, those first books, I read the first night. I asked HelperFriend to bring me more books, and he brought me armloads of books. Just about as fast as he could bring them, I read them. Of course he had other things he must do, and so there were times when I simply waited for him to bring more books."

"*Ah! Amazing!* Amazing, Lady Gervi. Quite phenomenal. Are you certain you want to leave the castle?"

"To be truthful, I'm torn. But I must be about this business. The dome needs to be reconstructed. The morale of The Folks will be much stronger when the view is familiar."

"Very true," Heart agreed. "But when the dome is reconstructed, then you and Yippee must come and be my guest." Heart saw Violet hopping toward them. "Where have you been?" She called to the little lavender rabbit.

"I might ask as much of *you!*" Violet retorted, sounding hurt.

"Oh! Violet, come here."

Juicing it to the limit, Violet dragged her rabbity feet toward Heart, ears flopped over her eyes, head hanging.

Chuckling, Heart picked her up and hugged her. "You are a silly little rabbit."

"I *am not*. Well, yes, I am, a little bit. Never mind me, did you see the wonderful thing HelperFriend has done for Lady Gervi?"

"I have! It's so thoughtful of our HelperFriend." Heart gave Lady Gervi a sad little smile. "Well, I'm unhappy to learn that Lady Gervi and sweet Yippee are leaving the castle to stay in the dome. And no doubt, they will work far too hard."

"Oh!" Violet said, shocked, "Just like that? You're leaving? I hope it's not because of anything I may have said or done."

"No, not at all, sweet Violet. You've been a radiance in our lives, isn't that so, Yippee?" Lady Gervi said.

As usual, any question directed at Yippee resulted in an avalanche of vocalizations that everyone but Heart, so it seemed to her, understood.

Jackson came striding up to them. "What is the dog going on about?"

"Waxing poetic on Violet's many charms," Heart surmised.

"Which I never tire of hearing," Violet sang from Heart's arms.

"Which she never tires of hearing," Heart confirmed.

"Wonderful contrivance, that wheel, Lady Gervi," Jackson observed. "Was it your idea?"

"No. It's the brilliance of our ever-remarkable HelperFriend."

"Excellent. Well, I don't mean to be rude, but I *am* bio. I'm tired of being trapped in this suit, and I'm ravenous, so, into the dining hall I go. Are you with me, Heart?"

"I'm with you," she replied to Jackson's back. She turned to Lady Gervi. "I look forward to your next visit. Remember, all the books in the castle are yours to read."

"I'll remember!" Lady Gervi went spinning off on her wheel and leg to the industrious group at the dome.

Still holding Violet, Heart, with Equuleus, followed Jackson into her father's room, where Jackson pulled off the bulky, ill-fitting protective gear. "Whew! The best part of that thing is getting out of it."

"Yes," Heart appeared to agree. "Well, there's also that part about keeping you alive. That's perhaps worth mentioning."

"Right. The 'keeping alive' part, also good. *Let's go!* Starving." Jackson sped down the hall to the dining room, Heart, Violet, and Equuleus following.

Jackson found his place and, without ceremony, sat and began to eat.

Somewhat appalled, Heart exchanged a look with her father. He shrugged. "The warrior must be replenished. Don't be shocked, Heart. He's fully bio."

Jackson, both hands filled with breaking a small loaf of bread, looked up to see even Violet watching him with mystification. "Ah ... sorry. I left my manners on Earth."

"Clearly," Violet said. "Goodness, sir!" she remonstrated in her quirky little voice, which made everyone giggle.

Jackson put down his bread. "Thank you, *all Powers that Be*," he intoned, "for this nurturing feast, and for every Being at this table. I am truly grateful."

"Amen," Father Inventor said.

"Well said, Jackson," Heart added. "You are a mystification."

"I'm an Earth man, of The Periphery."

"Perhaps no more need be said," Heart's father observed, patting Heart's hand poised on her water glass.

"Perhaps." Heart nodded.

She looked at the beautiful arrangement on the table that HelperFriend had "whipped up" for them in short order. "Spectacular as always, dear HelperFriend. Thank you for considering each one of us and our various peculiar needs."

HelperFriend's eyes twirled as he looked bashfully down. "Thank you, Heart. It's nothing special. I just follow what I know, and hope it's right."

"It's quite special! *You're* quite special. While I'm thinking about it, it's amazing what you've done for Lady Gervi." She turned to her father, "Have you seen his inventiveness for her, Father?"

"No. What did you do for Lady Gervi, Helper-Friend? And, by the way, where is she?"

"She's decided to rejoin The Folks, and contribute to the reconstruction, thanks to HelperFriend's brilliance. He removed her damaged leg and replaced it with a giant wheel, attached to tubing, attached to her body. She's able to get about quite effectively now."

"Oh! Clever!" her father replied. But Heart could see he had much the same thought as she did, when picturing Lady Gervi with a giant wheel in place of her graceful leg.

"Was this your own idea, or had Lady Gervi thought of it?"

"Oh, it was my own idea. It grew out of my contriving to put the wheels on the chair. I thought, why put wheels on a chair? Why not put one on Lady Gervi? So I made a wheel out of scrap metals, and devised a means to attach it. Then I told Lady Gervi about it." As he talked, HelperFriend attended to everyone's water glass, filling each in turn.

"I told her how completely mobile she'd be, and she'd be able to join everyone in the reconstruction. Well, of course, she was all for that. So then I had her lie down and I sawed off her leg, and attached the wheel. And, as you see, she's getting around wonderfully."

"So," Heart's father asked, "You didn't actually *ask* her if she wanted to have her leg sawed off to be replaced with a wheel?"

HelperFriend stopped with water pitcher and water glass in hand. "Ahm ... noooo, I didn't actually ask her. Ask her ..." HelperFriend's eye and head gears twirled, but, otherwise, he completely froze.

"Oh dear, Father. I'm afraid you broke HelperFriend." Heart didn't know if she meant to be teasing, or if she'd said a truth.

"HelperFriend?" her father said. No response from the gear man. "HelperFriend?"

Everyone stopped eating. Everyone watched HelperFriend's eye and head gears spinning frantically in a loop.

"I think he's really shorted out," Heart whispered, now deeply alarmed.

"I fear you're right," her father agreed. "HelperFriend, attend!" he commanded.

Still the water pitcher and glass were held in mid-air, still, his gears rotated in a loop that now had an audible click.

"Oh, that can't be good," Heart said.

"No, it can't. I hate to take a stronger action, because it will wipe out some of his memory. In fact, I don't know how far-reaching it might be. But it looks like the loop is grinding deeper. I don't want him to burn out a circuit."

Her father got up from the table and walked around to HelperFriend. He tried to take the water pitcher and glass from his hands, but HelperFriend would not release them. He studied his pocket watch a moment, then held onto the pitcher and water glass and said, "Clockworks HelperFriend: X77X7, reset, 20 nil 20."

HelperFriend's hands fell to his sides, leaving Father Inventor holding the pitcher and water glass, which he placed on the table.

HelperFriend's gears became unstuck. His eyes twirled, and he looked bashfully down between his feet. "Thank you, Heart. It's nothing special. I just follow what I know, and hope it's right."

Then he noticed Father Inventor standing right before him and became confused. "How did you do that? You were sitting right there!" HelperFriend pointed to Father Inventor's chair.

"I surprised you!" he said laughing.

Confused, HelperFriend tried to laugh too.

Heart's father turned to her and advised, "No memory of subsequent conversation. Not to re-trigger." He quickly returned to his seat.

"Of course not!" Heart agreed. "I believe you were about to pour me a glass of water," she said, smiling at HelperFriend. "Yes, I say again, what culinary wonders you perform. We are all grateful, are we not?"

"Oh, yes," everyone chorused while, still appearing disoriented, HelperFriend filled Heart's water glass.

Heart leaned over to her father and whispered, "What might happen when he sees Lady Gervi?"

"I don't know, Heart. I'm relieved that he appears to be intact at this point. I've never had to do a reset with him, and, as we both know, he can be surprisingly sophisticated, with unanticipated learning and reasoning capacity. So, well, *I don't know.*"

"I guess it's good, then, that Lady Gervi has decided to return to the dome. He won't encounter her change right away. Of course, she or someone will reference what he did, and thank him again."

"You're right. We'll simply have to wait and see how it sorts out. HelperFriend is always most interesting. I learn as much from him as ever I teach him."

Heart chuckled, "I've said almost the same exact words to him myself! But, Father, where do you suppose the ... appendage is? If it's in his rooms, and he encounters it ...."

"Oh! Right! *Hmmm* ...."

"You keep him occupied after dinner—I'll go through his rooms and Lady Gervi's room, and hope to find it."

"Yes, that's a good idea."

"All right, enough whispering over there between the two of you," Jackson ordered.

"How rude of us," Heart laughed, exchanging a glance with Jackson. "Now I guess, we're even. Violet, Equuleus and HelperFriend appear to be the only folks with good manners at dinner tonight."

"No argument," Equuleus agreed.

After dinner, Jackson hied himself off to bed, with, again, nearly as much ceremony as he had dived into dinner. With a nod to her father, Heart headed for HelperFriend's rooms, Equuleus, with Violet on his back, by her side.

"Where are we going?" Violet demanded. You're going to the back of the castle."

"Yes, Violet, I am."

"But why?"

"I'd rather not chat about it, in case Helper-Friend is more hooked up to me than I know."

"Oh. Because, hmm, no, I don't know." Violet tugged on her ears with her little paws, showing her frustration to be left out.

"Use your logic," Equuleus suggested, with the slightest edge of irritation.

"I see, you've figured it out, all by yourself," Violet retorted.

"Yes."

"Oh."

"Get along, *or* be quiet. Or get along, *and* be quiet. Either way, b*e quiet*. I'm trying to think," Heart ordered.

"Sorry Heart," Violet apologized meekly. But then, unable to endure the fact that everyone but herself knew what was going on, she continued. "But, sorry to interrupt your thoughts Heart, but could you give me a clue, like, a tiny clue?"

"No. Hush. Hush, or I'll set you outside."

"*Oh!*" Violet hushed.

They'd come to HelperFriend's rooms. Heart hadn't even thought about the possibility that he might have them locked, with all his programming about security that she'd encountered with him before. But she was relieved when she tried the door and it readily opened.

Everything in his rooms was clockwork neat and organized. Spartan, with a couple of books on a small table. Heart glanced at the title of the top one, "Clockworks of the World's Most Famous Inventor," with a picture of her father standing by the clockworks moon, housed in The Museum of Scientific Improbabilities and Unpredictable Oddities.

The moon looked new and shiny, and her father, as well, looked younger.

"Ah," she said to Equuleus, pointing at the cover. "Long before my time."

Equuleus looked at the cover, then looked at Heart, somewhat strangely and cryptically, Heart thought. But her attention was directly taken by what she saw in her line of sight. There, quite unceremoniously, on the small desk lay Lady Gervi's leg, hanging over both ends.

"*Ohhhhhhhhhhh!*" Violet sighed with sudden insight. "Of course! You are so smart, Heart!"

"I don't know about that. But we do have to take care of our HelperFriend, don't we?"

"We do indeed," Violet agreed. "You too, Mr. Horse. Brilliant. What's wrong with me, I wonder, that I didn't figure it out?"

"Nothing's wrong with you, Violet. You're brilliant in your own way. Now, we'll just take this ...." Heart hefted Lady Gervi's leg. "Whoa, pretty heavy. Jump down, Violet."

Violet complied and Heart placed the disembodied leg on Equuleus's back. "Now, there's a weird sight, I have to say."

"Strange, yes, very odd," Violet agreed.

"All right, to my rooms with this to figure out a way to hide it for the time being, in case Helper-Friend comes into my rooms."

"What are you going to do with it, Heart. I mean, wouldn't you ... recycle it or something?"

"Eventually, yes, I imagine so. But not just yet."

"Oh, another plan. I suppose you know all about this, too?" Violet asked Equuleus.

"No. For once, I have no idea what she's contriving."

Heart kept silent.

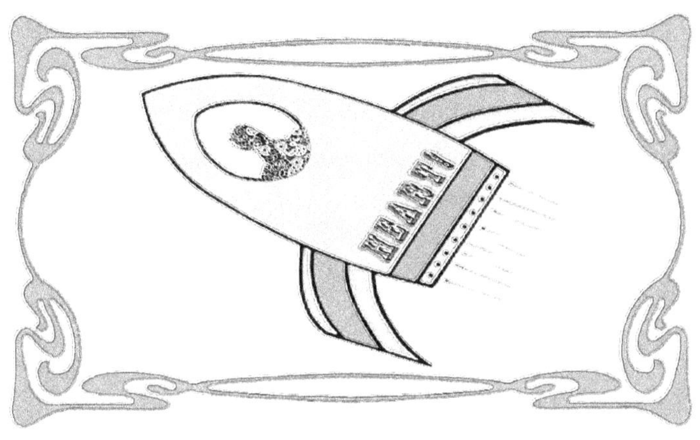

Chapter 7

The next twilight-y morning when Pink's moon rose, Heart stole from her bed, leaving Violet and Equuleus in stasis. She slipped over to the castle window. The smallest curve of Pink's moon began to crest the horizon.

The first moonrise carrying Xavier and flowers around Pink. She wondered if Xavier would show himself to her through the moon.

Her secret—her precious secret that let her carry on—was that Xavier remained with her. She knew she dared tell no one—even if she'd wanted to, which she did not. They would, everyone from her father to Jackson to Equuleus to Violet and even, probably, HelperFriend, would try to convince her not to believe this to be true.

But it was true. Though, with all the endless activity of the previous day there had been no communication from Xavier, she now needed him to talk with her.

So she watched as the moon's perfect sphere sailed into the sky. "Where are you, Xavier?" she thought. "Where are you?"

As the moon spilled the reflection of Earth's sun upon Pink in the light that passed for day, she felt Xavier moving about in her mind.

"There," she said. "There you are."

"So lovely and touching, what you and Father Inventor and Jackson and The Folks did to honor me yesterday. So sweet the words you said about me. Oh, my, so much more than I deserve. But, thank you."

"Not enough, Xavier, Not enough. But it is the most that we have and can do. So ... you're all right with ... with the shell of you placed in Pink's moon?"

"Yes. But more to the point, it doesn't matter. Doesn't matter Heart—except for those to whom it matters. The Folks, You. Father. Jackson. The Mystic, as you call her. Zack. It doesn't matter to me. The flowers, though, Heart, those do matter to me. Your thought, our connection, the flowers, yes, that is precious and generous."

"Not generous, Xavier. Flowers are for sharing and for remembering. I've never put flowers to a higher use." Heart watched the moon climb Pink's sky. "Jackson intends to give me flying lessons in the *Heart!* What do you think?"

"I can't think about such things, Heart. I'm fast upon creating my next life. What I fear—I fear you're becoming too dependent upon me. I've been willing to staying in the between but I fear it's not good for you. And earthly concerns are ... small to me now.

"I'm not without compassion. I just know that everything works out for the best. Eventually and ultimately, everything works out for the best. So, it's not right for you to keep yourself tied to me. I ... I'm not going to visit you anymore, now, Heart. In this moment, you need to be present there, not half there and half with me."

"No. It's all right, Xavier. It is." Cold fear rushed through Heart at the thought of Xavier fully removing himself from her.

"It's not all right, Heart. You're going to begin flying lessons with Jackson. You must be fully, fully present in the three dimensions. *Fully!* You can't have some sector of yourself off with an energy form in an external dimension. It was fine at first. We both needed it. But now, we both need—separation.

"My mortal shell has been laid to rest, and you must lay me to rest, too. Move forward with the amazing things you'll accomplish ... if you're fully present."

"I'll be present, Xavier. I promise. Just ... don't leave me! I keep losing everyone. But you and I ... you always said you would love me forever!"

"I do and I will. But that doesn't mean I'll always be present with you, there. Focus on what Jackson has to teach you. Focus on Jackson, altogether. He knows what he's doing, and he's carrying the burden of *The Cause of All Beings* upon himself. Don't make him do it alone. You are brilliant and loving, Heart. *Help him!*"

"I will Xavier, I will. Just. Don't. Leave. Me."

"I won't leave directly, Heart. But, I must be upon my own journey."

"*Oh!*" Heart whispered faintly, then returned to her thought-communication. "I'm being stunningly selfish—I'm not thinking about you! You have a journey to embark upon, and I'm keeping you from it! Why did I not realize this? All right, Xavier. I will become stronger. I will do as you say. I will pay closer attention to Jackson. I will ... I will begin to release you. But, please, let me do it in my own way. May I?"

"Of course, dearest Heart. I love you more than life itself. Well, life goes on forever, so I suppose one can only love *as much as* life itself, as they are one and the same. Now, please, dearest Heart, get upon your mission. It calls to you. I did, as Jackson has pointed out, lay down an important clue for him and for you, which, yes I had intended to reveal to you. But other events intervened."

"Will you tell me what I'll find if I go on this mission?"

"I'll not tell you the details, as the unfolding of life is its thrill. Even the narrow passages are part of the pleasure. But you're headed in the right direction, as long as you and Jackson *get along*."

"Good morning!" Violet called cheerily from the bed.

Smiling, but sad, Heart turned to her little friend. "Good morning, Violet."

Equuleus put his fourth foot down, stirring from his stasis. He whinnied affectionately. Heart went to him and patted his muzzle. "Big day today, dear Equuleus. *Flying lessons!*"

"Flying lessons. Play nice and listen carefully to Jackson, Heart."

"Oh, why do you even say that?"

"You know why. It's ridiculous the way the two of you waste so much energy sparring."

"Ah, Equuleus, don't you know it's not a was*te* of energy—it *inspires* energy? Keeps us going, matching wits."

"Interesting," Equuleus observed. "I'm glad you and I need not have such an interaction."

"Oh, *us*, Equuleus, we are one, that's different. Shall we fly down?"

"Let's!" Violet hopped off the bed and looked up expectantly at Heart.

She reached down to pick up Violet, then jumped on Equuleus. He trotted out of Heart's rooms and jumped from the landing. Around and around he flew in the castle's rotunda, in high spirits.

HelperFriend came into the foyer below, watching them while Equuleus gradually flew to the marble floor below.

"Beautiful, *beautiful* form!" HelperFriend exclaimed, facial gears clicking and spinning in delight.

When they landed, Heart leapt off Equuleus and gave HelperFriend a gigantic hug.

Grinning and hugging her back, he asked, "What's that for?"

"Just because you're you!" she answered, thinking of the close call they'd had the night before when it seemed, briefly, she might lose her friend.

HelperFriend hugged her some more. "All right. I like that reason. I'm hugging you more, just because you're you!"

"Will someone please hug me because I'm me?" Violet squeaked.

Heart picked Violet off Equuleus's back and she and HelperFriend both hugged her.

"All right, enough hugging. You're squishing me!" Violet protested.

"Now then, we must all hug Equuleus, because he's him."

"Ahm ... that's all right," Equuleus moved back a couple paces. "I get the gist. We have flying lessons to begin. As usual, we're waiting on the bio to get up and become animated."

"You talking about me?" Jackson said, coming into their midst, rolling his shirt sleeves up, biceps rippling, readying himself for a challenging day.

Heart looked hard at Jackson. Xavier had told her to pay attention to him. And so, she would.

"Are you ready, Heart?"

"Ready, sir!" She snapped a salute. Violet giggled and HelperFriend stepped back.

They made their way to Father Inventor's room, passing the dining hall on the way, a beautiful breakfast spread across the dining table.

"Are you not going to have breakfast?" HelperFriend asked a bit piteously.

"No time to sit down to breakfast," Jackson muttered, plowing ahead. "If you bring something to the *Heart!* though, it will be much appreciated."

"I'll do that!" HelperFriend said, apparently appeased. "Right now, or later?"

"Later. Right now, HelperFriend, I need you to help me bring the *Heart!* out on the plain. There are so many of The Folks running around, and so much reconstruction going on, I need you to make sure I don't damage anything or run over anyone."

"Good thinking, Jackson," HelperFriend agreed.

They arrived at Father Inventor's door, and Heart knocked. "It's us, your tribe," she called.

He opened the door, looking fatigued.

Heart's smile faded. "What's wrong?"

"I've been in communication with some of my … constituents. The Purists are on the move. They appear to be about ready to overtake The Darling Undesirables Facility of Eastern Shore."

"Oh, that's the one in the South," Heart replied, alarmed. "I haven't been there. I hear the keepers are generally nicer than the keepers I had to live with. What's happening?"

"Apparently a Purist movement attempted to breach The Darling Undesirables Facility of Eastern Shore. The neighbors, the people in the neighborhood, quelled them."

"*Really?*" Heart exclaimed. "Good for them! I hope no one ...."

"You don't want to know, Heart. But ... here's some 3-D." her father brought up a newshound story. "Brace yourself, Heart. You won't like what you're about to see."

Immediately there appeared a new generation of violent bots, looking slightly humanoid, with heads without features, and torsos, but, still, too many whirling appendages.

"No weaponry from them though," Heart observed.

"Trying to pretend they're staying within the limits of the law. But, of course, if they get a foothold ...."

As they watched the bots and The Purists, which, Heart was relieved to see, were not many, probably only about fifty people, but a hundred bots, converged on The Darling Undesirables Residence of Eastern Shore, people came out of houses and shouted at the Purists. They all ended up brawling in human and bot heaps, without weapons.

Before long, the People's Guards were on the scene, carrying away Purists, neighborhood residents and bots alike, piling them into several People's Guard Dark Energy Highway vehicles and whisking them off to who-knew-where.

"Was anyone there from *The Cause of All Beings.* Father?"

"It's hard to tell. Of course, some of the residents may be."

"It's awful. But it's also reassuring to see that people—ordinary people!—will protect *The Darling Undesirables.*"

"Agreed," her father said quietly.

"But?"

"But—it's not enough."

"No. It's not enough. What do you think, Jackson?"

He'd suited up and now stood by the exit door. "I think it's time to get at our flying lessons. We've no time to waste. This event shows us what we already know. Let's go."

"Yes, sir," Heart thought better of her snappy salute, which was, she had to admit to herself, just a tiny, little bit sarcastic. "Don't stress, Father. I've never seen you this peaked. It won't do us any good if you over-extend yourself so that you're not in the best possible position to advise us. We're counting on you!"

"Yes, of course, you're right, Heart. I must pay attention to self-care. I've always done that naturally, but now, the stakes are high. They revolve around you, my dearest. And, yes, I do become emotional. Not the best place from which to make strategic decisions. But now, go learn to fly the *Heart!* then come and show off for me."

Heart chuckled. Well, she didn't mind showing off her ability to fly the *Heart!*—the sooner she accomplished that, the better.

They made their way through the throngs of busy workers. Heart, thrilled to see the open infrastructure of the dome in place, with it now only needing to be covered. Then, the overall view would be almost as before the Bot Invasion.

Under the partially open dome, there remained much work to be done. Blackened and twisted metal hung about like giant cobwebs into the far reaches of the dome, while busy workers of all descriptions scurried about on them, bringing them down into heaps of scrap below.

Heart and her entourage wended their way to where the *Heart!* sat. Seeing it in its proper place gave Heart an unanticipated jolt. All the memories of her stowing away on the *Heart!* to go to Earth and save Eye came roaring up to the surface of her mind.

"Come along!" Jackson ordered, looking back at her as he stepped through the back hatch of the *Heart!* She'd stopped in her tracks without realizing it.

"Coming!" She hurried after HelperFriend into the *Heart!*, leaving Equuleus and Violet at the railing outside.

"HelperFriend, would you put your mind to rigging up something that will accommodate Equuleus?"

"Yes. Sure. All right. Ahm. Wait."

Heart sat in the copilot's seat beside Jackson. She turned to look at HelperFriend. His tone of voice sounded odd. His face and head gears spun. "Oh-oh, Jackson. Something's not right with HelperFriend."

"He'll sort it out. Now, pay attention. I'm going to go through everything on the instrument panel, and then I'll have you say it back to me. Please turn around and pay attention."

Heart unstrapped her safety harness and went over to HelperFriend. "What's wrong, Helper-Friend?"

"Heart!" Jackson commanded.

"Yes," HelperFriend agreed. "Something is wrong. I'm to determine a means of accommodating Equuleus. But, wait, there's something new. Must process."

"All right, HelperFriend. Take your time, sort it out."

Jackson sighed.

Heart gave him a "don't you dare speak," glance.

"*Oh!*" HelperFriend exclaimed. "I must ask Equuleus first. I must ask if I can make an arrangement to accommodate him here. I must not assume he wants me to."

"Ah!" Heart nodded, looking over her shoulder at Jackson. "I see, new learning. Well, we want you to be sure you feel great about helping Equuleus, don't we, Jackson?"

All but rolling his eyes, Jackson squeezed out a "sure."

Heart gestured to Equuleus through the viewport that he join them. When he did, Heart said, "Jackson has asked HelperFriend to think about an accommodation for you here in the *Heart!*, and HelperFriend has some new programming that requires him to ask you if you want him to do that."

"Oh!" Violet exclaimed from Equuleus's back, "Wonderful new programming, HelperFriend. Very thoughtful!"

"Yes, HelperFriend. I would like you to consider how I might be accommodated in the *Heart!*, which seems nearly impossible, as I look inside. But I know you'll come up with an excellent plan."

"I believe it would be better if I designed your accommodation for you sitting on the floor, rather than standing. I'm thinking of how comfortable you always look by the mantle, seated in your place, during dinnertime."

Equuleus nodded his head. "That's very thoughtful, HelperFriend, thank you. With that picture in mind, I know you will contrive something quite appropriate."

"I agree!" Heart added, relieved to see HelperFriend's whirling, twirling gears relax their frenetic whirring.

"I agree, too," Jackson said, less than patient. "May we move on?"

"We may," Heart had to clamp her lips tight to keep from appending, "Or we may not." Note to self, she thought, not necessary to add more irritation to the irritated soldier.

She returned to the co-pilot seat, HelperFriend's gears clicked contentedly as he measured the space with his calculator eyes, and came up with plans Heart hoped dearly would suit everyone.

Jackson named each component of the instrument panel adding a brief description, then asked. "How much of that sank in?"

Keeping a lid on her umbrage, Heart recited back to him what he'd said, word for word.

"Not bad," he admitted.

"Not only not bad," Heart quipped, "but very good. I'm giving myself the highest marks."

"Right. Let's see how you do, orchestrating the whole process."

"Ready when you are, my *capitan!*"

"'Jackson' will do just fine, Heart."

They taxied through the interior of the dome. Everyone stopped their work and formed a line on either side of the *Heart!* An undulating cheer rose up as they moved along the spontaneously formed path. In every mechanical, clockworks, bio or hybrid face, love, hope, trust, and adoration poured out to Heart and Jackson. HelperFriend came and stood behind them to take in the sight.

"Oh!" HelperFriend whispered. "Look, Heart."

"I know, HelperFriend. Love. Pure ... *love*." She glanced at Jackson, curious how he perceived this stark display of emotion. His furrowed brow said more to Heart than any flow of words. He appeared deeply touched.

The three of them remained silent as the *Heart!* moved slowly among Pink's population, many of the individuals broken and blackened like the very dome itself had been. They gave their all.

They cheered, they waved, they reached out, they cried. All of one mind, one thought, one goal. Love. Love of one another, love of their home, love of their life—they shared one heart—whether they had a physical heart or not.

Heart reached up her hand for HelperFriend. He took her hand, in his hand's whirring clockwork embrace, as they silently shared the moment.

Heart noticed Jackson glance at them, brow furrowing deeper, a longing fleetingly passing his features. Then they closed down again as he attended to maneuvering the *Heart!* out onto the plain.

At the end of the two lines of Pink's residents, Heart's father stood in his protective gear, hands clasped at his chest, face glowing with pride and love.

"Oh!" HelperFriend cried. "Oh, oh! *Too much!*"

Heart looked up at him, and his charming, funny, sweet metallic tears began to fall upon Heart and turn to little bits of copper, bronze and brass droplets. "Sorry, Heart, sorry. Oh, dear, I'm all too ... too ...."

Heart unlatched her safety harness, and made HelperFriend sit. "You needn't apologize, sweet friend. Your tears are touching, adorable." Heart gathered HelperFriend's tears and looking around, spied a small box wedged into a nook on the floor under the instrument panel. She pulled it out and opened it, stunned to see hovering there a 3-D of herself as a young child saying, repeatedly *"Stars! Stars! Stars!"*

Oh! Xavier! Heart thought, disquieted.

"Sounds like you, Heart," Jackson said, "on the 3-D interview with the newshound when you were a child."

"Um, it is." She poured HelperFriend's tears into the little box—how appropriate!—closed it and replaced the box where she found it. She felt, as HelperFriend had just said ... all too ... *too.*

Jackson stopped the *Heart!* on the plain when they'd moved a distance from the dome. "All right, Heart. It's time to begin earning all that display of faith in us we've witnessed."

"You're right, Jackson. Now, my friend," she said to HelperFriend, "I must have my place back, and you must get yourself situated. *We're going for the ride of your life!"*

"Oh, Heart—how exciting. Yes, yes, I sit, *we fly!"* HelperFriend leapt up, assisted Heart in fastening her safety harness, then retreated to the back of the *Heart!* and Heart locked him in place to the wall by magnetic force. *"Let's go!"*

"Watch carefully, Heart," Jackson said, as he flipped switches and pushed buttons, explaining the sequence of events as he went.

Suddenly, Heart became distracted by Equuleus flying by in front of them, Violet hanging on with all her might. Heart giggled, but she felt an edge of worry. Violet had never ridden solo on Equuleus, and Heart feared she could not hang on for long. But their show gave her a laugh, and, HelperFriend from the back of the *Heart!* joined in.

"Oh, they are too funny, those two!" he said.

"Yes, funny, but I hope Violet can hang on."

Violet hung on! Her lavender ears streaming out behind, her comical rabbity grin, and, at the same time, obviously chattering away, filled with glee.

"What next?" Jackson said under his breath, exasperated.

"I think the spontaneous show is over, Jackson," Heart laughed as Equuleus landed near her father, Violet jumping up and down on his back, plainly pleased with herself.

"Right. I shall start over."

"Let me, Jackson." Heart began flipping switches and pushing buttons in precise imitation of Jackson, and quoting him, word for word. She took the wheel as the *Heart!* began to move forward.

"Excellent, Heart," Jackson praised, obviously impressed.

Heart grinned. "Hear that, HelperFriend, Jackson just uttered the first 'excellent' in his life!"

"I heard it Heart. In fact, I recorded it."

At the top of her game Heart crowed, "Ha, Jackson, and so furthermore, you may never take it back."

"I don't want to take it back. But don't get too full of yourself. That's when errors ... remember The Tent...."

"Oh, yes." Heart sobered immediately. "You're right. You fly, I'll watch. I did watch very carefully when Xavier flew, so, I guess you might say I've cheated a bit because I already knew much of the basics, but now it's completely different. Instead of my begging him to let me fly, you're insisting I learn how to fly solo. I shall be a most attentive student."

"Glad to hear it," Jackson said perfunctorily. "Ready for take off." Jackson eased the *Heart!* into the sky, instructing the entire time. Heart paid careful attention to everything he said and every move he made.

Initially, he flew low over the endless pink terrain, then he began to explain and demonstrate ever more complicated maneuvers. "I don't imagine you'll ever have occasion to employ evasive maneuvers while flying the *Heart!*, but I may as well give you the full tour while we're at it."

"Absolutely, Jackson. And, you never know. We do not know what our future holds. I may find myself a mere soldier in the ranks of *The Cause of All Beings*."

"You may. Unlikely, but you may. Right. Now, your turn."

"Really? Already?"

"Yes. Show me what you've got."

"Sounds like a dare."

"If you like."

Jackson released the controls and Heart took over.

Finally! Finally, she was flying a spacecraft. Amazing! How different the power in her hands from the experience of riding Equuleus. The two of them were effortlessly one. *But this!* The power of the *Heart!* poured into her hands and through her body. She commanded the *Heart!,* while at the same time, the *Heart!* seemed to have its own mind, as well.

"Such power, Jackson! Almost ... unwieldy. Like ... challenging me. Testing me."

Jackson chuckled. He sounded pleased. "You've got it, Heart. The *Heart!* is not an easy ride. Xavier didn't just *make* the *Heart!,* he *created* it."

"Yes. Created it. Put his own intelligence, his own character into it." As the understanding grew in Heart that she held Xavier's creative genius in her hands, her intelligence and understanding reached into the powerful spacecraft and bonded.

"Right. Heart, right. Very good."

"Add 'very good,' to my score, HelperFriend."

"Got it," HelperFriend called back, almost giggling.

"You're sounding sort of giddy back there," Heart observed.

"I am!" HelperFriend replied, guffawing out loud. "This is astounding! HelperFriend, the Clockworks man in space flight. Oh, oh, history is written on Pink today."

"You might say!" Heart agreed. "Hang on!" She took the *Heart!* in a series of loops-within-loops that made HelperFriend laugh and laugh uproariously.

Then she straightened out and flew low over Pink.

"*More, Heart, more!*" HelperFriend begged.

"That's enough for today. I want to look over Pink's terrain, while we're out here."

HelperFriend sobered immediately when, even from his interior position, he saw the remains of several bots, scattered over the landscape.

"That's not funny," HelperFriend said soberly.

"No. It's not. Do you ... I don't want to, but do you think we ought to bring some of them back for Father to dissect and do whatever he might do with them? Or salvage components that might be usable in the reconstruction?"

"That's a practical idea, Heart," Jackson agreed. "But ... the timing ...."

"Oh, no, Heart, I'm trembling here at the sight of them, and I even know how important it might be for Father Inventor to have these remains. But the shock at the sight of them would strike a blow on everyone."

"Of course. What am I thinking?"

"You're thinking like Jackson," HelperFriend observed. "And, Heart, *Jackson is thinking like you!*"

"Oh, dear!" Heart quipped. "That will never do."

"I am *not* thinking like Heart. I'm being pragmatic."

"Oh, HelperFriend, do you hear that? Jackson does not think I'm pragmatic."

"Well then, he doesn't know the real Heart."

"Thank you!"

"You're impossible," Jackson mumbled. "The both of you!"

Despite the macabre environment, Heart and HelperFriend burst into gales of glee.

"You're impossible, HelperFriend," Heart said in an exacting imitation of Jackson.

"No more than you! *You're* impossible," Helper-Friend retorted, bettering Heart by using Jackson's actual voice.

"Oh no! *Soooooo funeeee!*" Heart laughed.

"*Do not do that!*" Jackson commanded, ever more serious.

"Order acknowledged," HelperFriend replied in his own voice, as, given the order, he could no longer use Jackson's voice. "Might there be an occasion when using your voice would be useful?"

Jackson reflected for a moment. "Perhaps. I amend my order. You may not use my voice to make fun of me or otherwise undermine my authority."

"Amendment to order acknowledged," HelperFriend said. "He certainly knows how to take the fun out of a moment, doesn't he?"

"I have observed this trait in Jackson, yes."

They both waited for Jackson to retort, but he remained silent.

"Silence is acquiescence," HelperFriend noted. "I learned that in my reading."

Heart nodded. "Back to the castle?"

"Right," Jackson concurred.

*   *

"We may as well leave the *Heart!* out here on the plain," Jackson suggested as the dome came in view. "No point interrupting the work taking it to its stall, when you'll soon be logging more flight time."

"Very good." Heart brought the *Heart!* to a stop, then shut down the engines as if she'd done it her whole life. Jackson climbed into his protective suit muttering and grumbling about it, then the three of them disembarked and trooped into Father Inventor's room. Heart's father, Equuleus, and Violet waited for them.

105 – Blythe Ayne

"Show off!" Violet exclaimed, pointing at the replay of Heart's thrilling loops. Heart watched, fascinated. "Hey! Not bad for a new girl," she crowed.

"Don't get too full of yourself," her father advised.

"There's an echo here," she laughed. "I've been duly advised, Father, to not be over-confident. Even though it's that over-*something* driving me to do much of what I do. Like leaving The Darling Undesirables Residence of Long Prairie, like shapeshifting when I went to The Museum of Scientific Improbabilities and Unpredictable Oddities, so I could stay to get close to Equuleus, like going back to Earth to save Eye. If I weren't driven, if I didn't believe in myself ...."

"We know, Heart. But we don't want you crashing the *Heart!*"

"Note to self, try not to crash the *Heart!* while believing in yourself," she teased. "Aside from pointing out to me not to crash the spacecraft, do you have any other observations or advice?"

"I *do* have an observation," her father said solemnly.

"Yes?"

"Bravo and well done, my girl! Was that really you at the helm?"

"It was."

"Stellar! I'm so proud."

"Thank you, Father. Whew! I'm racking up the points today, aren't I, HelperFriend? Did you get that recorded as well?"

"I did. It has gone into your personal record."

"However, Father, I want to mention to you all the remains of bots lying about out there. I thought to bring some of them back, but Helper-Friend reminded me it would be too shocking for ... everyone. I thought you might be able to dissect them, or they might have components you could put to good use."

"Excellent thinking, Heart, you're right on it. I have a few bits and pieces of the bots here in storage. But the ones who got here were destroyed by Xavier's troops and, well everyone. We'll have to give your idea some serious consideration.

"HelperFriend and I will figure out a means of keeping them here in the castle, and then the three of you can go out and retrieve a few of the more intact bots and bring them directly to my door so The Folks don't have to witness them."

Heart nodded. "That might work. Although I hate to ask HelperFriend to go on that mission, as it would be distressful for him."

"Distressful for *me*?" HelperFriend protested. "Many times more distressful for *you*, Heart."

"Well, I can be philosophical about it. I could have collected them today, as squeamish as the idea makes me."

"Then I can be philosophical, too, Heart. No matter how squeamish the thought makes me, it's for a greater good. What's more important is that if there are any—*any!* components in the bots our wounded might be able to use, that would be a sweet revenge."

"Sweet indeed, my HelperFriend," Heart agreed.

Chapter 8

Heart's father and HelperFriend set upon building a cryonic tank for the bots. Then several dusky, shadowy evenings later, she flew the *Heart!*, with her two accomplices, to the open terrain where the bots lay strewn, and set down in the *Heart!*

They gathered half-a-dozen of the repugnant, sickly gray bodies of the most intact bot carcasses. Having brought only a pair of gloves for the noxious project, Heart, for once, envied Jackson's full body protection.

After they returned to the castle, both Heart and HelperFriend couldn't get to their respective self-cleaning receptacles fast enough. But her father's pleased response made it all worthwhile.

Beyond that, Heart became obsessed with flying the *Heart!* Jackson told her not to go out alone, and she agreed, telling herself she had Equuleus to fly out with her. On the third afternoon in a row that she'd waited until Jackson had his back turned to scurry off to fly the *Heart!* without him, diving, looping and practicing a variety of edgy, if not downright dangerous, maneuvers, she was jolted out of her reverie at the sound of Jackson's voice.

"That last move, Heart, is not to be duplicated."

She looked all around for him, and finally saw his spacecraft on the far horizon, apparently silently watching her.

"Have you been there all along?"

"I'll be the one asking questions." He jetted up to the *Heart!* "Set down."

"All right." She couldn't see Equuleus and realized he'd removed himself from the soon-to-pass confrontation. Heart landed the *Heart!*, engines humming, while Jackson landed nearby.

He turned off his engines and came out the back hatch. Heart opened the hatch on the *Heart!*, waiting for Jackson, with his anger in tow, to enter, and give her a blow-by-blow critique of what she'd done wrong while secretly observing her.

Not fair! she thought.

She waited a long time for him to appear, but finally, he came through the hatch.

"What took ...." She stopped. She could not quip lightly about his dark visage. *"What's wrong?"*

"*You're* wrong, Heart. I'm having serious, and I mean, *serious*, second thoughts."

"About what?"

"About having you help *The Cause of All Beings*. About you coming to Earth. About you flying the *Heart! About—you*."

"But ... why?"

"Because, Heart, though you are brilliant, though you are talented, though you are loving, though you want to help, *you are a maverick*. A loose cannon. You are disobedient, challenging, willful—and, because of all these traits and behaviors, *you are frightening*."

"Frightening? You? Frightened? *Of anything?*" Heart's voice raised with each punctuated word.

"Do you not understand that your inability to follow a simple direction stands to destroy—well— *everything?* There's too much at stake. Yes, I need someone who has your background, intelligence, perceptiveness, and caring. But I need someone who is intrinsically different from you. Will you ever stop thumbing your nose at me? I think not."

"What in the name of a dozen heavens are you going on about, Jackson?"

"All I have hoped to see, these last three days, when the evening before I told you not to go out on your own without me, that just one time, you actually did as I requested."

"Demanded," Heart corrected.

"Demanded, ordered, entreated, plead, bid, desired, appealed, adjured, dictated, insisted. Use any damn word, Heart. You always do exactly as you please, so don't let me get in your way. I shall do the same. You are making my mission beyond extremely difficult. I now give up. I simply cannot have you on Earth, roaring around in the *Heart!*, thinking you have all the answers, thinking you know everything. *When. You. Do. Not.*

"Is there no limit to your ego? You have made me want to either throw away my well-worn and marked-up copy of *OurBook*, or begin to look for someone else that it's referring to. Because you appear not to be 'The One.'"

Shocked and recoiling, Heart unlatched her safety harness. "Damn you right back, Jackson. I've always *said I'm **not** 'the One.'* Hateful, hateful concept. Hateful book, for that matter. People, and I mean people I respect, like the residents of The Periphery, have wrapped that damnable book around me, and held me prisoner with just as much of a chokehold as The Darling Undesirables Residence of Long Prairie ever did.

"Criticize me, condemn me, leave me out of your precious plans and sure-as-sure, yes, please-and-thank-you, leave me out of your margin notes in your copy of *OurBook*. Could anything make me happier? Do you think I care about that? No. Just in case you were in any way unclear as to my feelings about it.

"If I go to Earth, it's for one reason and one reason only! To protect Darling Undesirables everywhere. There you are, a beautiful specimen of a being that's one-hundred-percent bio. You don't have any notion of what it is to be me.

"I will happily continue to *not* 'obey' you, to not jump at your commands, to not behave like all your military-minded bio pets you call soldiers. Whatever. You'll plan your maneuvers, you'll fight your battles, you'll be the ruler of your successful or failed kingdom. But, whatever you do, you'll be doing it without me.

"You won't be telling me what you won't have me do.

"*I WILL TELL YOU!! I WILL NOT HAVE ANYTHING TO DO WITH YOU.* For God's sake, or anything that resembles it—*talk about ego! Yours ....*" Heart sputtered, unable to discover words. "I need to get flight time in. I know my strengths and weaknesses. I know what I must accomplish. I know what I want, and I know what I have to do.

"I told you I want to stay here and protect my Father and pull Pink together. If those slimy, pasty beasts come in droves again, I'll go down like Xavier went down, but doing what I know I must and for whom I must. You forced me to join you. I did not sign up. I am not one of your compliant, panting-for-your-approval, wannabe soldier-types. Get over yourself, you pampered, egotistic, megalomaniac.

"So now, you will kindly leave me alone. Well, more to the point, go back to Earth. You've thrown your weight around here enough. Go where every-one obeys you and *leave me alone*. I have things to do. Furthermore, unlike you, I do not have an army. I have Equuleus, and HelperFriend. And ... a rabbit."

Heart, who had stomped up and down three strides in the *Heart!* exited out the back hatch and started to stomp toward the castle. "Have fun bringing both the spacecraft back. Oh, yeah, that's right, they'll do as you tell them, so I'm sure they'll come right along at your command, no doubt."

Heart had never, ever been this angry in her entire life. Nor had she ever been so severely crit-icized in her life. There were occasions when one keeper or another had said negative things, but their words never phased her. The keepers didn't know her. The keepers were not as bright as she was. The keepers were—keepers!

But Jackson. No, she'd never experienced any-thing like this. She wondered what Xavier would have said, had he been there. Would he take her side? Would he take Jackson's side?

Jackson flew overhead toward the castle in the *Heart!* What would he do? Would he complain to her father? Would he be gathering himself, getting ready to return to Earth? Would he be standing there, ready to launch into her again?

She hated the image of all of these pictures as they passed through her mind.

Finally, she arrived at the far edge of the dome. Everyone waved at her and smiled, though with apprehension in their look. Well, here she was, walking, Jackson having brought back the *Heart!* Why did she leave the *Heart!*? Because there stood Jackson, and she had to get away from him. Just … whatever it took!

She waved back but didn't engage in any chatter. *No talking!* She wanted to be in her rooms, alone, shut up and trying not to think.

As she began to stomp toward the front entrance of the castle, HelperFriend hurried out from her father's room, rattled and confused. "Heart!"

"Yes?"

"Heart, Heart!"

"Yes, HelperFriend, what is it?"

"Oh, alarmed, I am. I am … no, never mind that. Your father wants you to come in his room."

"Not right now, HelperFriend."

"Well, yes, he does want you to come right now."

"But I don't want to."

"You don't want to. You don't want to. That too has never happened. I don't have a database for this eventuality, Heart. I am your friend, but your father ordered me to bring you, and I fear if you don't come by yourself, I will take you."

"You will take me, HelperFriend?" Heart stopped in mid-stomp. "Against my will?"

"You will recall I did it one other time, and, well, yes, I will do it again. Heart, your father is very unhappy. Not good Heart. You must come."

"Very unhappy? He told you that?"

"He needn't. It's quite observable. Facial expression, body position. Frown. Sunken shoulders. Funny little sounds."

"Funny little sounds?"

HelperFriend produced a series of "tsks" she'd never heard from her father, but sounding like his voice, for sure.

This moved Heart. "Oh, that's not good. He doesn't deserve ...." Heart returned to her father's door baffles, and entered, HelperFriend close behind. Jackson stood, head hanging, refusing to look at her.

"You may go, HelperFriend."

"Yes?" HelperFriend became more confused. "I may go? Is that a directive, or is it my choice? I may go, therefore, I may, also, *not* go."

"Sorry, HelperFriend, I was not clear," Heart's father said in a voice she'd never heard, resembling the sound of the "tsks." "Please leave the room. I'll summon you if needed."

"All right. I'll be nearby." HelperFriend went into the hall toward the kitchen.

Agitated, Heart stood by the door, ready to leave if asked. Then it came to her that her father might ask Jackson to leave, and, as he stood there, still in his protective gear, it would be an easy exit—if she wasn't in the way. She moved into the room.

She watched closely as her father looked from her to Jackson, and back to her again, his face cryptic but—stoic, braced. "Disappointing. Very disappointing. Both of you. Your entire interaction blasting into here through the 3-D, with HelperFriend and Violet becoming steadily more and more upset, soon joined by Equuleus, returned from the war you were putting on.

"Do you not *BOTH* realize that what's at stake is far greater, far more grand than either one of you? Than both of you put together?

"You know you are both entirely precious to me, and I don't say that lightly." He turned his back to them, distraught with emotion.

"What's coming through now to our home planet is beyond your comprehension. It's a shifting of the mind of Earth." He turned back to face them. "The prevailing mind, contrived by every single individual, grows, too, into an independent mind of its own. It's spiritual and intellectual evolution of a profound order. Not that I expect either of you to understand that.

"But I do expect you to *KNOW* there is something so vital going on, a leap of growth, or at least the potential of a leap of growth so acute, that everything will *be different* in a wonderful and evolving way. A way you cannot hope to comprehend right now. I trusted the two of you to be wise and kind and caring enough, spiritual enough, to take your part seriously.

"Do you not see that each of you is reacting to the thing in the other that *is in yourself?* You have deep-seated similarities. First of all, you're both orphans. Heart, left on the doorstep of a Darling Undesirables facility with a unique physical anomaly. Jackson, parentless and raised, or cared for at least, when anyone could get near him, by loving inhabitants on the far side of The Wall. You are both brilliant, resourceful, strong, good-hearted and loyal.

"At the same time, you both hate the sight of the orphan in the other. You don't like to see this aspect that looks like rejection. You both think everything has to be your way. *You are both willful.*

"Well, I have news for you both. Neither one of you will get your way. Whether you decide to not have anything to do with each other from this point forward, or whether you decide to act slightly more mature than five-year-olds and continue your work for *The Cause of All Beings*, as you've been called to do, you will not get your way. You will have to compromise. You will have to take direction.

"I really never thought I'd be saying this, but I'm ashamed of both of you. You each said things that cut deep to hurt the other, and what do you have to show for it?"

What truth in his words, Heart thought. Everything he said, exactly, *exactly* right. She didn't know Jackson was an orphan, but it made perfect sense. It was true, she'd hated appearing to be an orphan, living in The Darling Undesirables Residence of Long Prairie. So, of course, she would hate that energy in someone else, if she didn't know that's what riled her up.

They both had a place deep within where they felt powerless. They both had invested their energies into developing power. They were both used to knowing things before other people knew them, and taking actions meaningful for others.

They were both used to being in the vanguard of any situation that needed a vanguard. Now, with the biggest issue of all time, working toward the goal of granting a life of freedom for all beings, they were snarling and biting one another. Each furious that the other dared to attempt to wield power over them.

"Can you not, Jackson, allow Heart an awareness of her own style of learning, and let her do it as she must, in order to be prepared in the way she knows best, and the way *you need her*?"

Her father then turned to her, "And can you not, Heart, allow Jackson to give you directives when it's necessary, as he may have a vision encompassing more than you might see at the moment. Will you not trust him?"

"Well, father, truthfully, it's not easy. But as you request it, from your wisdom, I will do as you request, if Jackson understands what you're asking of him and if he will do as you request."

Jackson looked at Heart and then her father. "I will do as you request, sir, with respect and willingness. I ask your forgiveness that I disappointed you.

I do know someone—although I don't know who— someone watched out for me all the time of my lonely, and sometimes very frightening childhood. To repay that unknown person, I will now work to think and behave more maturely. I know my socialization is poor. It's pretty much self-taught.

"I believe Heart had someone watching out for her too, all the time she lived at The Darling Undesirables Residence of Long Prairie. We might both be grateful for our overseers."

Heart couldn't believe this last from Jackson. Why would he say that? Did he actually know something she didn't know? Or was he being intuitive? Or simply placating her father? That last seemed extremely unlikely.

She'd never felt watched over or protected. She'd always been aware of her obligation to, and her love for, Eye. She'd been the watcher. She *had* a watcher? Strange thought. Strange contemplation.

"Very good," her father said, sighing deeply. "Very, very good. I take your comments as your word. As a promise from each of you. We're back on track. It's obvious that Heart is a natural pilot— more time spent practicing is wasted time. Let us prepare for the two of you to go to Earth."

*　*

As soon as Heart could slip away from everyone, and as soon as it became as dark as ever it became on Pink, Heart crept outside, out behind the castle where she'd rarely been. She wanted to be sure she'd be completely alone. Completely.

She walked a good distance from the castle then sat on a little hillock, waiting for Pink's silver moon to rise. Finally the brilliant curve of its sphere crested Pink's horizon. The light that reflected off Pink's moon from the sun ran across Pink's surface and, eventually, washed over Heart.

She looked up at the moon, imagining Xavier looking down at her, hoping he was not too disappointed in her. She wanted to sit quietly, meditatively and ask nothing of herself nor of Xavier. But she couldn't still her mind. She could not release her miserable, guilty, still angry, feelings.

"I know you want me to become stronger and more balanced, Xavier. But I'm so ... so self-loathing right now. To have disappointed my father ... or maybe I don't even deserve to think of him as my father anymore, to have disappointed him so profoundly that he had to address me in that way.

"Yes, I've frustrated him before. He's reprimanded me before. But this! This is different. I felt he might truly disown me. I didn't have to react to Jackson. Why didn't I let him rant and let it go? He wasn't entirely wrong.

"So what if he *was* wrong? I didn't have to react."

As Heart berated herself, looking at the moon, surely Xavier's features faintly began to glow on the moon's surface, and she heard, "Dearest Heart, be kind to yourself. You and Jackson both must do this bit of growing up. It's dramatic, yes, but don't make it harder on yourself than necessary. Don't let it damage your sense of self.

"Stay centered. No matter what happens, no matter what shock, no matter who seems to be different from the person or being you thought they were, *stay focused*.

"I send you my love, Heart. But your strength is your own."

Xavier's face faded as slowly as it had materialized.

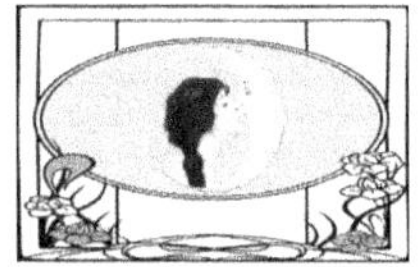

Chapter 9

That evening, HelperFriend installed a perfect nook for Equuleus in the *Heart!* which had been returned to its usual location in the dome while HelperFriend worked on it within easy reach of his tools and other materials.

He had to take out a half wall, and Heart, standing nearby, chatting with him while he worked, recalled the giant box of colorful candy Xavier had placed behind the half wall, that she had jettisoned in order to hunker down there herself when she stowed away on the trip to Earth. Sadness swept through her at that recollection, followed by the comfort of knowing Equuleus would be with her on this trip. They would be together all the way.

She asked HelperFriend to build a shelf above Equuleus's enclosure, and gave him its dimensions.

"Why, Heart? Why do you need a shelf precisely that size? It's a bit long for the space. It'll fit, but, it's tight. And it'll hover over Equuleus. When I presented the plan I came up with for him, it didn't include this."

Heart stepped through the hatch to address Equuleus. "Is it all right if HelperFriend puts up this shelf for me, that will be over your space?"

"I don't mind. I'll be sitting."

"Thank you!" She stepped back inside. "He said ...."

"He's all right with it. Then, all right!" HelperFriend began whistling—or something like whistling, if a tsunami could whistle—while he worked.

*   *

Later, in the middle of the twilight night, Heart and Equuleus stole down to the *Heart!*, the dome altogether silent. The gigantic aspect of the reconstructing had been completed, and most of the residents of Pink were taking a well-earned evening off, recuperating and preparing for the following day, when Heart and Jackson would leave for Earth.

With a large box on Equuleus's back, they stepped through the hatch. Heart placed the box on the shelf HelperFriend had built to her specifications. She turned on the magnetic code she'd installed within the box that both held it in place on the shelf no matter what maneuvers the *Heart!* might engage in, and that also prevented the box from being opened by anyone other than she, herself.

As she crept back out of the *Heart!*, she thought she heard someone call her name. After Equuleus came through the hatch, she gestured for him to be still, while she listened.

"Heart," she heard faintly.

"Do you hear that?" she whispered to Equuleus.

He nodded.

They waited.

"Heart."

It seemed to come from the wall itself.

"Is someone there?" she breathed.

"Yes."

"Where are you?"

"In the wall. Under the stairs."

Heart went under the stairs and stood before the wall.

"Is the wall talking?"

"No. It's Geometria. I'm ... I'm stuck in the wall. If you will kindly run your hands over the wall below your waist height, I can connect with the energy from your hand and come through."

Heart reached out, but hesitated. What if ... well, what if so many things? What if it was not Geometria? What if something hid in the wall about to pull her through, and *she* would be trapped in the wall?

But she'd been watching for Geometria since the Bot Invasion, not wanting to ask if he'd been destroyed, hoping he was somewhere safe. As he was so small, she kept telling herself, he probably stood right there among everyone, and she merely had not seen him.

"Is it really you, Geometria?"

"Yes. Really me. Remember when we met, my sacred geometric box became a pyramid? There's a strong energy between us. I've been hoping you would come without anyone else, well, except for Equuleus, of course, that goes without saying. I didn't want anyone else to see me come through the wall. They'd be wanting me to teach it to them."

"Interesting," Heart replied. She reached her hand toward the wall, moving it around, but still without touching it.

And, *then!* She felt a charge of energy. "All right, I'm trusting you," she said as she touched the wall, prepared for something terrible and dramatic if Geometria were to come tearing through the metal of the wall.

Immediately, Geometria stepped through the wall as if through an open doorway. Sighing deeply, he bowed to Heart. "Thank you, Miss Heart. I had begun to prepare myself to be in the wall for a long time, given that you're about to take off for Earth."

Heart sat on the metal stairs and gestured for Geometria to sit by her, which he did, barely a foot tall beside her when seated, his sacred geometry box a glowing white pyramid.

"How did you come to be in the wall? Why were you waiting for me?"

"Geometria nodded and looked up at her. "I have these answers and more, Heart. I came to be in the wall because when the Bot Invasion began to destroy the dome, I knew I must not be destroyed, so I intended to put myself into an inner wall, the most likely to survive the onslaught, and, further, I came here, to the *Heart!* And by the empowerment of certain sacred geometric gestures, I took myself into the wall.

"I brought myself here, in particular, trusting that sooner or later you would come to the *Heart!* And, that what just transpired would transpire. I knew you'd be able to bring me back through the wall because of this energy we share." He held the white-light pyramid up, "and also because of your shapeshifting abilities, which is low-level sacred geometry. Without study, you have knowledge of the basics of sacred geometry."

"I see," Heart said thoughtfully. "So, why is it so imperative that you not be harmed? Of course, I don't want *any* of Pink's residents harmed, but tell me about you, in particular ...."

"I advise your father in important, multi-dimensional ways. I am closely attached to dark energy and am composed, in part, of dark matter. But even more important is my interdependence with other dimensions."

"I think I understand," Heart mused, gesturing for Equuleus to stand near her by the open stairs. She reached out and stroked his neck. "Equuleus and I relate profoundly in the three dimensions, but also, I'm certain, in realms beyond."

"That's true, Heart. Well, I will tell you, I'd love nothing more than to sit here on these cold, rough metal steps talking with you throughout the ages, but we are still in the realm of time, and it is swiftly passing. So for now, beautiful young woman, thank you for assisting me. You were lionhearted, as always, though—*and wisely so!*—trepidatious.

"What I must tell you ...." Geometria turned his attention to his sacred geometry box, which, with his directed attention, melded into a sphere, into which he peered. "I scry to advise and suggest, but not direct. But only if you are interested."

Heart became mesmerized, slightly hypnotized, studying the roiling, turbid movement within the sacred geometric form in Geometria's small hands. "I am interested ...."

"I see," he said, studying the shifting forms. "Oh! *Hmmm* ... goodness."

Heart resisted the urge to ask "Goodness, what?"

Geometria looked up at her. "Well, I am only going to tell you this—you will discover some amazing things. I may not tell you more. I am out of bounds with much higher energy. An image of *Ourbook* floated to the fore and blocked my quest, so I will leave it at that. But I advise you to trust Jackson. No more petty bickering ...."

"Yes, we got that lecture from my father. Duly noted."

"You will likely chafe at the bit, so to speak, but if you relax and follow the directives of others, it will work out. It may not seem like it on occasion, but it will.

"You must go, now, and get ready for your departure. *Ah! Heart!*" Geometria exclaimed. His sacred geometry box returned to its pyramid shape, the turgid forms gradually overtaken again by a bright white light, sending rays out to touch both Heart and Equuleus.

"My light blesses your stunning, astounding light, Heart and Equuleus. You may always call upon my eternal strengths if you so desire. I will add them seamlessly to yours."

He hopped up from the steps. "Off I go now, to continue my work with the rebuilding of the dome."

"Continue?" Heart queried, wondering how he'd helped thus far, from inside the wall.

"Yes. Continue. How do you imagine the infra-structure," he pointed up to the maze of triangles of the infrastructure, upon which everyone had begun to attach the exterior sheeting the previous day, "was raised and stayed in place while all the workers crawled over the open, sky-held tubing, welding it into place? *I* hold it in place."

"Oh! Do they know that? Do they know you do that, and yet, they're not able to see you anywhere?"

"Most of them do not know that. They take it as an intrinsic dynamic of the physics here on Pink. Well, it is. Because of me!" Geometria opened his arms and Heart reached down to give him a big hug.

"Bye now! Travel safely. Oh, what an adventure you are about to have," he chatted as he disappeared into the cavernous darkness of the far reaches of the dome.

Heart looked at Equuleus. He shrugged. "Curiouser and curiouser," she muttered.

Equuleus nodded, having nothing to add to Heart's succinct observation.

They left the *Heart!* and came around the front of the castle. Heart gestured to Equuleus that she would step inside to give and receive a blessing from her flowers. Stepping through the baffle, she immediately noticed that the flowers had taken on a darker hue, more vibrant, less pastel.

The plaid among them vibrated, clearly defined. Furthermore, Heart noted, their plaid was identical to the plaid of one of the outfits Martha had made for her.

She thanked the flowers for their good cheer and the pleasure, peace, and joy they gave her. She told them how much she loved them, then she stepped through the back baffle and into the other greenhouse.

Much to her surprise, she witnessed the same plaid here, when, previously, the plants in each greenhouse had flowered into distinctly different plaids. She thanked these flowers as well, mentioning she would wear the plaid *they* wore. Walking through the greenhouse, she resisted her desire to sit down among the flowers to drink in their calming, delightful aroma. Then she passed through the front baffle, where Equuleus stood.

"Amazing, Equuleus! Same plaid among the flowers in both greenhouses."

Equuleus snorted.

"I know. They've never done that before. Unmistakable plaid, and it's the plaid of the outfit I've worn the least. I love any plaid pattern, but that one feels uncomfortably strong. When I look down at it, it seems to demand my attention. Really *demand* my attention. I guess it's time to give it my attention, even if I don't know what it means. Not the first time I've been mystified by something."

"No, it's not," Equuleus responded.

"You don't have to be so ready to agree," she teased as she stepped through the front door. The environmental locks shunted, and she stepped inside. Then Equuleus took his turn behind her.

Fly me up, my friend." She jumped on Equuleus and they flew up in the rotunda, landing gracefully at the door to Heart's rooms.

They heard a keening from the other side of the door, and Heart quickly opened it. Violet stood in the middle of the narrow bed, weeping and wailing.

"What's the matter?" Heart asked, looking around the room to see if anything could possibly be causing the little rabbit's distress.

"What's the matter? How can you ask this, Heart? *What's the matter?* You're going to Earth again. Of course, that's what's the matter. The last time you went, you came back all but a corpse, and now, off you go again as if you haven't a care in all of Pink."

"Goodness!" Heart sat beside Violet and held her on her lap. "Really, Violet. Calm yourself. You know perfectly well I didn't know, the last time, I could not be that far from Equuleus for so long, and that he's coming with me this time."

"Leaving me completely alone, on this whole entire moon. *All alone!*"

"You're such a liar—you are not alone! You spend more time with Yippee than me of late, and you know it!"

"That's only because you're always too busy, and off running around, and flying the *Heart!* and so on and so forth and etcetera and etcetera and etcetera, and all what have you ...."

"She's got you there, Heart."

Heart wrinkled her brow at Equuleus. "I don't need you making it worse!"

"Sorry. I'll just step over here out of the way of the histrionics."

"Less drama, all right, Violet?"

"But ... I am afraid you won't come back."

"I'm coming back," Heart countered, having no way to know if she told the truth.

"Promise?"

"Well, ahhh, Violet, I can't make a promise about things I don't know. But, I promise I have every intention of coming back, and, barring events beyond my power, I *will* come back."

"*WAAAA!*" Violet cried with renewed intensity. "Now I'm more scared than ever. You sound like ... like you ... *waaaaa!*" Little lavender teardrops fell onto Heart's plaid pants.

Heart watched as several white centers of plaid became lavender. "Look, Violet, you're changing my plaid. I think it's an improvement. Look at your lavender tears." She pointed at the several squares that had neatly turned lavender.

Still in the midst of her last "*waaaaa*," Violet looked down, intrigued. "Hey, that's pretty! I did that?"

Shaking her head, Heart looked up at Equuleus, "Just dangle a piece of colored glass ...."

"Yup," Equuleus agreed.

"What's colored glass?"

"Oh, it's a metaphor. Anyway, dear Violet, do you feel a bit better? Everything is fine. You'll be fine. You'll hang out with Lady Gervi and Yippee and HelperFriend and Father. It will all be so interesting, and you'll have a great time."

"I don't suppose you'll promise that, either," Violet said, somewhat disgusted.

"I can't promise anything about your choice of mood, my rabbity-eared friend. You must choose your mood for yourself."

"I don't know why I even talk with you!"

"Now what?"

"You never promise anything."

"Well, you won't have to talk with me for a while, will you?"

"*WAAAAAA* ...."

"All righty, enough over-indulgence. I must organize myself. You can either help me, or I'm setting you outside the room. I have to be able to concentrate."

Violet clamped her mouth shut mid "*waaa* ..." looking up piteously at Heart as if to say, "you wouldn't set little me outside, would you?" Her ears fell down alongside her face and she drew her little mouth down. "What can I do that would be helpful for you?" she said quietly.

"Much better." Heart gathered a few things. As before, she needed little. She pulled out the outfit that bore the plaid her flowers had shown her. She remembered the first time she wore it. Her father, HelperFriend and Equuleus had responded instantly and positively to it. She felt it made her look different. Stronger, less soft, slightly ... imperious. Not her style.

But then she reminded herself of her diatribe that she let fly at Jackson, and thought, maybe there is a bit of imperious in me. Not that he hadn't earned every word I said to him, she silently argued. However, her respect and love for her father outweighed everything else, and she would do not only do as he bid, but as now, Geometria, too, suggested.

Maybe I can use a tempered imperiousness on this trip, she thought. Just as long as I keep my emotions in check with Jackson. He's working hard for the two of us to get along, and I must do the same.

Whatever it took.

She studied the plaid again, then slipped into it, like a new skin.

Chapter 10

When Heart, astride Equuleus and holding Violet, came around the corner of the castle rather regally, she thought, all The Folks were gathering around the *Heart!* and Jackson's spacecraft. Both vehicles sat, side by side, out on the plain, ready for whatever mission they were about to be called upon to do.

Heart felt a deep pang of disquiet. *Would she return to Pink?*

Expecting a cheer to rise up at her arrival, she became somewhat nonplussed by their murmuring quiet. All eyes were upon her, but no cheer. No exclamation.

The baffle to her father's room opened and Jackson and her father, in their protective gear, and HelperFriend stepped out. They, too, stopped and stared at Heart, making her begin to wonder if she'd sprouted another head, not visible to her.

"*Wow!*" Violet whispered.

"What?" Heart whispered back.

"They are ... it's like ... so moved ... reverence. You must ... there must be a light coming off you."

"*Heart, Heart, Heart,*" The folks began to chant, making her ever more uncomfortable.

She looked over to her father, with a similar expression. She slid off Equuleus and, putting Violet down, went up to her father.

"I don't understand ...."

"You are in a supernatural light, Heart. Can't you see the glow around you?"

"No. But, why? I'm just me." She looked down at the new, bronze and golden plaid and then she, indeed, saw the glow coming off her.

She moved to stand before the gathering. "I am your own Heart. I love you all, every one of you. If I'm glowing, it's only a reflection of the love you are sending me. This is not my glow, *it's your glow*.

"I'm going to Earth in the name of your courage, your freedom, in *The Cause of All Beings*, with our one mission statement, to love and to honor all expressions of consciousness, however embodied, in all beings, unconditionally. I take your love with me as my only weaponry. I believe in it, and I know it will prevail."

Then the cheer broke and broke wildly. Wonderman One and Wonderman Two began their amazing gravity-defying dance, Lady Gervi, pulled by Yippee, practically flew about on her giant wheel.

HelperFriend began to play a new, haunting piece of music with a melody that crawled into Heart's deepest recesses. She knew he had composed this music just for her. The sweet, vulnerable, sadness pouring through the sounds was how he saw her, how he loved her, how he championed her.

Heart looked at HelperFriend, her hands in prayer to her face, touched beyond words. His tears of brass and copper and bronze bits of metal fell to the surface of Pink, making a small mercury-like pond at his feet.

Her gaze moved to Jackson. He stood stoic, at attention, unflinching. He'd shifted his focus from Heart to the horizon. Heart had a sudden profound insight about him.

He wasn't so very cold. He was too hot. He had to shut himself off from emotion, or he'd not be able to function at all. She felt a rush of protective sentiment for him. Then, everything in her shifted.

Looking up at the moon, she couldn't see Xavier's face, but she could hear the echo of his voice.

The two of them, she affirmed, she and Xavier, would protect Jackson as much as ever he had protected them.

She moved to stand beside Jackson, and, for reasons that somewhat mystified Heart, this made the roar of approval augment a multiple of decibels.

"Are you ready?" she asked him.

Without looking at her, he nodded curtly and moved to his spacecraft. Heart walked to Helper-Friend and, not wanting to disrupt his amazing music, patted him on the shoulder, mouthing, "love you!" in an eye-to-eye gaze.

Then she went to her father, who was holding Violet, and embraced them both as if she would squeeze their love right into herself. Then she, with Equuleus, headed for the *Heart!* The hatch stood open, and they entered. She made sure Equuleus became settled and locked in, then did the same with herself.

"Prepare for take off," Jackson's voice came into the *Heart!* Heart flipped switches and pushed buttons.

"Preparation complete. Mind if we give them a tiny bit of a show? They've worked hard."

"Right. Slow taxi, three matched heart loops, and we're outta here," Jackson commanded.

Heart grinned a secret half grin. *Perfect!* She couldn't have asked for more. "Got it."

As they slowly taxied by the many expectant faces—bio, clockwork, mechanical, hybrid, whole

or shattered, they held one expression in common—
TRUST. Love? Yes. Faith? Yes. But most of all, she
saw *trust*.

They trusted with all their united energy in
Heart and Jackson to defend *The Cause of All Beings*.
They trusted with every fiber of their belief that
their cause would triumph.

Heart *almost* believed as they did. Not quite,
but almost. She had seen the relentless tenacity
of the Purists force their way upon everyone,
while *The Cause of All Beings* was the opposite—
to not force any *way* upon any *one*. To have an
appreciation for those who contributed to the
betterment of all, but no critique or negative
comment about anyone's individual ideology.
Or lack of ideology!

She pocketed The Folks open and guileless
trust in her soul, and, following Jackson's lead,
began to gather speed. Just as the *Heart!* lifted,
she saw, at the very, very end of the line of Pink
residents, Geometria, with his sacred geometry
box. It had formed a glowing golden pyramid.
Golden now, not white. She exchanged a look
with him, with the wonder of why gold in her
mind.

"White is pure spirit. Gold is strength," came
back to her, audibly, in the *Heart!*

"Who's talking?" Jackson asked.

"You heard that?"

"Of course."

"It was a message to me from Geometria."

"Who?"

"Ah! You didn't have the opportunity to meet him. A quite impressive being here on Pink. I thought his message was psychic."

"Maybe, but also audible. All right, into the air." Jackson thrust ahead, zooming up into the air. Heart met him in tandem, at the bottom point of the heart, then side by side, they flew upwards, around and curving and back to center again, forming the first heart, then forming another heart on top of that one, and a third above those two. By then, they were far from Pink, but close to Pink's moon.

Heart couldn't help giving it a good study, this close. Yes, she saw the colors of her flowers faintly but sweetly, and then, as Jackson bolted nearly out of sight, she waved her wings at the moon, at her flowers, at Xavier, and, intrepidly followed Jackson toward Earth.

They were all, Heart, Jackson, and Equuleus, strangely silent for most of the journey. Content to be left with her thoughts, and always knowing what Equuleus had on his mind, she enjoyed the calm, quiet camaraderie. She knew it was usual for Jackson not to speak unless something of particular importance arose. So, if he wasn't speaking, it meant all was smooth sailing.

She found herself imagining the near future of her sweet reunion with Martha, Key Man and Peter, after they touched down at The Museum of Scientific Improbabilities and Unpredictable Oddities. The last time they'd been together, she had been at death's door. They would love to see her whole and healthy. A special delight for them would be to spend time with Equuleus.

Just as she reveled in the depths of this pleasure, Jackson's voice entered the *Heart!* "You'll be setting down in *The Periphery*, at The Mystic's cottage."

"What? We've been planning all along to land at The Museum of Scientific Improbabilities and Unpredictable Oddities. Why the change?"

"I've been planning all along that the *Heart!* would land in The Periphery. I let you talk your talk because I didn't want to get into an argument."

"I—I don't think I would have argued ...."

"What's this that we're doing right now?"

"Discussing. You're telling me that you didn't tell me your true plans before, letting me sort out in my mind my maneuvers in a landing location I'm familiar with, and, shortly before we land you tell me you intend for me to take a spacecraft into a forest, which I've never done, and land. I don't know the terrain in the least. Landing at the museum is familiar to me. I'm not out of line to express concern with my ability to safely land a spacecraft on dirt, in a forest."

Calm, calm, calm, she thought. Just stay calm. Jackson knows what he's doing.

Jackson hesitated. Did he hesitate, trying to keep calm too, but actually, becoming angry with her for "arguing" when she really did not feel she was? Or had he become quiet, thinking over what she said, realizing she might be telling him an important truth?

"Zack will be there to fly you in. They've cleared a runway, but still, with forest canopy, it's true, to keep the *Heart!* hidden as much as possible. I believe in you, Heart. I know you can do this. You're right. I made an error in judgment, trying too hard to fulfill Father Inventor's directive that we not argue. Yes, we ought to have done some simulations at least.

"You can do this Heart. I know you can. With Zack on the ground, talking you in, you'll be fine."

"Won't you be there too?"

"No. There's no room, and I don't want to draw more attention than we will already. I'm hoping to slide in without external observation."

"Where will you be?"

"I'll continue on and land nearby. It'll be a couple hours ride for me back to The Mystic's cottage."

"How will you get back?"

"Amdrona is en route with Molly & Lolly and the wagon right now."

"I see." Heart thought hard about the new picture, trying to see herself landing in the dense forest.

"I have to say, Jackson, I've never felt this kind of fear that I'm feeling right now. You're asking a lot."

"You're right. I am asking a lot."

They both fell silent, but a few moments later, a 3-D map appeared before Heart. Jackson had drawn an animated line on it, showing her trajectory, with even an image of Zack on the ground, pointing the way.

Heart looked back at Equuleus, who studied the map as intensely as she'd been. "What do you think? Do I have the skill to pull this off?"

"You do, Heart, barring your own lack of self-confidence. It is a tall order, though, out of nowhere." His frustration came across, undisguised. "Of course, there's an alternate plan."

Heart took in what he meant. "Well, yes. But no."

"He's certainly asked for it."

"I'm a bit surprised at your willingness to be vengeful, Equuleus." Heart shut off audio communication with Jackson. "And, anyway, if you and I were to leave the *Heart!* mid-air to crash who-knows-where is not only irresponsible, but could, of course, do huge damage. Start a forest fire in the Periphery. Kill people."

"True."

"I wish there were a way to employ that option, though, if it looks like I simply cannot accomplish the landing. It's a terrible dilemma to have placed me in. If I release you from your security, you could really get injured, Equuleus. But if I leave you attached to your space and the *Heart!* crashes, you, just about for sure, will get seriously damaged."

"Heart!" Jackson's voice resounded. "Your audio is dead. Check for a malfunction in your audio system. It must be found. You'll need audio contact with Zack and me."

She flipped the audio back on. "Test—audio on."

"Right," Jackson replied. "What happened?"

"Private chat with my crew."

"Equuleus?"

"Trying to decide if I ought to leave him magnetically attached and strapped in or release him, in case I crash. We're trying to decide which is likely to be better for him."

Another long silence from Jackson. "Equuleus ...." More silence. "Unstrap him, but leave the magnetic attachment on. That way, you can push the release button on the magnetics in a moment. Open the hatch, Heart, as you head in. Absolute worst scenario, you two can escape and let the *Heart!* crash."

"That's what we were discussing. But I don't want to hurt anyone or start a forest fire if the *Heart!* crashes."

"I intend, and I assume you intend, not to crash the *Heart!* Right?"

"Right, Jackson."

"So, we're contemplating backup maneuvers in case of the worst—*unanticipated!*—scenario. No one wants a forest fire or injuries. But—you and Equuleus are more important than the *Heart!*, obviously.

"I'll tell Zack to mobilize a ground team. But, Heart, I really believe in you. You're skilled and intuitive. You and Equuleus contemplate the map and discuss strategies. But, mostly, concentrate on success."

"Will do."

"Signing off." Jackson's audio went dead. Heart knew he didn't want her to hear his conversation with his cousin, Zack.

"Well, there's no reason not to imagine a perfect landing."

"Agreed," Equuleus said. "He's right. You're skilled and intuitive, you'll do fine. A bit dicey, maybe. But it'll give you an edge when you pull it off."

Jackson clicked on. "I heard that."

Equuleus whinnied.

Heart clicked off her audio and looked over her shoulder with a big, "*he-he!*" grin.

"But think of it, Equuleus, to see Zack and The Mystic and Amdrona and ...."

"Butterfly, yes, but mostly, Eye."

"Yes, Equuleus. If I don't kill us, I will soon actually get to be with Eye. Briefly, I know, but ...."

She hadn't thought of this for one fleeting moment. There'd been nothing in their plans about being in The Periphery. Now, that's where she must land.

"*Oh!*" she said softly, as the very thing she had hoped and hoped for rose up in her immediate future.

Chapter 11

The features of Earth rapidly took shape. Heart realized she could have suspected Jackson had something up his sleeve all along as they were coming in during the late afternoon. Of course, they preferred to arrive at The Museum of Scientific Improbabilities and Unpredictable Oddities under the cover of dark.

She could only blame herself, not noting the irregularity. But they had so little time to plan, and now she feared this might not be the only detail that had slipped between the cracks.

She got up and unstrapped Equuleus, patting him affectionately. "Here we go, my friend."

Equuleus nodded his mighty head.

Heart returned to her seat, clicked on the audio and strapped herself in. "Let the show begin! Did you connect with Zack?"

Jackson clicked his audio on. "Right. Ground team mobilized, everything looks good."

"Good. I know you've kept in mind, Jackson, that we have to enter *The Periphery* well behind The Wall, or all other plans will rapidly become irrelevant."

"That base is covered, Heart. Both to avoid detection, and to avoid you encountering the dark energy of The Wall, we're entering on the far side. Interesting to me, as I've never seen that terrain from the sky."

"Don't get us lost now," Heart teased.

"*Har-umph!*" Jackson replied with mock indignation.

Heart grinned. They were both in good spirits. That's the way to do it, she thought. The map before her took on a near ground appearance.

"In we go!" Jackson said. "Follow close, watch the map, look for Zack. We'll go in low and slow. If it looks like you can't make it, circle around, try again. Relax. Take it easy."

"Right, right, right." Heart answered. The beauty of The Periphery's forest took shape below. "Oh! So beautiful!" she uttered.

"The map, Heart."

She nodded, even knowing Jackson couldn't see her. The map seemed almost to rise up itself like the forest below. There, she saw Zack, a tiny figure, waving with wild abandon. The map showed she would have to make a 180-degree turn to come back on the clearing.

"Tight turn, Heart, to avoid the possible energy of The Wall."

"So I see. Added pressure." She slowed to a crawl, so it felt, and banked the curve. But she could not make it 180 degrees. She would miss the landing.

Below her, Zack waved and smiled and gestured for her to go again. He didn't look the least bit disconcerted. Where was Jackson?

"Where are you, Jackson, where are you? I have to go around again."

"I see that. I'm out of your way, don't worry about me. Take your time. You handled it well, You did great!"

"I missed it!"

"That's fine. You're handling it just fine. Go again."

Frustrated with herself, she flew hovering over the forest to some distance. "What's my problem? I've done many trickier maneuvers."

"In Pink's open sky, with no one around. Not over Earth's forest," Equuleus answered.

There, far from everyone, she practiced the 180 degree turn. "Perfect!" she crowed.

"Perfect," Equuleus agreed.

Feeling much more confident, she returned to the clearing, came in close, Zack all smiles and thumbs up. She banked tight, and lowered, lowered.

Yes! Right in line, everything clear. Buzzing below the tree line, she slowed and touched down on the earth. She felt it give. She felt the *Heart!* jerk. She braked and the *Heart!* began to nose into the dirt. She saw herself and Equuleus going end over end with no opportunity to escape, but the *Heart!* settled back, and came to rest, right side up and intact.

She heard a roaring cheer come up from the forest and she simply could not wipe the gigantic grin from her face as she released her safety harness, then released Equuleus's magnetic security.

"Let's show off," she said.

"Let's!" he agreed.

They exited the hatch and Heart jumped on his back. He leapt up into the sky, then flew back toward The Mystic's cottage. Out in the forest all along the clearing, shouts and cheers rang up.

"Thank goodness we landed as we did. We would have taken out folks left and right, otherwise. Why didn't Zack tell them to stay clear?"

"I'm sure he did, and I'm sure they ignored him!"

Heart laughed. "No doubt, my friend!"

Equuleus flew high and circled, then dove, performing his midair pirouettes that Heart so loved. He extended his amazing wings to their full, glorious width, and then abruptly pulled them in. He appeared to stand on the air, pawing at the sky, spinning and plummeting, then extending his wings again.

A breath-taking display, Heart knew. Even at their height, she heard gasps and exclamations from the gathering below.

"All right," Hearth sighed, "I guess that's enough grandstanding."

"If you insist." Equuleus floated down toward the ground like a supernatural eagle feather, landing deftly before The Mystic's cottage.

Predictably, a crowd waited for them. Heart did not recognize most of the people who cheered and chattered, closing in on Equuleus and herself. She searched for the faces she longed to see.

Zack jostled his way among the throng. He'd grown taller since last she'd seen him, and his beautiful muscular shoulders rose above almost everyone. His eyes fixed on Heart, a smile as wide as his handsome face.

What a sight to behold, Heart thought.

Picking up on her fascination, Equuleus whinnied.

"Hush!" she warned him.

Before saying a single word, Zack grabbed her, wrapped his arms around her and gave her an extended and affectionate hug.

Heart let him.

The crowd cheered ever more delightedly.

Finally, he pulled back from her and gave her a good looking over. "More beautiful than ever, if at all possible."

"*Ahhhh!*" the crowd sighed.

"Thanks," Equuleus said, which made everyone giggle like kids.

"Well," Heart returned, "You haven't lost any ground, either. And ... you're taller!"

"I believe I am," he agreed. "As for you," Zack added, turning his attention to Equuleus, "you're ever the epitome of ageless beauty."

Equuleus extended his right front foot and bowed deeply, muzzle to hoof, wings pointed up toward the sky. This sent the crowd into a frenzy of delight.

"Ah! *Ahhhhh!* It's so good to be here!" Heart exclaimed. "Oh, the way it feels ... I can't express."

"All right you all, move back!" Heart heard The Mystic at the edge of the crush of people. As she worked her way to the center of the crowd, everyone took a step back. Finally, she came face to face with Heart. "Goodness, you'd think these provincials had never seen a flying clockworks horse."

Everyone's glee rose to an entirely new level, because, of course, none of them ever *had* seen a flying clockworks horse! Though a few of them who had, years previous, lived freely on the other side of the wall may have seen Equuleus, inanimate and inert, in his showcase in The Museum of Scientific Improbabilities and Unpredictable Oddities.

"Everyone, go find things to do," The Mystic said, shooing them off. "A bunch of you, go out and see to the condition of the *Heart!* I should imagine it's up to its belly in dirt."

"Almost," Heart agreed. "I thought for sure we were going to go tail for beak, but, somehow, we managed to stay upright."

"Yes," The Mystic agreed. "So I saw."

"How? I landed far out in the forest."

"I have my ways."

Heart thought twice, recalling the golden scrying mirror above The Mystic's mantle. "Yes, of course. What am I thinking?"

A number of people broke away from the crowd and ran off into the forest to attend to the *Heart!*, which relieved Heart immensely because she'd already been imagining the frowning critique she'd receive from Jackson if the *Heart!* was, in fact, damaged. It didn't look too bad, but it was definitely buried in the dirt.

The rest of the crowd moved back a little but refused to disperse altogether. The Mystic waved her hands about, wordlessly insisting everyone else get about their business. "For pity's sake, you'd think nothing ever happens here."

"*Hmmmm* ...." Zack wordlessly suggested.

"Enough from you!" she retorted.

"I said nothing!" He grinned at Heart, winking. *Oh heaven save me*, she thought.

The Mystic began to amble toward her adorable, storybook cottage, and Heart, all too happily, practically danced along with her. "Where's Jackson?" she said, looking up into the sky.

"Oh, he went on. Not even bothering to see if you survived, I might add," The Mystic said. "But, of course, he knows your abilities."

"I doubt it since I've been whining about his expectations that I land in a forest! Without any training, not even a flight simulation! On dirt! More likely he didn't want to witness my destroying the *Heart!*"

The Mystic laughed. "Such hyperbole, my girl! We both know he had you on his radar, as well as trusting his cousin and all the folks out in the forest."

"Yes!" Heart exclaimed. "Risking their lives, so innocently, with me roaring around in the sky and on land. I'm sure glad I didn't run over anyone."

The Mystic almost giggled, an incongruously girlish sound. "*So are we! Tee-hee!*"

As they approached the little arched door of The Mystic's cottage, Heart became nervous. She sighed deeply.

"He's not in the cottage, Heart." The Mystic said, reading Heart's thoughts.

"Oh?" Heart didn't even attempt a coy, "who?" Everyone knew who she meant.

"He's been stirring around like a caged cat since we knew for certain sure you were coming here."

"Oh!" Heart uttered again, at a loss for any single bit of vocabulary.

"He and Butterfly are in the back, with the flowers. But come in and say hi."

"All right," Heart agreed, wondering who she'd be saying hi to, as Amdrona was on her way to get Jackson, but happy to chat for a few minutes while gathering a strange, anxious courage to visit the flower garden.

Surprised, she discovered she had to noticeably stoop to go through The Mystic's front door, The last time she'd been here, she'd only had to stoop a little bit. Inside, a charming, subdued light relaxed her.

Heart became accustomed to the shadowy light while watching The Mystic busy herself putting a kettle over the fire. "I'm so grateful, brave, amazing, Amdrona, saving Eye and Butterfly. Saying thank you to her will never be enough!"

The Mystic chuckled as if Heart had said something quite amusing, but replied, "Amdrona only did what any one of us would do."

"Perhaps," Heart conceded, "But Amdrona *did* it. And she can shapeshift."

"All right, all right, enough accolades for someone who's not even here," a familiar voice growled.

Shocked, Heart turned to see Swen! Right there before her! Coming out from under The Mystic's tiny table.

"Oh! *Oh, oh, oh!*" Heart became seriously reduced to her single syllable. She took two steps and fell to her knees, "*Swen!*" He came into her embrace, and she hugged him as if he spouted a fountain of Life Force. He returned her affection.

Finally, she pulled back from him and said simply, "You're here!"

"So it would seem."

"I ... you ... you're here!"

"Hmmm, Heart, what has the environment on Pink done to you?" Swen said in his gravelly, and emotion-filled voice.

She laughed. "Not funny!"

"You're laughing."

She hugged him again and stood. "You've always been quite astute." It felt grand to spar with her own, dear Swen!

"Indeed, I am." He nodded his head most emphatically, his long floppy ears performing a counterpoint.

Equuleus, standing outside the doorway, chuckled. Heart, picking up on his amusement, laughed too.

"What's so funny?" Swen demanded.

"You ... you remind us of a friend of ours on Pink."

"*Hmmmm,* lots of dogs on Pink?"

"This made Equuleus snort and Heart almost guffaw. "Well, one. But that's yet another story."

Heart sat at the table and waved Swen to come by her. She patted his head while saying, "It's strange to think of my life there that no one here knows about. Father wants to keep it as 'cloaked' as possible."

"For good reason," The Mystic acknowledged.

"Yes. For good reason."

A silence fell around them as a variety of thoughts passed through their minds. Pictures of what Pink might actually be like, which only Heart and Equuleus knew. Thoughts of The Purists. Thoughts about the very real and dangerous reason Heart now sat in their midst.

There rose a collective sigh, while Heart leaned over and hugged Swen tightly, whispering in his ear, "Thank you, my beloved friend, for being here."

He nodded softly.

She stood "Well, now …."

"Yes," The Mystic agreed, "Well now, time to go admire the flowers …."

Heart stepped through the even tinier side door, then stretched, flinging her arms wide, breathing in the forest air, breathing in the lengthening shadows of the gorgeous Spring evening.

Breathing in the soul-deep truth: *there was no place like HOME!*

*   *

Heart recalled the lay of the land from the brief 3-D Jackson had brought to Pink to share with her of Butterfly and Eye, safely ensconced in their new—and much safer!—life at The Mystic's cottage. Around to the back of the cottage, and at a short distance, Heart saw a rock garden, not entirely unlike the one Butterfly had brought together, with her tiny but authoritative voice commanding other Darling Undesirables to "move this here," and "put that rock there!"

The memory made Heart smile. She gathered yet more courage—how strange! It was Eye! Her sweet brother-friend, Eye. It felt like forever and a day since she'd seen him. But it was only a short while since she'd seen him—with Butterfly—sleeping like two little babes in what had previously been her own bed.

Thank goodness for Butterfly! What might have happened to Eye had she not been there to help him process the traumatic void when Heart left?

Enough reflection and procrastination, she commanded herself. She stepped around the corner of the cottage. At a distance, Butterfly sat on the ground in front of Eye, himself sitting on a large, beautiful, flat rock. Butterfly talked with him, and most sweetly, kept watch on the corner of The Mystic's cottage.

Butterfly saw Heart, and they exchanged a look of love and, perhaps the slightest edge of jealousy, each to the other. After all, they each felt Eye was "her" Eye.

Heart immediately released this feeling. Not only did she have the greatest love and respect for Butterfly, but, she thought quite distinctly, there was enough Eye to go around.

In fact, this thought felt like his and not hers!

His smile widened. Ah yes, her Eye—thinking to her, proving his point, that there was, *for sure!*, enough Eye to go around.

Butterfly leapt up, and, always fairy-like, giving the illusion of flying, she moved delicately and rapidly on the very tips of her toes, her fabulous golden hair catching the evening sun rays—*gorgeous!* Heart felt sad that Eye could not see Butterfly in this moment. Exquisite. Strong. Petite. Purposeful. Quaint. Kind. Self-aware. Shy.

"Heart!" she whispered with her fairy voice. *"Heart!"* Shy but sure, she threw her arms around Heart, and Heart reciprocated.

"So perfect to see you here, Butterfly. As if you've always, always lived here."

Butterfly stepped back fairies, and looked to the forest. "I know the forest is my true home … I'm certain my experimental DNA came from here."

Heart knew well Butterfly's belief in fairies and her belief that one had been captured to use in the endless experimentation with various biologic materials that produced The Darling Undesirables, and that resulted in the wingless fairy who all but fluttered before her now.

"We'll talk later," Butterfly continued. "But right now, Eye is waiting for you." Without pause, Butterfly flitted off and passed through the back door of the cottage.

Heart took a deep breath, then went to meet her life-long, precious friend.

She sat on the ground before Eye where Butterfly had been, saying nothing. She took Eye's hand and made their sign for "love you" in his palm. He took her palm and returned, "love you more!"

"*Oh! Eye*," she whispered. "Eye ...."

"*Heart!*" The sound broke through as if from some great distance, with a voice that stunned Heart, and even made her lean back. "Oh, my! Your voice. You're becoming a man, my little friend. Goodness, what a beautiful sound, your voice. But what a shock!"

Eye laughed with pleasure. "That's exactly what Butterfly said would be one of the first things you'd say to me. My voice, beautiful but shocking!"

Heart laughed too. What a mixture of emotions! Here, finally with Eye. Completely familiar and entirely unfamiliar.

Eye became silent. "Thank you, Heart! Thank you! Thank you for bringing me here, of course, my dearest friend, thank you. I am so, so grateful you made arrangements for Butterfly. I don't know how you knew to do that. But ... thank you."

"I ... well, when I stowed away on the *Heart!* with Xavier and came to Earth, I came to see you. Just to know that you were safe. That you were all right.

"I made everyone alter their plans to accommodate me, to let me go to The Darling Undesirable

Facility at Long Prairie. Which I did in the middle of the night. Once there, and under the fence, I shape-shifted all the way, stealing upstairs to look in on you. I only needed to see, as I say, that you looked all right. And to confirm you were still in your same room.

"Well, you know what I found. *No Eye!* You can imagine what I went through. Oh, my mind ran wild with terrible thoughts. But then I settled down because I saw all your things in your room. They appeared organized, as always, and—it simply felt like you'd been there recently and regularly."

"I stepped back out, puzzled, and upset. I had a plan to have you removed as soon as possible— if I didn't know where you were, how could we accomplish that?

"At the same time, I couldn't stop my curiosity about who might be in my room now, enjoying my star dome, if anyone. I felt very, *very* guilty opening what used to be my door, but it opened easily, and there, I saw two little babes, sweetly dreaming. But-terfly's delicate arm around you, so protectively, so … so …."

"So?" Eye asked softly, holding onto Heart's hand tightly.

"So, just right, Eye. Everything about the energy between you, everything felt and looked sweet and right. I'd already been told that Butterfly had bonded closely with you when I 'disappeared.'

"At first that news shocked me. And that night, when I saw you and Butterfly in my little bed, that shocked me, too. I'm not going to lie, I was ... not quite jealous, exactly. Just ...."

Heart sighed so, so deeply, throwing her head back, looking up into the most perfect color of blue anywhere in all of the Universe in the sky above. She tried to pull her hand away, but Eye would not let go.

"I felt *afraid*, Eye. Afraid. Afraid that I would really, truly lose the only person who is my real family. Like, you are my whole family and Butterfly might take you from me.

"All wrong, wrong, wrong, of course. But, still, that's what I felt. Even while incredibly relieved and grateful that the two of you became close. I didn't have to worry about you, every minute of every day. I only had to sort out the horrible feeling of having lost you.

"Of course, my life is so full! I have Swen, I have Equuleus, I have my father. I have a slew of new, amazing and wonderful friends.

"But family is something else."

"You haven't lost me one little bit, Heart," Eye said. "You're my sister. My big sister. You will always be my big sister. No one is my family like you, Heart. In fact, if I lost you, I'd be losing much more, because now you have Father Inventor, your father. Your actual father."

They sat quietly holding hands for a few moments, then Eye continued, "But now—now you're all right about Butterfly? You knew, that night, you knew for sure, we'd become so close. And you ... ahm, approve of Butterfly?"

"Oh, yes, Eye. Yes! Who else? No one else. Eye and Butterfly. It even rhymes. Yes. I feel ... this is part of what I told myself, that if I truly loved you, I would want you to have a companion. Absolutely true. Then I thought about how wonderful that it's Butterfly. I grew up with her, too. I know her very well, to her depths. I know she's transparently fierce, loyal, reliable, trustworthy, affectionate, intelligent. And she loves flowers, like you and I do."

"Well, more than we do," they said together, which ignited a giggle-fest neither of them could stop.

"Let's walk a bit," Eye said, as the giggles kept rolling over them in waves.

"Love it!" Heart jumped up and Eye stood right with her. Just as if he had eyes. He knew where he stood, and where he was going.

They wandered, hand in hand into the forest and along the clearing that had been made for the *Heart!*

"Oh, Heart, I felt panicky when you flew in. I could hear it wasn't right the first time. I sat here and prayed you would not try to make it work. I cheered when you accelerated again, and took another turn at it. Then, sure as sunrise, you were on it. To a hair's breadth! I never saw anything so perfect."

"*Wow!*" Heart murmured. "I know when you say you saw something, you really saw it—like no one else could see it."

"For sure. I even saw it would nosedive, and I prayed you wouldn't hit a pocket of soft dirt, or you'd go spinning. I could hear, by your speed and the sound of the earth under the *Heart!* that there would be no avoiding it digging in, but you handled it to perfection."

"Thank you, Eye. That means a lot to me. So much. Especially considering Jackson told me just a short while ago, as Earth became bigger and bigger through the *Heart!*'s viewport, that I would not be landing at The Museum of Scientific Improbabilities and Unpredictable Oddities like we'd planned, but here, at The Mystic's cottage, with not even one single simulation, or not even sitting and talking it through."

Eye stopped in his tracks. "Why? Why would he do that? It's ... why?"

"Oh, because we had a ridiculous, but nonetheless huge, fight. And, and, well, my father gave us the lecture of our lives."

"Worse than any you received at The Darling Undesirables Residence of Long Prairie?"

"Much, much worse. Because, first of all, I care what Father thinks and feels. He's always gentle, always kind. Hates confrontation. Ironic, no? He's the center of the world's biggest confrontation. Anyway, he gave us a lecture like we've never had. And, oh, I felt *soooooo* bad ...."

"I can imagine," Eye said, squeezing her hand. "But, what does that have to do with Jackson risking your life?"

"Since our 'lecture' where my father said he would scrap this whole mission if we didn't immediately behave more responsibly, we've been overly circumspect with one another. A bit too distant, a bit too polite. A bit too afraid of ourselves that we'll go off on each other again.

"So when I told him that not telling me about this landing could be life-threatening, not only for Equuleus and myself, and not only for the residents, but it could also start a forest fire, he realized he'd made a bad decision.

"The first and only bad decision, I dare say, he thinks he's ever made." She chuckled. "Anyway, he spent some time talking me through it. Bottom line, because of you and your prayers, I think, I made it."

Eye shook his head. "My prayers were with you, but you did this on your own, Heart. I believe my prayers are likely better directed to getting Jackson to chill."

"Not a bad idea." Heart laughed.

Eye stopped, cocked his head and inhaled deeply. Then he leaned over and deftly picked a single, pristine, perfect, white trillium. "For you, Heart, a perfect trillium, Faith. Hope. Love.

"But the greatest of these is *love*."

Part II

Chapter 12

Heart and Eye wandered among the wildflowers, chatting about a myriad and one bits and pieces that fascinated them, from the trillium to The Purists, from Heart sharing a tiny bit about Violet and HelperFriend—she couldn't be with Eye without telling him about her two wonderful new friends—to reports of strange goings on at The Darling Undesirables Residence of Long Prairie.

"Interesting," Heart said after Eye gave her a thumbnail sketch of an apparent lockdown only two days previous. "What's *that* about? Maybe there's really something going on, or maybe it's a way to get press."

"With the two of us, here now—*oh, Eye!*—this is *almost* my dream become reality. The two of us here, in the forest, chatting. If only—if only this *were* our reality, instead of a passing moment. Though I'm happy to have this precious moment. Oh, goodness, I've babbled along, I forgot my point ...."

"The two of us here," Eye recapped, "instead of at The Darling Undesirables Residence of Long Prairie. And someone there perhaps making it their mission to get the focus back on *them* by posing a lockdown, rather than it being the truth."

"Yes, dearest Eye, that's my point, precisely. My, my, how well I present it, too!" She laughed, while at the same time keeping silent about her mission— to go where angels feared to tread.

The thought of there being a lockdown at The Darling Undesirables Residence of Long Prairie, when there had never had been one the entire time she lived there sobered her.

"What, Heart! *What?*"

Of course, Eye saw right through her silence.

"Can't say, Eye."

"Can't say? *To me?!?*"

"For your own good, dear. For your own good."

He became still, holding her hand, trying to read her mind pictures, she knew. "Don't, Eye. I must be about my business. All I need from you is your love, your emotional support. Your prayers."

"Yes, Heart—you have them, you know you always have everything I have to give. But ...."

Swen loped up to them. "Sorry to interrupt your cherished tête-à-tête, but Jackson is near, and with

Peter, too. Jackson wanted to talk with you. He sounded, well you know Jackson ....”

“Indeed I do,” Heart agreed.

“Anyway, he sounded somewhere to the left of happy not to be able to talk with you. Right here. Right now.”

“Ah me, oh my,” Heart sighed, turning and heading back to The Mystic’s cottage, still holding Eye’s hand, and refusing to rush. But she stopped in her tracks. “Wait! Peter’s coming! How wonderful, but ... hmmm, not Key Man and Martha?”

“No. Not Key Man and Martha.”

“Then, why Peter?”

“Well, he has, that is, he is ....” Swen stuttered.

“The newshound stutters,” Heart teased, feigning shock.

“Yes. Well, I leave it to others to fill in where I’m now leaving it off.”

“Leaving what off?”

“This subject.” Swen trotted ahead. “You coming?” He glanced over his shoulder.

“Yes. Sure. Coming.”

Heart and Eye continued ambling to the cottage. They both stooped through the little side door, following Swen. Everyone in the cottage stood poised, waiting for their return. Heart went up to Butterfly and put Eye’s hand that she still held, into Butterfly’s, then stooped down and gave her a kiss on the cheek. “Thank you for loving and caring for Eye, sweet Butterfly,” she said simply.

Butterfly looked down, shyly. *"Oh, Heart!"* she exclaimed.

"Jackson is quite anxious to speak with you," Zack said. "I told him to let you have a few minutes, which he begrudgingly granted. He'll be here shortly, along with Amdrona, Peter, and of course, Molly and Lolly—who, I must add, will be happy to see you!"

"Oh!" Heart cried. "I'll be delighted to see them, as well. Do you think they'll remember me?"

"To be sure, Heart, they'll remember you!" Zack smiled at her endearingly.

"It's lovely that Peter is coming as well."

"Lovely, yes," The Mystic said. "But pragmatic."

"Pragmatic?" Heart became even more mystified. "I don't understand ...."

Equuleus, standing at the door, whinnied.

Heart exchanged a look with him. "Here they come."

She stepped outside, and, as the little cart ambled within hailing distance, she walked, with Equuleus, to meet it. Peter, sitting on the little rustic seat beside the beautiful Amdrona jumped down from the seat and rushed up to Equuleus. "How are you, my friend? How are you?" He reached out and patted his forehead.

"I am well, Peter."

Heart watched, curious, as she saw Equuleus process something. "You look drawn, Peter," Equuleus observed.

"Do I? Perhaps. There's a lot going on."

"True." Equuleus agreed, nodding.

Stunned by this interaction, and by the obvious fact that the two of them had much knowledge between them she was not privy to, Heart whispered, "Strange."

"Let's get at it," Jackson ordered, jumping down from the back of the cart, roaring up to the cottage, past Heart and Peter and Equuleus.

"Let us share a few moments," Peter serenely suggested.

Heart, stunned yet again, as she watched Jackson stop short in his tracks and turn on his heel to face them.

"Right," he said, frowning slightly, not relaxed, but with his hands folded behind his back as if at attention.

Heart moved from the mounting weirdness toward Amdrona and Molly and Lolly. The moment, she decided, needed some femininity to balance it out.

"Hey, Molly, hey Lolly," she called softly to the two adorable donkeys plodding the last few feet to the cottage, patting the nearer Molly on her forelock. "Hi, Amdrona."

"Heart!" They had reached the cottage, and Amdrona stepped gracefully down from the small cart.

Heart went to her and hugged her, whispering to her, "Thank you for saving my Eye and Butterfly."

"Oh, no, Heart," Amdrona demurred, "I did no more than anyone would do."

"Just as The Mystic said!" Heart chuckled. "But *no one* could do what you did. Going to a place you'd never been, not taking a single false step. Shape-shifting, getting them out of the building, through the garden, under the fence and to the spacecraft, undetected."

Zack came to the cart, and he and Amdrona unharnessed the donkeys, who plodded dutifully to their little shed, Lolly reaching over and giving Molly an affectionate nuzzle as they went.

"Let's go inside, shall we?" Peter suggested.

"Let's," Jackson agreed, leading the way.

Or, leading the charge, Heart thought, watching his almost robotic movements as he ducked into the cottage. Heart let everyone go before her, and tagged along behind with Amdrona, thinking about the crowded interior of The Mystic's little cottage, and trying to picture how, quite frankly, they would all fit.

But, as had happened before, which seemed so long ago, in the days when Heart was innocent of all her life would soon become, she now stepped through the little modest door into a space The Mystic brought into being for this, clearly auspicious, event.

Gone was the cozy, shadowed room. Heart entered a glowing hall, lit with long tapers, along walls that reached up to the sky, with but a canopy of the forest trees for a ceiling. The shadowed evening light mingled with the candle glow in a swirling, whirling matrix overhead, while the light from the tapers shimmered and glimmered on everyone in a pastel flow.

"Ohhhhh!" Heart sighed, drinking in the supernatural sight. The Mystic stood at her little door, waiting for Heart, and yes, Equuleus, who could barely pass through, to enter.

She turned to The Mystic, and somewhat teasingly asked, "Do you know Geometria?"

"But of course," The Mystic replied, shutting the door firmly. "Though I've not met him in 'the flesh' as saying has it. We are good, old, old, friends."

The Mystic gestured to Heart to join the others, who flanked either side of a long, dark oak table, each standing behind a beautifully carved oak chair. Heart moved to stand along the side of the table, but there were only two chairs available—at the head, where she stood, and at the foot, where The Mystic moved to stand, herself.

Somewhat uncomfortably, and feeling very much in the dark about, well, everything, despite the stunning and mystical light, Heart stood behind the chair at the head of the table. Equuleus situated himself to her right. Swen came to her left. Peter stood at the chair to her right, beyond him stood Eye, then Butterfly. Then Jackson stood at the chair to her left, next to him, Zack, then Amdrona.

Heart took in every movement, nuance, and aspect of the proceedings, fully aware that something huge, something perhaps world changing, transpired.

Everyone, *even Equuleus!* knew something she didn't.

Ah! she thought, I've no doubt entered a scene straight from *Ourbook*.

The pause extended. No one moved or said a word, not even Jackson, who had been so antsy moments before. She now understood, he'd needed to get to this moment.

But ... what was everyone waiting for? She hadn't stood at the head of the table because she wanted to. They had, by default, intentionally placed her there.

She made a small throat-clearing sound, then dared to say, "I suppose you're all wondering why I asked you here."

Much to her surprise, they laughed joyously, pulled out their chairs, and became seated. She looked to her left at Swen, chortling and nodding, baring his teeth in a wide grin, eyes closed in mirth, and, to her right, her own Equuleus softly whinnied, eye gears whirling in amusement.

When they were all seated, and the mysterious gaiety had settled, they each turned expectantly toward her. She pulled her chair out and sat, then took in each person in turn, slowly and patiently.

The energy of every individual swirled with the otherworldly light that infused the space, as well as a light unique to each. As she beheld the swirling energies, she saw the immensity of each being, how much more amazing each one was than the small-but-beautiful bodily container before her.

Breathing deeply, she worked her gaze around the table, filled with wonder. As her study finally came around to rest upon Equuleus and Swen, they, too, each had their own unique, swirling Light of Being, extending far beyond present time and space.

Finally, she decided to attempt to look at herself, but for this, she closed her eyes and peered at the young woman at the head of the table. Her light, like all the others, extended beyond the body sitting calmly among her friends and protectors. She felt, as she imagined love for herself, her light extend to everyone at the table, she saw a glowing thread come from her and work its way around the table, through everyone in turn, like a necklace of power that would not be thwarted, and returning to her-self.

When Heart opened her eyes, the white-light thread continued, visually apparent.

"We are the necklace of goodness, power, and love," she said. "We are eternal beings, in the midst of a 'time-event.' We have only one mission, to be the ambassadors, the messengers of love. There are no accidents.

"As I sit here with each of you, and we bond in this metaphysical moment, I see now the remarkable intention that I, myself, put into motion when I became inflexibly determined to seek my destiny, with a clear vision. That destiny being that all Darling Undesirables be treated with love and respect, that all Beings, whatever the spark of cognition may be within them, however, it may be sparked, to honor the fact that every single being and creature has a purpose.

"It is *our* purpose to protect *their* purpose.

"I don't know how to direct, or even suggest, how we proceed. I can only give you everything I have to give, my devotion, my strength, my curiosity, my determination, but most of all, my love. My undying, my powerful, my gentle, my protective, love. May we each keep our vision clear and focused upon our goal."

Around the table passed a prayerful murmur of approval and agreement.

Then—the planning began in earnest.

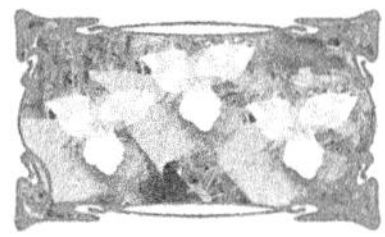

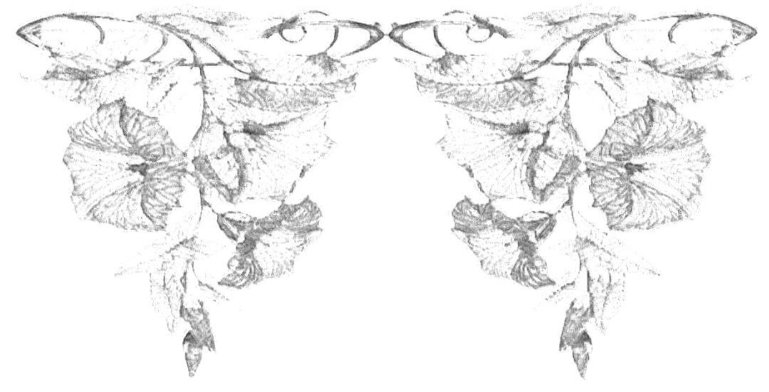

Chapter 13

While Jackson and Peter dove into plans they had, somewhat obviously to Heart, been developing for some time, The Mystic rose from the far end of the table and retrieved the kettle she'd earlier hung over the fire. She brought it to the table. Starting with Peter, she filled the pewter goblet that stood at each place and, Equuleus and Swen's beautiful pewter bowls.

Heart watched in fascination as the elixir pouring from the kettle flowed like molten gold. She wondered if the liquid itself was golden, or if it appeared golden, reflecting the golden, swirling lights. However, she couldn't keep her mind focused on the thought and gave up.

She watched as everyone, including Equuleus and Swen, sipped at the beverage, and, finally, took a sip herself.

Such a flavor she had never known! Seeming more a sensation of touch than flavor, though it did have a flavor as well. One thing for sure, it opened and relaxed her mind.

She'd been listening without much perception to Jackson and Peter, overwhelmed by their exacting subtlety regarding the movements she and they would take. Intense planning had never been a skill she resonated with. Intuition served her.

On the verge of suggesting they stop batting her name about like a playing chip in some sort of game, the touch of the elixir brought before Heart a vision shared by everyone at the table. The confusing details suddenly took form, hovering over the table, a translucent 3-D vision of their planning.

"*Ah!*" Heart exclaimed, "this is a field I can become involved in." At present, it had little detail, composed primarily of colored lines, which she took to represent herself, Jackson, and apparently Swen, although she wasn't clear on that point. Thus far in the planning, no one else, not even Peter, appeared to be involved. She pointed at a rectangle in the midst of the projection. "Is this meant to represent the garden shed at The Darling Undesirables Residence of Long Prairie?"

"That's right," Peter nodded.

"Let's give it some distinction." Heart thought into the projection, and the charming little building materialized.

"Oh!" Butterfly gasped.

"Well done," Eye said.

"Can you see this?" Heart asked.

"Probably better than all of you. You've perfectly captured the garden shed, Heart, roses and all."

"Thank you, Eye." Heart beamed, proud of herself.

"Right," Jackson interjected. "Not a game here, Heart. This is serious business."

Frustrated, Heart kept her mouth shut.

"Jackson, you must release control," Peter reprimanded.

Heart looked at Peter, grateful that he defended her. Then she understood, once again, that considerably more was going on than she at first perceived. She studied Peter's face.

Something wonderful had come upon Peter's face, and she saw now that he, usually, cloaked himself, shapeshifting in his own way. She suddenly realized that, if she'd been asked to render a drawing of Peter before this moment, it would have no distinction. But now, the strength in his face matched the power of his calm, yet forceful words. She found herself focused on a faint but jagged four-inch scar along his jawline.

She'd never noticed this scar, in all the time she'd known him, and all the time she'd spent with him.

What event did this scar represent? What battle, what bravery? Peter—"her" Peter, was not merely the doorman at The Museum of Scientific Improbabilities and Unpredictable Oddities.

There was more to him. *Much, much more.* There arose in Heart, who thought she could "read" anyone, a serious doubt in her abilities. If, in all this time, she hadn't "seen" the real Peter, how could she possibly imagine she could do all that they expected of her?

A silence hung in the air after Peter's reprimand.

"Thank you, Peter, I agree. I don't mean to criticize you Jackson, and considerably less want to. But, please do relax. It's quite stressful feeling like one is never coming up to your standards," she said softly.

Swen made a small throat clearing growling sound, wordlessly agreeing.

Heart patted Swen as the two of them recalled shared memories of Jackson's harsh treatment the first time they ever met. "Please, Jackson, make an effort to attune yourself a bit more to my energies.

"I believe what's being planned here is, in the end, primarily dependent upon me. And yet, I remain unclear as to what, precisely, the mission is. I'm not communicated with in a transparent and candid way. I say, that must change.

"As I understand it, point number one is that there is some reason to believe that Xavier intentionally placed the four magnetic resonators of the Moons' protective shield where he placed them.

"Point two, the center of the cross of those four resonators happens to be at the garden shed of The Darling Undesirables Residence of Long Prairie.

"Point three, somehow that shed is related to our quest for my father's cloned brain.

"And point four, since I lived most of my life there, even though I've never been in the garden, as is true for all Darling Undesirables, since Keeper A, beautiful outside, mean and selfish inside, would never let a single one of us stroll upon the garden path—that by my stealing into the shed, unobserved, or so we plan, I will discover something.

"We don't know what!—but I'll discover something about this clone from within the garden shed, that will assist *The Cause of All Beings* in revealing the clone brain's whereabouts, so that it might be seized and put out of commission.

"Whereupon, The Purists will have lost their most sophisticated component in their grassroots war against all who are not fully bio.

"Does that about sum it up?"

Jackson looked at Heart much as though she'd just appeared out of thin air. "Yes," he muttered.

"Excellent!" Heart became filled with an inexplicable joy. "*Excellent!*" she repeated. "Well, then, why all the ceremony? Let's get on it. I'm to shapeshift, go into a little shed I passed more times than I care to count the first fifteen years of my life, and look for something, a map or some such that says, 'Here's the box that holds Father Inventor's clone brain.' Then we all engage in a treasure hunt."

"Hmmm," Peter said, shaking his head ever so slightly. "One extreme to the other with you two. Do not get too flippant, Heart. There are a considerable number of details you don't know about. Jackson *does know* aspects of this operation that you do not.

"Balance, you two. *BALANCE!* The varying nature of your perceptions is necessary to accomplish our goals. But it will go down in failure if you both insist upon not honoring the other's way of perceiving. In short, we need you to work in harmony. Make music, not noise!"

"He started it," Heart, feeling the reprimand, said in a tiny, little voice, looking at Peter out of the corner of her eye with an impish grin.

Peter chuckled. "Amusing, and ... true!" He turned his attention to the vision space between them, which had all but melted. "Now look what we've done. Focus please."

Within moments, the vision returned.

"Fabulous," Heart breathed. "All right now, what is it that Jackson knows, that I don't? I'm not inclined to have any more figurative *or* literal landings in dirt up to my waist."

"Anything you aren't told, Heart," Jackson said in a subdued voice, "is for your own peace of mind."

"My peace of mind! Strange thought with all that's boiling up. Never mind my peace of mind, Jackson, which you cannot hope to fully understand, anyway. Tell me what's at stake, tell me what's going on behind the curtain that I don't know."

Jackson sighed deeply, exchanging a look with Peter, then looking at the far end of the table at The Mystic. He apparently received approval from both.

"The most pressing issue at this moment, as of but a short while ago, is the news that The Purists have figured out a means of a single flash trajectory, with which, they say, they intend to capture Father Inventor on Pink and bring him to Earth."

"I don't believe it," Heart protested.

"Neither do I," Swen agreed. "You can never trust the news."

Heart looked down at him, "*Ah!* This from a newshound."

"*Former* newshound."

"They're not releasing this bit of their story to the public," Peter added, "but the underground notes that it has become possible because of the ever-growing genius of Father Inventor's clone brain."

"*Hmmmm.*" Heart glanced around the table, then addressed The Mystic. "Why not put your powers into making short work of all this confusion? I somehow feel that you could."

The Mystic smiled at her, with mischief in her eyes. "This is a learning within the three dimensions, Heart. If I—or anyone who might have certain potential powers—took it upon themselves to foist their values on a situation such as this, and it came out cheerful and sweet, without anyone having to go through any tempering fires, then what would be the point of the three dimensions?

"Every one of us at this table has remarkable powers, but it's up to each of us to take our own journey, to learn our own learnings, to help one another when together, to stand strong when alone, and, dear Heart, to learn the highest lesson, that cuts through all dimensions. You know this perfectly well."

"To love, and to be loved ...." Heart replied.

"Yes. To love and to be loved."

Heart drank down the remains of whatever it was in her pewter goblet.

Amdrona and Butterfly rose and went into the little kitchen which reappeared behind Heart, and began to make a modest luncheon for everyone. When Heart looked back at the table, it had diminished the length of the two far seats.

"Shall we leave directly?" Heart asked.

"After lunch, yes," Peter agreed.

Zack and Eye stood. "We must attend to the creatures, we'll be back shortly for lunch."

Again the table reduced in size, bringing The Mystic across from Heart at a cozy table with Jackson and Swen to her left and Peter and Equuleus to her right.

The open night sky closed above to the interior thatch of the cottage, and the little living space seemed never to have changed.

"Now, for the specifics," Heart said, her arms around Swen and Equuleus. "How am I getting to The Darling Undesirables Residence of Long Prairie? I know it's closer to us here than to The Museum of Scientific Improbabilities and Unpredictable Oddities, but I'm not sure how much closer, as I made that journey with my loyal and life-saving friend here, on foot."

"It'll be like the last time we made this trip," Jackson said. "In my vehicle, with Swen. Equuleus will stay here. The *Heart!* will remain here. We only brought it so you and Equuleus could return to Pink."

"So, a simple in and out, with grand and high hopes that I'm some kind of wildly successful at discovering where my father's clone 'brain in a box' might be. It's hard to understand why or how an important component of The Purists movement might be at The Darling Undesirables Residence of Long Prairie. If they have such a footing, why do they not destroy it?"

"Hiding where one is not imagined to be found has always been the way hide and seek is played," Peter observed.

"*Of course!*" Heart felt more than a little dense for having asked such a silly question. "Sometimes you have to hear your words out loud to discover how inane they are!" she laughed at herself.

The Mystic joined in heartily. "A good bit of wisdom, that!" she exclaimed. The lines in her face danced with merriment at Heart's erudition.

"Next serious question—and this one really is serious, if we're to fly over The Wall—with all the precaution we took flying in, will we be able to fly high enough to prevent my meltdown, or whatever it is that happens to me, as we fly over the wall?"

"Now, that's an intelligent question," The Mystic said.

"Indeed it is." Peter waved away the last traces of the vision field still hanging between them like softly colored cobwebs, then reached behind him to a pack he'd brought. Heart had noticed it, but paid no particular attention to it. With ceremony, he brought it to the table, then waved his hand over it. Heart heard a slight "*shush!*" as its magnetic locks released.

He reached inside and pulled out a carefully wrapped package and handed it to Heart.

She unwrapped it, her fingers tingling from whatever lay inside. "*Oh!!!*" Heart sighed. "Oh, my precious paisley blanket."

"Yes. your life-saving paisley blanket," Peter said. "Waiting in our little hidden room in the museum for whenever you may need it again."

Heart hugged the paisley blanket close, and a note fell out from its folds.

My Dear Heart,
I know if you are holding this blanket again,
you are upon a truly great mission. I'm sad
I'm not with you at this moment—but trust
that I am with you in spirit!
All my Love,
Martha

"Oh, Martha!" Heart sighed. "Tell her I return her love, will you, Peter?"

"You know I will, Heart."

"The paisleys are moving," Equuleus observed.

"Yes. They are pleased to be in my hands." As she felt the energy shared between the amazing fabric and herself, she knew—as if she had any doubts, which she didn't—that the perfect moment for the mission had arrived.

Especially if there was even the slightest possibility that her father's clone brain had contrived an energy burst that could capture him and bring him to Earth. After all, she and Equuleus had been transported to Pink within her father's Aurora Borealis in a short span of time. It seemed not beyond the realm of possibility that his clone brain could work this out as well, and, further, such a burst may travel through the shield.

But with her paisley blanket in her hands and the amazing energy of everyone around her, Heart felt strong. She felt centered. "Ready to go when you are, Jackson," she said softly, smiling at him.

And, wonder of wonders, he returned her smile.

*   *

Everyone stepped outside to share their luncheon in the glorious afternoon warmth. They would spend the rest of the afternoon together, waiting for the shadows of dusk to fall. Then Heart, accompanied by Swen, would shapeshift and steal to the little garden shed in the middle of Keeper A's showy flower garden at The Darling Undesirables Residence of Long Prairie.

As she stooped through the little side door, Heart was surprised and pleased to see the *Heart!* nearby, in a copse of alders, shiny clean, and looking in perfect condition.

She turned to The Mystic gesturing to the *Heart!*, "Please tell everyone I said thank you."

"Not to worry, dear, they hear you now themselves. I told them they had to stay clear so you could eat in peace and gather your thoughts. But they're right out there."

Heart heard giggling—yes behind and among the trees, the residents had been outed.

Heart smiled a long slow smile. She seated herself on a rock and began devouring the wonderful fresh made bread, thanks to Amdrona and Butterfly, and fresh cheese, and a giant glass of spring water.

Eye sat down beside her on another rock, and Butterfly flitted to his other side. Everyone else found a place to sit on a rock or the ground, completely comfortable in the moment.

The bluejays and robins sparred with one another, the flowers nodded their elegant heads in the spring breeze, while the breeze whispered in the fir trees high overhead. The fresh aroma of nature, of fir trees, of flowers, of the gentle zephyr, was spellbinding. All of nature orchestrated to make Heart long, deeply but privately, to Just. Stay. Here. To be like a child without a care.

But she could return to this place in her mind whenever she wanted, whenever she needed, she reminded herself. This moment would live forever and forever in her mind, hers to bring out and hold, like the vision in a crystal ball.

* *

All too soon the shades of twilight braided and wove among the group, bonding their reverie and companionship. She and Jackson exchanged a "the moment has arrived" look, which rippled among them all.

Eye grabbed both of Heart's hands, writing, *etching*, his love into her hand, and telling her other things as well, so that she could store them away. Deep in her soul. He closed his soliloquy with writing, "You have been my eyes for nearly all my life, and I have never wanted nor needed eyes. But I wish I had them now, so I could cry. *Oh!* Could we not all live together, quietly, humbly, in peace?"

Heart couldn't prevent a small sob from escaping. "Keep that dream alive, my precious friend," she wrote back. "Our *DREAMS!* Keep them alive!" She kissed his beautiful hands, then placed them in Butterfly's hands, stood abruptly and headed for the *Heart!* without a parting comment to anyone.

Jackson, Swen and she would fly low to Jackson's vehicle, only a few minutes away by flight. There they would leave the *Heart!* and take Jackson's vehicle.

They quickly transferred from one vehicle to the other, while determining the best way to assure Heart was completely cocooned in her beloved paisley blanket. They finally decided she ought to lie down in the back seat. Jackson wrapped her up and tied her down with the safety belt, while Swen "supervised."

"Every inch, Jackson, you know. She must be completely covered."

"I know Swen," Jackson answered with, Heart thought, a stunning amount of patience.

"Don't put the safety belts too tight, she has to breathe."

To which Jackson replied under his breath, "I'll let *her* breathe. Wouldn't mind strangling a bio-mechanical dog, though."

"I heard that," Swen said, insulted.

Heart stifled a giggle. Just like old times! she thought.

Everything secure, Jackson, with a sigh of relief and exasperation, as it audibly sounded to Heart, got into the pilot's seat, charged up the engines, and they were off. He flew back over The Mystic's cottage, where everyone below sat in the evening air, waiting to wave good-bye and good luck.

Jackson rose his vehicle high above The Wall before reaching it, then dove across, flying above the Dark Energy Highway. "Everything all right back there?" he finally asked.

"Everything's perfect back here. Are we beyond the wall? Can I come out now?"

"It's looking good," Swen said.

Heart came out from under her blanket and struggled to release the safety straps. "Wow, Jackson, Swen had a point. I almost can't get loose." At the same time, she heard clicking from somewhere else in the vehicle. "Oh, no, Swen! You're not latched in."

"No, afraid I'm not. You know, it's the old no opposable thumbs problem. These latches are not made for such as me."

Heart reached around to the front and slipped the two components together. "There now!"

"Thanks, Heart. I feel much safer."

"Now, me," she said, latching herself in.

"Excellent. Now that everyone is latched in, we're about to come in for a landing." Jackson flew down to the Dark Energy Highway, and slipped onto it, staying in the flow of traffic for a few minutes, then veering off, smooth as silk.

"Great driving, Jackson," Swen said. "On and off the Dark Energy Highway like nobody's business."

"Thanks," Jackson answered, his tension palpable.

Why, Heart wondered, why was he more nervous than she? All along, something about this mission had him uncharacteristically keyed up. Did he have yet more information he didn't share with her? Always a possibility. If not a probability.

Moments later, they hovered over the open field next to The Darling Undesirables Residence of Long Prairie. A horrible feeling overtook Heart as she recalled the last time she'd been here. With Xavier. She'd been so cold to him. And now ....

She dared not let her mind wander to those sad thoughts. This mission was so different from the previous one, when her entire focus had been upon saving Eye. Now, well, now! *The Cause of All Beings* counted on her to successfully find out something— anything!—about her father's cloned brain, and the Pacifists plans.

She couldn't get a bead on what she might find. The garden shed was a tiny, little bone-colored building, with a tiny, little, cute second story, hardly big enough for a person to stand in. The shed had a cupola and pale green shutters. Keeper A's cool colors, bone-white and pale green. Just like her, so cool and cold.

Though Heart felt a deep sense of anticipation, it didn't seem logical that there would be anything in the little building other than, depending on the season, bulbs that needed planting, yard tools, and the like.

They landed with a soft thud in the field. Heart smiled—Swen called it right, nobody came anywhere near Jackson's ability to handle a vehicle.

"Right. Ready?"

"As ready as ever I'll be, I suppose." She checked again that she had her communication device, a thumbnail-sized 3-D camera, a few small tools, and other bits and pieces in her backpack. That was it. Going on an info search, hoping not to be seen as she shape-shifted through the grounds, or, literally be sniffed out by Keeper A.

The three of them ran across the field. Then Heart ran along the side of the tall fence enclosing the back of The Darling Undesirables Residence at Long Prairie, to where Swen had first helped her cross, that night, ever and ever so long ago now, it seemed. That night when Keeper A put Eye in the sensory deprivation chamber, and Heart had snuck back and forth across the fence to check on poor Eye.

That amazing day when she met Equuleus, and then that horrible night when she thought she might lose Eye.

"Here, where you first helped me, Swen," she whispered when they were bunched up together on the outside of the fence. "Although there's not close access to the garden shed, this provides the most cover. I can slink around a couple buildings, then dare to cross the garden fence in the back, as far away from Keeper A's residence as possible. I'll shapeshift and hope for the best. I guess the two of you will stay here."

"No way," Swen protested. You shapeshift, and look as invisible as possible, but, I'll come along and if your motion is detected, which is likely when you cross the garden fence, I can look like a dog loping through the garden, and no one will think anything of it."

"Why we didn't talk about this before I don't know, but, Swen, I don't want to risk you."

"He's right, Heart. The garden fence will have a lot of motion detecting devices on it since Keeper A is so precious about her flowers. Swen's plan is perfect. He can meander through the garden, looking like a big, dopey dog ...."

"I beg your pardon!"

"Well, that's the objective, isn't it?" Jackson countered.

"Well, yes ...."

"You and Swen are in audio contact. When you're ready to come out, Heart, then have the big dopey dog wander back through the garden."

"Just hoping there's actually something—anything!—there to justify this much intrigue. Oh, Xavier, be with us now! All right my-beautiful-canine-definitely-not-dopey-friend, lead the way."

"I'll be right here," Jackson whispered.

In moments, Swen had dug a tunnel for the two of them to pass under the fence, and they were inside.

Ah! Would it ever come about that she never needed to be here again? Heart wondered. Whatever she might be looking for, may it become immediately obvious, like a map on the wall with a big sign overhead: "Here Is That Which You Seek."

Heart shapeshifted into the buildings and the trees that they swiftly passed. Next, the four-foot tall fence that looked utterly benign, climbing roses growing charmingly all over it, accompanied by the sweetest aroma. But, as Jackson had said, no doubt with plenty of surveillance.

With Swen by her side, Heart took a running leap and sailed over the fence. Swen remained in perfect tandem with her. She felt proud of him, knowing that his magnificent dog senses told him precisely where she was, although he could not see her shapeshifted form.

She slowed to a walk, staying on the narrow path, utterly beguiled by the stunning, fragrant flowers. This part of the garden was forever hidden from the view of the Darling Undesirables by hedges and dense climbing vines. Heart had never realized the astonishing extent of the exotic, aromatic flowers and plants.

But it made sense, given Keeper A's bionic scent implants that these exotic aromas would be worth collecting from the world's gardens. And, Heart thought, even without scent implants, this is heaven.

Swen looked in her direction, probably knowing why she dawdled, but concerned about her nearly halted progress. She inhaled deeply. Then, with resolve, moved on. A few feet further she came to the back of the garden shed.

She was surprised to see a narrow louvered window on the back of the building. With a "what's there to lose?" shrug, she pushed on it. It swung sideways readily. Wedging herself sideways, Heart barely managed to slip through the opening.

The ground receded at a sharp angle below her feet. As she descended, she discerned that she'd already gone below ground level, looking out at the floor of the shed at eye level. Some sort of scrim hung before her, and she realized that anyone coming through the front door of the little building would see whatever was on the front side of this scrim. Heart felt fairly certain it depicted the inside of the back of a little garden building, showing realistic three-dimensional images of yard tools.

She took note of the fact that the louvered opening she'd slipped through would not accommodate anyone at all larger than her own slender and agile self.

Thus, anyone familiar with the setup would know they must push aside the fake back wall to access this steep decline. After reasoning that out, Heart understood that she stood on a path considerably more relevant than a map on a wall. She stepped another step down, now fully underground. She cautiously sent a message to Swen and Jackson.

"Think Violet's home. Over. Out."

Step by step, Heart descended deeper into the Earth, moving through a narrow passageway. Small lights at her feet lit faintly as she moved, though she would much prefer if they did not. All around her it remained strangely quiet and Heart chuckled inwardly, somewhat droll, at the thought that it was—well, like a tomb.

She took another step. Suddenly, bright lights came on all around her, and she found herself in a huge, open cavern. She looked around frantically, hoping to find a spot to hide, but immediately saw that was not an option. Strange glass-like walls surrounded her, so shiny and reflective that she saw faint replicas of herself in every direction as she turned in a full circle.

Mystified by why keepers or gardeners didn't practically come out of the walls to nab her, she all but fainted away in shock to see her father hurrying toward her from the far end of the glassy chamber.

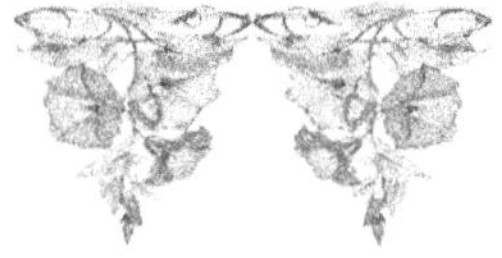

Chapter 14

"**F**ather!" she cried, without a second thought. They must have succeeded in stealing him from Pink after all, and in very short order!

"Heart!" he called to her, still approaching, but seeming to make little headway across the chamber.

Heart then realized that the peculiar quality of the reflective walls themselves created the illusion. She rapidly figured out that he was actually traversing several similar caverns, as he steadily approached.

Heart did not move toward him, still trying to sort out the dynamics of the space she found herself in, and keeping in mind she now stood closer to the exit than if she moved farther in. Once her father reached her, assuming nothing came between them, she would escape with him.

Certainly, that would not be readily permitted, but she'd put up a fight. She grabbed her communication necklace and snapped images of where she stood hoping the peculiarities of the place translated—if her communication escaped this place at all.

"Father is approaching me," she recorded. "Passing through chambers. Strange illusions of ice walls."

Finally, it appeared he had made it to the "real" chamber where she stood. He came through the huge cavern, smiling. Which seemed strange, under the circumstances.

Then the puzzle pieces came crashing together.

My father's clone is not a computer, nor some sort of contrived "brain in a box," Heart thought. *This is* my father's clone, this embodied being, right before my eyes, in this strange place where the very walls reflect copy upon copy of the two of us.

"Heart!" The replica of her father said again. *Oh! His voice!* It left her speechless. "You've come! I'm so delighted. The talks we'll have, I can't wait!"

He came up to her. Heart stepped back. Studying the face before her, she looked for any mark or clue that it was *not* her father. There was none.

"*You're the clone,*" she said quietly.

He chuckled wildly. "Oh, so bright! So bright, Heart! Just like everyone has said. Do you know how long I've waited for this moment? The moment I get to meet you, Heart! My daughter!"

"I am not your daughter."

"Of course you are." He reached out to take her hand. She jumped back.

"You're the clone," Heart said again, not able to find any other words. It was her responsibility to—to—decommission him. How could she do it? How could she even hope to do it?

"Why does no one know of this space?" Heart asked, waving her hand at the glassy walls, while hundreds of pale Hearts waved in tandem.

"These walls," Her not-father replied, waving also, "one of my crowning achievements. Nothing gets through them, neither in nor out, except where and when I want." He smiled warmly at her again. "Well, Heart, I know, this is a big shock. I've done a good job of keeping my physical self secret, haven't I?"

"Yes. But—how is it that you *have* a physical body? I've studied everything I could get my hands on about the illegal clone downloaded so many years ago. That's all that has ever been mentioned—that the clone is nothing more than a download."

"True! In the past, true! But, Heart, I am a clone of the me you're more familiar with, the two of you living together there on Pink. I have steadily invented and created myself. I'm quite impressed with my work, I must say.

"The greatest frustration of my life is that I've almost no one around me, because of your father's indiscretions, and the readiness of the world to incarcerate him. Thus, I cannot go out and move about in the world. I cannot be acknowledged for my own brilliance. I've done endless genetic testing, endless bio reversals, endless mechanical experiments. Nothing with clockworks, they are entirely outmoded. I've accomplished amazing research with dark matter.

"The only area where 'the other' Father Inventor continues to be ahead of me is with Dark Energy. I cannot seem to unlock this secret. But I will. Especially with you by my side."

"No." She backed away the way she came. I'm in extremely real danger, Heart thought. This clone has the genius of my father, but he is mad. Mad and frightening.

"You're the one responsible for the Darling Undesirables!" she cried with lightning insight. *"Oh! Monster!"*

Her outburst delighted the clone, and he broke into laughter.

"Really, truly, what fun you and I will have! Hyperbole. Goodness, a bit dramatic, yes? I've

improved the world tremendously for all human-
ity."

"But ... you are not, properly speaking, a human.
Why do you care?"

"All good roads lead to serving me," he said
with quiet confidence. "Humans are great, but, still,
they are inferior to me! That includes my own bene-
factor, the original Father Inventor. I'm superior to
him in every way, including my brilliant experiments. You Heart, you! So far, you are the most
amazing being alive, because of your dark energy
component. Nothing can destroy you ...."

"That's not quite true ...."

"*Pah!* The small glitches, such as your brush
with permanent stasis due to being at too great a
distance from Equuleus, is small, is irrelevant in the
larger scheme. All steps to higher learning along the
way."

"But," Heart dared to argue, "it's horrible to
selfishly create sentient beings that are defective
and broken, like the Darling Undesirables."

"A beautiful cake contains a number of broken
eggs. It's the price of upward motion. Which, you,
my darling, epitomize."

"Stop saying that!" The realization hit her
like lightning. Her father would be absolved of
the accusations of his worst crimes, if the world
only knew that here, before her, stood the criminal

they've pursued. Her father could live freely, wherever he chose.

Heart continued to try to visualize her immediate escape, while a myriad questions surfaced.

"Here you are, under The Darling Undesirables Residence of Long Prairie, apparently for a good, long, while," she observed, "are you aligned with those who protect and defend The Darling Undesirables? Or are you aligned with The Purists?"

"Don't be mystified, dear Heart." He reached out and pushed an invisible button, a luxurious, deep blue divan glided right through the glassy wall. "Shall we relax?" He seated himself and patted the place beside him.

"I'm fine, right here," Heart answered, impatient to have more understanding.

"As you please." He pressed upon the arm of the divan. A delicate china teapot painted with intricate pink rose blossoms, with the sweet aroma of rose water tea rising from it, and two dainty, pink rosebud painted teacups appeared at his side.

"I do wish you'd join me. This is the most precious rose tea in the world. I contrived the recipe myself, with a careful harvest of the fussiest roses, and an exotic process of extraction and infusion. Another invention of mine, adding to the exquisite quality of a life well lived by intelligent and creative beings.

"That's you, my Heart, and that's me! I've waited forever and forever for you to come voluntarily to me ...."

"I've not come voluntarily to you! I've come voluntarily to protect all beings, whether intelligent or ordinary or handicapped."

"*Ah!* Beautifully said." He sipped his tea. "I see you still anticipate an answer to your question. I see you still don't quite realize who I am, and how I plan the best for the best.

"I am aligned with *myself*. I put in with whoever serves *my* cause and contributes to *my* intentions. Interestingly enough, sometimes that's The Purists, sometimes it's those who defend and support The Darling Undesirables."

"Why do they put up with it?"

"Because no one really quite knows what's going on. No one is as smart as me."

"The crowing rooster may well get shot," Heart said, disgusted with the megalomaniac before her. In this regard, he could not be more different from her father. Opposites. Which, she intuited, was perhaps the way it must be.

"Oh, I see your thoughts. Good Father Inventor, bad Father Inventor. No, you've got it wrong. And, over time, you'll come to believe as I do."

"I. Shall. Not," Heart said firmly, quietly.

"We. Shall. See," He said with imitative punctuation.

Glancing around again for any being or mechanism that might try to impede her escape, Heart leapt up the incline she'd just come down.

Behind her, she heard the clone sigh deeply. "Oh, my why do you have to do this? I had so hoped not to traumatize you, but you bring it upon yourself."

She'd not gotten three steps when the dark and close wall beside her opened, issuing her worst nightmare.

Bots! Horrible, slimy white, maggoty-white, giant bots. Worse than ever, with rudimentary, featureless, heads, appendages slightly resembling arms and legs, yet too many, all of which were ill-formed.

"*Augh!*" Heart cried as the first one grabbed her with ... well, she couldn't tell how it managed to hold onto her. Some slimy magnetic force.

They kept coming out of the walls, eight, ten, twelve of them, gathering around her and bumping into one another, with their only goal being, apparently, to touch her.

"That's enough," the clone said calmly. Back to your rooms. Everyone except ***XLG. Good job my pet!" He stood and patted the slimy brute.

The gelatinous mass quivered at the positive words. Heart saw, then, that the bots had feelings. The bots were sentient.

She must find in her some form of empathy and compassion.

But—the bot still held onto her, and she wanted that to cease immediately. "All right. Obviously, I'm not going anywhere right now. Will you please have it stand down?"

"I'll have him escort you to your lovely room that has been waiting for you for years. With a fairly recent update since you left The Darling Undesirables Residence at Long Prairie. I hope you like it."

"Like? Oh my, no response required. I'm not only at The Darling Undesirables Residence of Long Prairie, where I'd hoped never to be again in my life, but I'm in the bowels of it, with a—whatever you are—an insane being and his pet."

"I'm not insane at all. And, if it's a choice between this thing and you, you are, Heart, my very favorite pet."

"*Ick!*" she said without further comment. She walked ahead of both the inventor and his invention, following the lights that came on along the floor, which appeared to be directing Heart where the clone would have her go, and, in preference to being touched by either of them, she went without dissent.

The narrow hall widened. Overhead, bright lights came on, revealing yet more glassy, reflective walls. One function of these mirroring walls might be to keep her from escaping, she reasoned. So many images of herself moving about would trip alarms everywhere.

Directly ahead a door slid open, revealing to Heart her accommodations—her *very own* accommodations.

Chapter 15

In the room she found her furniture from her room, more recently occupied by Butterfly. There were her star maps on the walls. As she passed through the doorway, she spied her writing materials, her own 3-D player, her knick-knacks. The entire room an exact replica of her room in the building not so far away, right down to the location of the closet and bathroom.

She stepped into the bathroom. There she saw her personal items, and in the closet, all her—far too small now—clothes. She snickered wryly and turned to her captor. "One thing you will never do is grow. These clothes—I have no use for them. I've outgrown them, along with my life here."

Her father's clone remained at the door, not even crossing the threshold. The "grub-man" as Heart decided to name them—was nowhere to be seen.

"I'm well aware of that, Heart. Still, I made the decision to have every item of yours placed in this room. Your room. For your enjoyment, if you derive any. Perhaps, even though the clothes don't fit, some of them were gifts that may offer you pleasant moments of recollection. In any event, they are yours to do with as you please.

"Also, I apologize for the absence of your star dome, which I realize is the most important component of your room.

"However, aside from installing something fake, just for the appearance of it, I haven't yet sorted out getting a star dome to work in this subterranean space. But I *am* working on it." He turned and headed back down the hall.

"I'll leave you to yourself for a while. I'm sure you know it's futile to attempt escape."

While Heart stood in the doorway watching him recede, a door of the shiny glass-like surface slipped shut. She stood, face to face with her own vexed reflection. She listened closely as the door closed in its frame. Yes, there were magnetic sounds of locks being set in place. Despite his admonition, she immediately pushed on the door, to see if it had any give in the frame. There was none.

Now she had to think, and think hard. How long would it be before Swen and Jackson attempted to find her? How much danger would they be in?

No, they would not come roaring in. In response to her one small note, that she had gone into a place like Violet's home, Jackson, no doubt this very moment, was working out how to determine exactly what sort of rabbit hole she had fallen into.

Maybe he'd even have an idea of what she ran into. He'd been so cryptic and strange, maybe he had a *very* good idea of what—or *who*—she ran into.

In the meantime, she decided, she would do well to be as quietly observant, as cryptically agreeable as she could summon herself to be. One thing for certain-sure—her father's clone was, as he openly boasted, a genius to be reckoned with.

What would she call him? She didn't want to use the word "father" in the same sentence when referring to this other—being. She decided she would simply keep calling him "the Clone." In her mind, to his face, and to anyone else—if there *was* anyone else. It seemed unlikely that she'd be having conversations with the grub-men.

She turned and let her gaze take in the room, little by little. A plethora of thoughts and feelings washed over her. Most of them having to do with time spent in the space much like this one—with Eye, studying, dreaming, laughing, bonding.

She moved to sit on the bed, then wrapped the blanket around herself and leaned against the wall, replaying the wonderful time she'd just spent with Eye. Well, if she was captive, and she had nowhere to go, she could replay and relive the walk in the forest with her dearest and oldest friend.

"Oh!" she exclaimed reaching into her shirt pocket and pulling out the trillium Eye had given her, which still held a gauzy remnant of the scent of fir trees. With all she'd been through, the little flower remained, almost magically, in pristine condition.

She folded her hands and bowed her head over the little flower. She thanked all the *Powers that Be* for the time at The Mystic's cottage. Then she sent, with every scintilla of her energy, a picture of her current predicament, wrapped in an image of Faith. Hope. Love. Affirming that the greatest of all was love.

The Clone may have a dark agenda for everyone but himself, but Heart peacefully affirmed:

Love.

Will.

Prevail.

*   *

Curiously, she fell asleep in that seated position, holding the precious wildflower, thinking to The Mystic, to Eye, and, of course, to Equuleus her circumstances.

She awakened in the replica of her childhood room, straightaway from a dream of being in the forest outside The Mystic's cottage. The walk in the forest had been so real and sweet and relaxed, much more real than this horrible reality.

As she meditated on the rejuvenating dream-walk in the forest, the door slid open.

In walked Loruza. Her own Loruza, the Keeper who had sat at the head of her dining room table the whole of her life at The Darling Undesirables Residence of Long Prairie. Loruza, who had calmed and soothed her when other Keepers abused her.

Loruza, who had listened to their study projects, who had offered suggestions of flowers to plant in their garden. Loruza who had protected Eye, and defended her, time and again. Who had seemed to care about herself and Eye.

Of all people, Loruza was the one person Heart would have imagined being farthest from The Clone's dark inventions.

Although, that time when she had faint echoes of mistrust, and had told Eye to remain aloof with Loruza, now came to mind.

Heart didn't say anything, waiting to see whatever was Loruza's business with her, here and now.

"Well, there she is," Loruza's sweet-tempered voice came out sarcastic. "Heart! Ummm, holding a little flower. Charming. So charming."

She moved about the room, touching one thing and another. "I see that you'll not be able to squeeze into a single thing in your closet. But, there you are, big as life, in plaid, as always.

"I thought your plaids were shamanistic, or mystical, or something like that. But here you are! Captured! *He-he*! No more flying horses for you, broken, inadequate girl! No! Your life is now a round of experiments, to get at how dark energy works in you. When we figure that out, the world will be ours!"

"Whose?" Heart asked quietly.

"Mine and the being who ought to be thought of as the real Father Inventor. Do you not find him charming?"

"No. I do not. And what has he *done to you?*"

"Nothing. Well, that's not true. He's made my life unbelievably better. And I've improved his." She grinned widely. It was not a good look on her face. "And, as I say, you'll improve both of our lives."

Heart refrained from retorting, "I doubt it," although she did doubt it. The emotion pouring off Loruza exceeded the moment, as emotion-packed as the moment might be. "Have you always hated me?"

"Rather," Loruza answered transparently. "I did a good job of disguising it, didn't I?"

"I will grant you that, Loruza," Heart said, carefully pocketing her precious flower. "However, I wouldn't get carried away patting myself on the back if I were you. I was a child, in a monumentally sheltered environment, with overtly difficult adults all around.

"To have someone treat me politely and with interest, and, much more important than that, treat Eye with respect for those few minutes during meals—it's not difficult to understand why I might have been willing to accept your fake kindness."

Loruza shrugged—letting Heart know she didn't care what Heart thought.

"Are you ... are you a Purist?"

"You might say. Or, others would likely say. But, much like Father Inventor's Clone, I am about making things work for myself."

Heart stood and moved toward the still open door.

"*Shut!*" Loruza commanded. The door slid shut and Loruza rushed at Heart. "Understand? *Do you understand?* I don't care what anyone around us calls themselves, and I don't much care what they call me. Just as long as I get to where I'm headed."

"Where's that?"

"First, *and most importantly*, to a world free of deformed Darling Undesirables. Secondly, into a world of plenty and comfort. But most of all, a world where I don't have to hear 'Heart this and Heart that.'"

"Why are you hearing 'Heart this and Heart that' so much?" Heart asked, mystified.

"Because Father Inventor's Clone is obsessed with you. I can't wait to tear you component from component. Twice the happy for me! Finding out how to incorporate dark energy into myself, and good riddance to heartless Heart!"

"Wow," Heart breathed, taken aback—not easy to be this close to such intensity of hatred directed at herself.

"Yeah. Wow. Well, that's enough for now. I only wanted to see you for myself. Caught the little fish right in our net, so amazing! Too smart and yet not smart enough for your own good, right?"

"The game is not over," Heart couldn't resist retorting.

"Ah! There's still fire in you. Well, we will see how the game plays. You may consider yourself a force to reckon with, but you still look to me to be a force of one. And we, well, we're many.

"Enough sparing now. I'm to bring you to dinner. Just like old times. Try not to be too shocked with the sudden change in how I present." She turned to the door, "Open!" she commanded.

"Another thing, dear Heart," Loruza's tone changed already, "do not attempt to escape. You have the luxury of freedom right now. For your own good, don't make us shackle you."

"Lovely," Heart said under her breath, awash with irritation, disappointment, and disgust.

Heart followed Loruza down the glass hall, which opened at Loruza's approach. The Clone sat at a little round table, set for three. He stood smiling as Loruza and Heart entered.

"Allow me," he said, looking at Heart and gesturing to the chair to his right, which moved away from the table of its own accord, apparently responding to either his words or gesture or both.

Reluctantly, Heart seated herself.

Turning to Loruza, he smiled, and gestured to the chair on his left, "And you, my dear," as the chair slid out.

Loruza returned his smile, saccharine deceiver, and sat, inching her chair closer to the Clone.

"Did you two girls have a nice chat?"

"Lovely chat," Loruza nodded. "Almost like old times. But, Inventor, dear, our Heart has grown so tall! None of her clothes fit."

Inventor, dear!, Heart thought. All right, he'd named himself "Inventor." Seemed about right for his megalomania.

"This is true. We'll have to do something about it before long, I dare say."

Loruza nodded her agreement, smiling across at Heart. "Ah, yes, so like old times. If only Eye were here with us."

Heart clenched her jaw tight. Do not mention his name! she wanted to shout.

"Have you seen him of late?" Loruza asked.

"Please refrain from asking personal questions," Heart said in as even a tone as she could muster.

"Oh dear, Loruza, Heart is not happy with us," the Clone observed.

"No, she's not."

Oh! Madness, Heart thought. *M-A-D-N-E-S-S !*

A slick-icky grub-man entered, awkwardly carrying a tray in its three handless appendages. Setting it down, it seemed to look at the Clone for further direction

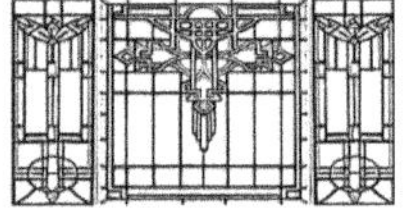

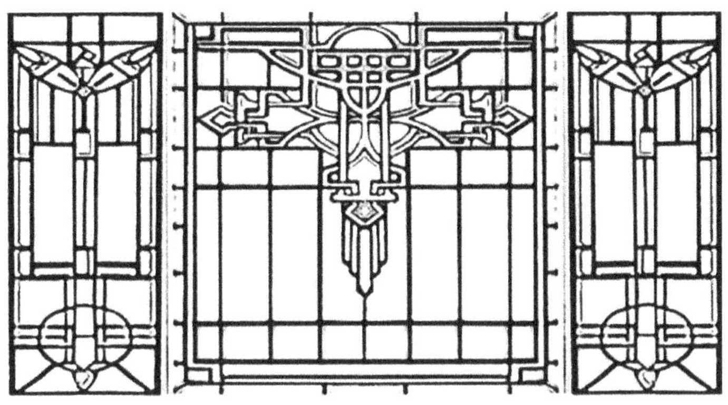

Chapter 16

Heart scoffed at herself. As if anything Keeper A might have in mind for her would outweigh Loruza's promise to "tear her component from component." Looking at the faint replica of herself in the weird door, the impenetrable door, the impossible door, she wondered if the Clone and Loruza and Keeper A and their grub-man minions could succeed in tearing her component from component.

Heart suspected she had incredible resources of physical strength, which, she further suspected, she'd never absolutely fully called upon in her life. If it came to a flat out, hand-to-hand, fight for survival, she would not go down easily. Of that, she felt certain.

She prowled around her all-too-familiar prison cell, curiously studying each object in turn. These relics! Exhumed from her history, her past—now impossibly remote.

The 3-D star maps were nice, she wouldn't mind having them, not for any sentimental reason but only because they were beautiful and informative. The little things on her desk, the knickknacks and such? She had no use for them. They only made her a bit uncomfortable, having upon them the stamp of a life she'd managed to escape. Everything in the closet, of course, needed to be given to Darling Undesirables who could fit into them.

The only tender, nostalgic feelings she possessed were those she felt for Eye. The only thought that anything brought up worth keeping were moments of love and joy with Eye.

A tiny 3-D album stood on the little bedside table. Heart sat on the bed and turned the album on, fast forwarding through the images, stopping to study the ones with herself and Eye. Many of the images had been taken at huge public events, the sort of thing various Darling Undesirable facilities would either put on themselves, individually or jointly, or participate in, produced by big business, to generate funds.

It disgusted her anew, just as it had when she'd been required to go to these events and perform. She and Eye were little puppets, set upon the world's stage to perform, to "sing and dance" to the tune that would make people feel just guilty enough, and entertained enough, to cough up their funds. It served as people's hedge against the hand fate might deal them if they didn't give something in return for these children, the result of experiments driven by the covetous desire for their own longevity.

There, in the image of one of the huge media events, when she and Eye were literally on a stage, she saw, in the front row of the audience, Swen! There was Swen, looking up at her with interest and adoration, like everyone else, but somewhat unlike the other newshounds in the throng. Something else lingered in his look, something else in the big, sad, down-turning eyes of her dear friend, years before they ever met.

If anyone could read Swen's expressions, it was Heart! There, in Swen's eyes, with his focus on her, she saw the determination to protect her.

To protect her! Ah! Swen! Ever faithful. Ever sure. Faithful long before she knew he existed. Her smile of affection turned to one of concern, then alarm. He would do anything to protect her. And she'd never needed protection like the present moment, when being torn limb from component had been promised.

Oh, Swen, she thought to him, please do not risk yourself! Losing Xavier is enough. She returned her attention to the images, looking for other times, other places when, perhaps, Swen had been there. There she spotted him, in other images, with crowds pushing about, trying to get Heart's attention, smiling adoringly at her, wistfully, guiltily. Except for the children. They guilelessly loved her. There Swen patiently stood.

She was surprised to see, though, that Swen was *not* to be found in the crowd as much as she expected, now that she'd spied him. Then the realization hit her that he'd been the newshound snapping the images. It was, after all, his job, that granted him the means to go to the events where she would be.

Why, she wondered, had he never told her of his life following her every move? She would ask him one day.

Then Heart had a startling observation, another thing she'd never noticed in her young life. In the background of far too many of the pictures, stood Keeper A, either watching the crowd intently, or eyes riveted upon Heart. She was not readily recognizable, wearing dark and somber, nondescript clothing, instead of her usual form-fitting eggshell and pale green outfits, and, somehow, toning down her rare beauty. And yet, once Heart detected Keeper A's presence, she found her in many images.

A chill ran through Heart. She hadn't even known Keeper A went to these events. She'd always believed she loathed leaving her luxurious office and home, her—right above Heart's head at this moment, ironically—precious garden of exotic and rare flowers.

Keeper A's rare flowers. Just like the Darling Undesirables. Each one an exotic and rare flower. Never mind that many of the Darling Undesirables were so broken as to almost not be recognized as beings of any sort. They were each one-of-a-kind. Unique. And, by that virtue, precious. The most unique, the most precious of the precious, Heart knew, was herself. A Darling Undesirable who lived and breathed without a heart.

Well, not quite. With a heart housed in a virtually indestructible clockworks horse. A miracle of invention and creation, wrought by her father.

Here. There. Everywhere, she now saw, near or far, Keeper A in the images. Overseeing Heart's Every. Single. Move.

She had her own agenda regarding Heart. She had an agenda, kept close and secret, all Heart's life that would probably put to paltry shame the wildest thoughts of the Clone and Loruza.

But, Heart saw, Keeper A would cleverly play along, and even contribute to their plans, developing her own, far more sophisticated plan whatever that might be.

Now! A sensation much like fear ran through Heart's mind and body. She must escape! Keeper A would not hesitate to fulfill her—at the moment unrevealed—dark and frightening plan.

Not only for herself. She must escape from what the evil in this pseudo-glass cavern represented. From what that evil might wreak upon the whole of Earth if the secrets that Heart contained were unlocked by this conniving, treacherous, vile and malevolent darkness.

Some noise from the other side of the door took her attention. Were they coming for her now? She must prepare herself. She slipped the little 3-D album into her pocket with the precious trillium, then moved to stand flat against the wall alongside the door.

As she stood there, listening intently to subtle noises on the other side of the door, and, so it seemed, far down the hall, she looked around the room and thought, one of these things is not like the others.

The walls of this—her—room appeared to be made of the same sheeting as her childhood room. Only the door had the glass-like matrix. Otherwise, the room represented a precise replica of her little room in the building but a short distance down the path that passed in front of the garden. Heart wondered if this strange glassy reflective matrix lined the walls behind the interior sheeting.

The commotion outside stilled. Heart turned to pry at the edge of the wall along the door frame, but it would not budge. She'd had a small dark energy operated toolkit in her desk, but surely it would not still be there.

She opened the desk drawer. On top was a notepad with the scribbles of a poem she'd begun and had never finished. She shoved it aside, *yes!* They—and she wondered who "they" were— whoever they were, they'd moved all her things from her room to this subterranean place, had moved her desk, and didn't even go through the drawer. It remained exactly as she'd last seen it, her little dark energy operated tools under the notepad.

She took out the tiny saw with a circular blade about the diameter of her little finger, She'd used it in a woodworking class she'd loved. However, since Heart was the only student, the instructor left after three sessions.

She began to cut into the wooden door frame, running crosswise for a short distance, then making a similar parallel cut a short distance above it.

Turning the tool off, she tugged at the door frame and the strip she'd cut broke away in her hands. Disappointed, she discovered that, indeed, the glass-like matrix hid beneath the sheeting.

"What did you expect?" she asked herself. Maybe a dirt wall, instead of this weird reflective matrix. Not that she could tunnel through in a short period of time, even if it were dirt.

But! what about ....

She looked up at the ceiling. Except for the missing star dome, it, too, looked identical to the ceiling of her childhood room.

Before going any further, she must sort out where the spying 3-D devices were. She found two of them, somewhat un-cleverly, exactly where they'd been in her room. She thought there must be more, but couldn't find a trace of even one. Well, they needn't watch her, in this glass cage.

She put one in image capture mode, put it on a short timer, then lay down on the bed with her back to the room, counted to six, got up and retrieved the image, then she had the 3-D device project her image onto the bed.

There now! It looked like she had gone to sleep. She shut the audio off on both devices.

Next, she put the chair on the desk and began sawing at the ceiling. Even if beyond the ceiling she encountered the same strange glass-like matrix as the walls, she would be much, *much* closer to escaping by going up—the outside world right above her head, she reasoned, than going sideways through the wall.

As the floor of the little shed had been right above her head when she came into the Clone's subterranean habitation, she'd now be beyond the shed.

She had another *aha!* realizing that was why the walls were made of the strong, weight-bearing glass-seeming matrix, to assure that the world above did not come caving through a thin layer of earth. The flowers outside only needed enough depth to grow.

But how would the reflective matrix hold up against impact? Or small but mighty dark energy power tools? Reaching up, Heart cut a circle in the ceiling material big enough for her to pass through, grabbed it as it began to fall and dropped it to the desk.

She wished she had something to protect her eyes and face as she began attempting to cut through the glass-like material. She remembered the funny-fun star-shaped glasses someone had sent her after her childhood claim of her love of stars. She jumped down and rummaged through the closet, coming out triumphant, with glasses in hand.

Returning to stand on the chair, she put on the glasses, then braced herself for any result. Reaching overhead, she began attempting to saw through the glassy surface, which seemed to be impenetrable, when she heard someone call her name.

Chapter 17

Someone very familiar, in fact.

"Heart," Jackson whispered through her audio necklace. The necklace the Clone had pointed out would not work in this place.

She pushed send on her necklace. "Jackson?"

"Heart, where are you?"

"Where are *you*?"

"I'm in. I'm under the shed."

"Oh!" That's why he could communicate with her. "Watch out for the bots, Jackson."

She heard the walls moving. "They come out of the walls!"

Then she heard a skirmish. She had no idea what was happening, as Jackson, a man of few words on a good day, said *nothing* under attack.

Then she heard Swen begin to howl like she'd never heard him howl.

Throwing anything resembling caution aside, Heart renewed her assault on the ceiling. She thrust the little saw into the reflective material.

At first, it refused to do anything but throw sparks. Then she saw that the heat from the spinning blade, more than its teeth, appeared to have an effect upon the material. The ceiling began to soften and distort.

Heart watched in dismay as her little tool became mired in the syrupy matrix. She feared that if the material cooled, her tool would be caught in it, and if it dripped onto her hand holding the tool, she could well be trapped, hand overhead, if the substance cooled.

She pulled at her little saw. The material, still slightly pliant, had solidified enough that, continuing to hold onto her tool, she leapt from the chair to the floor. Or tried to. She ended up hanging in mid-air as the motion itself cooled the substance enough that it instantaneously solidified.

She hung onto her tool, the tool mired in the hardened, dripping matrix. But her hand remained free, and even *more importantly*—she had produced a hole, when she jumped, in the ceiling!

Heart redoubled her efforts as the wordless sounds of struggle came through her necklace—the unmistakable, slimy thwacks of a slew of grub-men thrashing about, Jackson's labored breathing, all accompanied by Swen's intensifying wail.

She jumped back up on the chair and beat furiously at the bit of dirt now exposed. The hole in the reflective matrix was too small for her to get through. But first, she reasoned, she'd make a hole through the dirt to the outside, to determine the thickness of the matrix and dirt, then sort out what her next step might be.

While she contemplated the dirt and roots overhead, the earth gave way of its own accord, piling down upon her, followed by thorny roses, stabbing and scratching her.

Heart laughed, delighted. Never had getting hurt felt so wonderful!

She looked at her little, intrepid saw, hanging, stuck for good, within the cold matrix. She grabbed onto it, and swung on it with all her might, pushing her feet into the wall, back and forth, more dirt pouring down upon her.

Finally, she paused to look up. *Yes!* She'd managed to make a small tear in the matrix. She climbed back onto the chair to study the tear—just long enough that if she could bend the glassy matrix a little, she believed she might slip through the hole.

She hopped down from the chair and grabbed a couple garments from the closet. Then, back on the chair, she wrapped the fabric around her hands to protect them as she seized the edges of the matrix and began to hoist herself through the small hole.

Much to her surprise, the ceiling gave away, and she, along with a giant heap of ceiling materials, glassy matrix bits, dirt, and thorny roses, tumbled to the floor.

The night sky looked down upon her.

"Well! That should do it!" Heart laughed and sprung to her feet, climbed onto the dirt-and-rose-covered chair, then pulled herself up into Keeper A's beautiful flower garden—now with an unsightly, gigantic hole into an underground world.

"Sorry, Keeper A," she said, just a wee bit sarcastically.

She rushed through the front door of the little garden, looking for anything she might use in self-defense, grabbing a long-handled spade. She didn't want to harm anyone, not even the grub-men. But she *would* protect Swen and Jackson, come what may.

Shoving aside the heavy scrim, she jumped through the hole, down into the glassy-matrix caverns below where the clashing sounds of combat rose to a fevered pitch. She scurried along the hall, no longer narrow, as the dark walls had opened wide, letting out the grub-men—the terrible, terrifying, bots.

Dreading what she might encounter, she ran, unhesitating, into the large, brightly lit cavern at the precise moment that Jackson, wounded and bleeding, slashed Father Inventor's Clone in two.

"*Ah!*" she cried in shock as she watched the two halves of her father's Clone fall to the floor, the reflections repeating the shorn halves, again and again. She couldn't help the jolt of terror the sight triggered in her. Jackson, now fending off bots, didn't even know she stood there.

The piteous sound of Swen's wretched whining finally fractured Heart's shock, returning her to the moment. Looking around, she saw Swen cowering under the little table, where Heart had so recently sat with her father's now cleft-in-two Clone and Loruza.

Heart experienced another shock as she saw Swen's front leg torn from his body, his shoulder clockworks spinning madly, while profusely bleeding pure hound blood.

"No, no, no!" she cried, rushing to him.

She was knocked to the floor from behind. Turning, she saw Loruza raising a figure eight device over her head. Heart intuited it to be a weapon invented by the Clone.

For reasons Heart didn't understand herself, she thrust the spade she still held into the midst of the figure eight and twisted with all her might.

Screaming in pain, Loruza released the device, running into the depths of the cavern, screaming, "You killed him, you killed my beloved Inventor!"

Heart returned her attention to Swen. "Why did you come in here, Swen? Why? You know you're not equipped to fight!"

He looked at his leg, at some distance from his body, and cried, unable to express himself beyond that.

"Do you have something in your backpack I can use as a tourniquet?"

Swen nodded.

"Heart!" Jackson called.

"Here. With Swen. Wounded."

"Right. Look, you gotta get out of here. I've decommissioned the Clone, which seems to have the bots in confusion. They're thrashing at each other. But The Purists are mobilizing and we must get out of here."

"All right, Jackson. Triage here. Then I'm carrying Swen out."

"And my leg," Swen panted.

"And his dismembered leg." She thrashed through Swen's backpack, found a small red box, "Newshound first aid" written on it.

"Wow!" she said, surprised.

"Newshounds are often in the middle of dangerous events," Swen squeezed out.

Heart opened the newshound first aid kit, grabbed the cord lying in it, and wrapped it around Swen's shoulder. "It'll be all right," she whispered, scared beyond fright for her friend. "It'll be all right."

"I know, Heart. You're with me now. It's all right."

"Right," Jackson said. "Peter will soon be overhead. I'll tell him to let down a travois for Swen along with something to collect this box of toys. Equuleus is hovering for you, Heart."

Heart's mind reeled from all Jackson had just said.

"Peter? Peter? Overhead in what?"

"In the *Gargantua.*"

"*What?*" She hugged Swen, then retrieved Swen's severed limb, put the first aid kit back in his backpack, and tied his leg to the backpack. "Ready?"

Swen nodded.

"The *Gargantua?*" she whispered.

She carried Swen back up through the cavern. When she came to Jackson, she watched him gather all the little bits and pieces of the Clone that had gone flying when cleaving him in two, and put every piece into two boxes. Off in the corner, the grub-men bots that were still on their feet thrashed around ineffectively at each other with their various limbs. Otherwise, the floor was strewn with bots and bot parts.

Heart exchanged a look with Jackson. "Did you do all of this?"

He glanced around. "Most of it. That dog there, though, he did his share. I am impressed with his valor."

"*Whoa!* From the dictionary of the words you never thought you'd hear." She hugged Swen even closer. "Oh, Swen! So heroic!"

"They were ... not to ... *it's my Heart!!* No hurting my Heart!"

"I am your Heart, Yes. Let's get you to—where's he going?"

"Peter will take him to The Mystic."

"Yes. That's good. He's ... he needs to be there soon."

Jackson shouldered the boxes. "Right. Soon as possible. Let's go."

Strange sounds issued from the boxes, but Heart chose not to pay attention to them.

"Equuleus is hovering for me?"

"Right." They left the bright cavern and moved up the incline toward the rose garden.

As they came to the place where she'd slipped through the louvered window, she saw the louvers removed, revealing how Swen and Jackson had slipped in.

"What's the *Gargantua*?"

They came out into the heady, rose fragrant night air. A penetrating humming issued from somewhere. Jackson and Heart stepped out into a bit of clearing away from the bushes and vines. Jackson looked up into the sky. "*That's* the *Gargantua*."

Heart followed his gaze. What was he referring to? She gradually realized she saw no stars—the sky above solid, dark, with the deepest darkness of night. "What?... What? ... I don't understand."

"The *Gargantua!*" Swen whispered. "A *theoretical* spacecraft."

"A *real* spacecraft," Jackson corrected.

Heart looked for stars, looked for Equuleus. Finally, at a distant edge of the darkness above, she saw a few faint stars, and, far away, Equuleus, fluttering, hovering, waiting to come to her.

That's when she realized that what she saw was a spacecraft of unimaginable size. And ... Peter? Peter was its captain.

"Pentagon-shaped, and nearly as large as the city," Jackson said. "Very difficult to distinguish, though, unless a person happens to be wanting to look at a particular star."

Jackson clicked on a connection on his wristband. "Captain, skirmish resolved. The Clone in parts, two boxes to be retrieved. One wounded."

"Who's wounded?" Peter's voice came clear and concerned.

"One valiant newshound goes by Swen. Needs immediate attention."

Out of nowhere, two gondola-shaped devices dropped, hovering before their eyes. They reminded Heart of Pink's hover rafts.

Without ceremony, Jackson plopped the two boxes on one, while Heart gently and lovingly laid Swen down in the other, hugging his face. "We'll see you in a while, dearest Swen. See you soon." She couldn't seem to let go of him. *Would* she see him again? *Would she?* He appeared to be in very bad shape, and she didn't know how much his clockworks and mechanicals had been compromised, along with his bio-components.

"Let him go, Heart. The sooner the better."

Heart nodded and stepped back. She heard a zipping sound, but could not see the little hovering gondola move. She looked up, and saw, with relief, a hatch open, a faint light behind it. The two gondolas slipped inside the great blackness above, and the small opening of light shut.

The humming augmented only slightly, then disappeared. Instantly, the stars shone above, with Equuleus coming directly toward her.

"The *Gargantua*," Heart whispered. "One must know more."

Equuleus landed neatly at her feet.

"You will learn more," Jackson affirmed. "But now you must get to The Museum of Scientific Improbabilities and Unpredictable Oddities before there is the slightest ray of dawn. And I must be about some extremely important business myself, so be off." He didn't even wait to see if she left, as he scurried across the garden toward his spacecraft in the open field.

Heart jumped on Equuleus. "You came for me!"

"Of course. Always, Heart."

"Let's make sure Jackson makes it to his vehicle, first."

Equuleus leapt from the ground, and they flew straight up high into the sky. She watched as Jackson, a tiny ant far below, jumped into his vehicle and zipped away from The Darling Undesirables Residence of Long Prairie.

"Let us do the same!" Heart said. Equuleus flew high above the Dark Energy Highway, the two of them sailing through the glorious midnight Earth sky. If only, Heart thought, she could feel as carefree as the wind through Equuleus's wings. But, at this moment, her thoughts were with her cherished friend, Swen.

Just as the sun promised to make another day, Heart and Equuleus came to The Museum of Scientific Improbabilities and Unpredictable Oddities.

At the back door with open arms, waited Martha, Key Man, Wonderman One, and Wonderman Two. Well, Martha and Key Man waited with open arms. The Wondermen were more stoic, but their eye gears spun with affection.

Chapter 18

"Come inside, come inside!" Martha waved, as if by the very gesture they would appear inside.

Heart didn't bother to dismount until they were all inside. Then she slid off Equuleus and embraced Martha while Key Man threw his jangling arms of keys around Equuleus.

"Equuleus," he said, choking up.

Equuleus curled his head around Key Man's shoulder, silently bonding with his caregiver of many, many years.

Heart turned to hug the two Wondermen, together and separately.

"Jackson let us know you were coming," Martha said softly.

"Swen," was all Key Man could utter.

"Yes. Swen." Heart moved to join Equuleus in giving Key Man some affection and support.

"Let us move into Peter's rooms," Martha suggested.

They slipped down the night-lit hall, Equuleus's hooves clacking on the marble floors. Martha inserted the key to Peter's rooms, and everyone, including the Wondermen, stepped inside. It was crowded, but as they were a small group, they managed to fit. Equuleus sat in the corner away from the table. The two Wondermen stood, stooping over considerably, just to fit in the low-ceilinged space.

"Why don't you two sit on the floor?" Heart suggested. "Next to Equuleus."

"Sit?" Wonderman One asked.

"On the floor?" Wonderman Two wondered.

"Yes. Sit. On the floor. Why not?"

"We've never," Wonderman Two said.

"Sat on the floor," Wonderman One clarified.

"Well, then, now's the time. You're clearly extremely uncomfortable standing. I believe if you sat in any chair in here, that would be the end of the chair. But you need to know what's going on, because you're healing powers may be called upon. And, well, sit!"

Yes, Heart," Wonderman One said.

"We sit," Wonderman Two agreed.

They both attempted to sit at the same moment, with the result that their hip gears became entangled with one another, and, so, for a few moments, they were Siamese twins. They managed to get their gears disentangled—*somehow!* thrashing in the small space.

"You must sit one at a time, not both together." Heart observed.

"Oh!" Wonderman Two said.

"Yes!" Wonderman One concurred. "You sit," he said.

"No, you sit!" Wonderman Two insisted.

Heart took Wonderman Two by the gear twirling hand and had him step aside. Then she pointed at Wonderman One to sit by Equuleus, which he finally succeeded in doing with great, but awkward caution.

Then she directed Wonderman Two to sit beside Wonderman One, against Peter's little, old fashioned, and probably virtually irreplaceable, kitchenette cupboards, as the entire museum came from a time long gone by.

Once seated, the Wondermen held their hands in the air over their knees, looking considerably more uncomfortable than they did standing.

"Relax," Heart instructed.

"How?" Wonderman One asked.

"Put your hands on your knees, lean back against the wall, and *relax!*"

They did as Heart instructed. Their facial gears began to whirl most contentedly.

"Quite nice," Wonderman Two said.

"Umm, yes," Wonderman One agreed.

"Very good! Now then ...." Heart turned to Martha and Key Man, who had, without ceremony, seated themselves at the little dining table. "No complications with seating over here, I see."

"No. No, we're good," Martha smiled, patting the seat beside her. "We're good. How are you? You look a bit scratched up, and, well, dirty."

Heart looked down at herself and saw that, yes, she was quite unpresentable. "I just did a jailbreak from a subterranean prison, digging my way up through the earth. But, more importantly, I know Key Man is waiting to hear from me reassurances about our dearest friend." She reached across the table and took his hands. "I cannot lie, dear Key Man. He's ... he's in bad shape."

"Jackson said he was taking Swen to The Mystic, rather than here to the Wondermen. I don't know the limits of her abilities, but I guess they're pretty strong." Heart tried to sound reassuring.

"I've never heard Jackson compliment anyone, least of all Swen, and he carried on about how gloriously he fought," KeyMan said. "But all I want to know is ... will Swen return to me?"

"I ... I believe so, Key Man, although I cannot promise. He ... I don't want to tell you this, but we both must be prepared. He lost a leg, and was bleeding bio blood. His mechanicals and clockworks were showing, and it didn't look good. I put a tourniquet on him. I don't know if I did right or wrong, good or bad. He didn't complain. He was amazingly valiant, it's true."

Heart's voice caught and she stood and turned her back to the room. "Why did he get into the fray with Jackson? Why? He's not trained. He could have—*should have!*—stayed outside."

Martha stood and patted Heart's shoulder. "What might have happened to Jackson if he *had* stayed outside?"

"I don't know. I wasn't there. I was working my strange way up through the earth, to escape. I could hear the fracas through my audio device. If only I'd been earlier."

"More likely, Heart, if you hadn't arrived when you did, that would certainly have been the end of poor Swen," Martha said softly.

Key Man inhaled abruptly. "Well," he added, "that's probably true. Probably true, Martha."

Martha led Heart to sit again.

"So," Heart asked, "what's the plan at this moment?"

"We're waiting to hear from Jackson," Martha said. "Or perhaps, Peter. Jackson said he's on a particular mission. And Peter is headed to The Mystic's cottage. So—we wait."

"We wait," Heart repeated. "Oh! Just a minute! What's ... I mean ... who ... I mean ... *the Gargantua!* Please, someone, anyone, tell me more!!"

"Under wraps," Key Man said. "Cloaked and under wraps for many years."

"Ummm," Martha agreed.

"Well, not now! There it hung, like some gigantic ... something ... hovering in the sky. Blocking out the stars, the moon and anything else that might be up there."

"True!" Martha agreed.

Heart looked from one to the other. "*WHAT?* Why won't you tell me?"

"There's really nothing to tell, Heart. You've now seen *Gargantua*. What more is there to say?"

"Who built it? Why is Peter flying it? What is its purpose? Etcetera, etcetera, and so forth and so on," she said, in imitation of Violet.

Martha ticked off the answers on her tiny fingers, smiling her round smile, her eyes squeezed down into half moons. For some reason, Heart could see, she was loving this moment. "*Peter* built it, with help from people in The Periphery. With a *lot* of help from people in The Periphery. *Peter* is flying it, because it's his machine. Its purpose is the same as the purpose of *The Cause of All Beings*, that we live in love and peace.

"It came in handy tonight, didn't it, Key Man?"

"Yes. Good timing? Not sure. But, if it saves Swen, then that's all I care about. Whether it's been sighted or not."

"Meaning?" Heart asked.

"*Gargantua,*" Martha explained, "was not to be 'exposed' until, well, until a later date. But given the discovery that Father Inventor's clone was right under our noses! and the shocking events that suddenly unfolded, with a regiment of one, well, apparently, two, including Swen, no, technically, three, with Heart taking action. Wait a minute, four, because Equuleus rescued part of our regiment ... anyway, with the surprise of the moment, Peter rushed to the rescue in what was available to him."

"I see," Heart said, feeling like somewhere in this talk there lived a big lie. "So, question one, does Peter fancy himself someone who would go into battle? and two, where, oh where, did he imagine he would put *Gargantua* down if he was really coming to fight with Jackson to immobilize the Clone?"

Martha laughed softly. "I guess, for the moment, the best answer to your question is: number one, yes, Peter does fancy himself someone who would go into battle. And the answer to your question number two is the *Gargantua* is quite capable of hovering where placed until commanded to do otherwise. It doesn't need to put down."

"I see. I see," Heart mused, thinking she could just as well say, "I don't see, I don't see."

In that pause, something on Key Man began to chime. He pressed a button on his wrist pad. Peter came through, loud and clear. "I know, my friend, you would want to hear as soon as possible about Swen, so I thought I'd let him speak for himself.

"*Swen!*" Key Man called, "Are you there?"

"I ... I'm here. I'm still here. Not that easy to get rid of, *he-he!*"

Heart gasped and laughed all in one breath. "Heart?"

Heart reached across the table and held Key Man's hand. "Yes, it's me. I'm not that easy to get rid of either! *He-he!*"

"You sound weak, Swen," Key Man said.

"No lie, I am. But The Mystic saved me. Well, first Heart saved me by putting me in that floating city, then Peter for bringing me in a twinkling, and now The Mystic with her magic. I'm a bit in pieces, though, Key Man. Dunno about this poor leg. The Mystic doesn't hold much hope for it."

"Don't worry about that, my friend, I'll fix you up with a leg. Just—we need you—bits and pieces or altogether, fine, fine. Just come back."

"I'll be back. Every decent museum has a watch-dog. My cousin, Barky, is here keeping me company. Say hi Barky."

"*Woof, woof, bark, barrrrrk!*" Barky said.

Everyone laughed, even Equuleus sniggered.

"Glad to hear it, glad to hear it," Key Man fairly sang, his face a veritable basketful of smiles. "Just, do whatever you have to do. See you soon! Love you!"

"Love you more," Swen said.

Heart couldn't resist playing, too, "Love you more, more!"

The connection broke and everyone sat with each their own satisfied grin.

"We ought to have told Peter we are tearing his place up," Heart said teasingly.

"Ah, missed a golden opportunity," Martha agreed. "He can be such a fussbudget."

"*Funn-eee* old-fashioned term," Heart crowed.

"Yep," Key Man agreed in great spirits now. "Just like Peter himself!"

The all tittered, happy and sad at the same time. They had not lost Swen ... he would not be the same.

"What's all this with legs all of a sudden?" Key Man said pensively.

"Oh! Was Peter able to ... in such short time? ...."

"Molly and Lolly were bringing Peter back here with Zack at the reins when Zack heard the message you sent to Swen and Jackson. So Peter, figuring you had stumbled upon something extremely significant, thus dangerous, thought it might perhaps be Father Inventor's Clone. Hiding in plain sight."

"Almost," Heart agreed.

"They happened at that point to be near the *Heart!* The Periphery has its own bit of underground, and the *Gargantua* lives under where Jackson parked the *Heart!* It looks like a meadow, but it's where the *Gargantua* has been being constructed for a good, long, while.

"Ever the one for details, Peter fulfilled your request, getting the big, rectangular box from the *Heart!,* he dropped it off on his way to The Darling Undesirables Residence of Long Prairie.

"I had just opened the box and begun to contemplate the details of fulfilling your kind request, when, Jackson told us about Swen."

"Then, of course, he couldn't create," Martha said.

Heart nodded. She understood.

"We could see what we can do about it now, if you'd like," Key Man said.

"Really? That would be wonderful, I'd very much like!" Heart jumped up from the table. "Much better to be doing something constructive!"

"Enough sitting," she said to Wonderman One and Wonderman Two, "let's be about our day."

"Oh! Just got," Wonderman One said.

"Used to it," Wonderman Two, added.

"Come on, come on, no whining, there's much to be doing."

Before the possibility of getting his gears caught up in the Wondermen's gears, Equuleus leapt up and Heart opened the door to let him out. "Wise move," she said. He didn't even look at her ... just shook his head.

"The last one sitting is the first to stand," Heart directed.

The Wondermen looked at each other.

"That seems," Wonderman Two said.

"Counterintuitive," Wonderman One concluded.

"Nonetheless, it's the best approach. The top gears should rise first, then the bottom one, so that the gears don't become entangled—*again!*"

Both of the Wondermen's face gears clicked and ticked.

"Yes, Yes," they babbled together. "She's right! Perfect logic!"

Wonderman Two attempted to rise, but appeared unable to gather the momentum needed to stand.

"Why can't I stand?" he asked.

"I don't know," Heart answered, puzzled. "I don't know. I'd give you a hand, but I'm pretty sure you'd pull me down before I'd get you up."

"They've never had this particular position before, I think," Key Man said. "Let's try some specific instruction. Wonderman Two, engage all gluteus gears, fully, to rise, followed by thigh gears, extend to height."

Following Key Man's directive, Wonderman Two soon stood.

"Now you," Wonderman Two said to Wonderman One, repeating Key Man, word for word. "Engage all gluteus gears, fully, to rise, followed by thigh gears, extend to height."

They patted each other on their backs, face and eye gears spinning joyfully. "Thank you, Heart," they said together.

"We love," Wonderman Two said.

"To learn new things!" Wonderman One said.

"Today's lesson, *Learning to Sit and Stand*," Heart chortled, thinking that a tutorial for clockworks beings about sitting on stairs and the floor was perhaps overdue. "Wonderman One and Wonderman Two, very, very good. Lesson well learned. We'll have to practice it again sometime soon!"

"Yes, let's!" they agreed in tandem.

Heart stepped into the hall, looking after the two, happy Wondermen.

The long rays of the early morning sun poured through the grating at the front of The Museum of Scientific Improbabilities and Unpredictable Oddities. Lines of sun and shadow crossed the rich marble floor like an arcane map, like her mystical plaid.

The map to the future, Heart thought. *Ah!* What all remained hidden in the sunlight and shadows?

She turned to Martha. "It looks like you'll be a bit short-handed opening the museum today." Heart grinned, knowing that however true that may be, she would not expect Key Man, on his mission of mercy, nor Peter, equally occupied, to be attending to The Museum of Scientific Improbabilities and Unpredictable Oddities this day.

"You're right." Martha nodded. "I'd better get at it!"

* *

Heart, Equuleus, and Key Man moved quietly, with but the muted clicking of Equuleus' hooves against the marble, to the end of the hall and stepped into Key Man's domain. Filled to the brim with broken, rusted, ruined, cannibalized, and otherwise damaged clockworks, it never seemed to become less full, though Key Man worked tirelessly, rebuilding and repairing clockworks donated to the museum from everywhere around the world.

Too long to be conveniently worked on by Key Man on his workbench, he'd placed Lady Gervi's mangled leg on the floor.

"This is an amazing piece of workmanship, Heart. Such a pity to see it destroyed like this."

"Yes," Heart agreed quietly, thinking of her kind-hearted but proud friend, at this moment moving around on a giant wheel instead of her two graceful gear legs.

"She must be a magnificent sight, this ... this Being."

"She is, Key Man. Magnificent, and intelligent, brilliant, and kind."

"Ah!" Key Man paused for a moment with Heart, picturing the divine clockworks creature. "She does not seem to be entirely clockworks."

"Really?" Heart had not been aware of Lady Gervi being anything other than clockworks. "Oh dear. Does that mean you can't ...?"

"I think I can. But there is this component of bio that was rather unceremoniously and ... ahm, somewhat unskillfully ... cut off. I hope you aren't the one who did this, dear Heart."

"Oh, no! I can't imagine I'd be able to do such a thing, even if I wanted to. I just about came unhinged picking up," Heart's voice caught at the image, replayed, of picking up Swen's severed leg. "Well, you know."

Key Man nodded, and gave her a big hug. "You're a softie for a tough guy, aren't you?"

Heart half-grinned. "That's me." She opened her hands to the mangled pile of gears on the floor. "So—what do you think?"

"Let's have at it! If you'll assist me, I think we might be able to ...." He interrupted himself as he got down on his knees and began going over the entire construction, cog by cog. He took 3-D images from every angle, had the simulation repair each gear and mechanical part, then animated the whole composite, and projected the 3-D for both Heart and himself to observe its perfect, intricate workings.

"Poetry in motion," Key Man said in a subdued voice of awe. "You see here, Heart," he pointed. "This is where the bio hooked up. I don't have bios. If ... if it's possible to develop another one of these," he circled the bio-component," this being will have a fully functioning limb. Without that, it will work, but less gracefully."

"Oh, Key Man! Really? How long will it take? How will we get it to Pink?"

"Why, you'll take it with you, of course!"

"Seriously?"

"If we start to work on it rather than talking about it, it will go much faster."

"You speak truth, oh wise Key Man!" she teased.

Heart loved being Key Man's assistant. She watched closely as he carefully took the leg apart. She wanted to tell him everything about Lady

Gervi. She wanted to tell him everything about her life on Pink, about her father, about her new friends ... but she knew that, for the time being at least, she must keep all this to herself.

Key Man hammered and shaped the gears that were salvageable into their previous shape, sanding them until they shined. Two of the gears were broken beyond repair. For these, Key Man took Heart out behind the museum to a long shed Heart had noticed before, but had never been in.

She gasped when they stepped inside. Every sort of gear in every size and every kind of metal, with every interval of teeth, along with other, apparently clockwork and mechanical, gadgets, apparatuses, contrivances, widgets, gizmos, and doohickeys—objects she could not guess what they were, even conceptually. There were mechanical parts stacked neatly according to size, and, Heart, supposed, function.

The thought of the many damaged and maimed Folks on Pink that this little shed could give new life and function to poured over her. She stood—and *with*stood—the mix of pain and excitement at the amazing sight.

Key Man had jotted down some notes and now muttered to himself number and letter combinations, looking for the two perfect gears.

"Ah!" he said, pulling out the smaller. "Perfection! Now for the big one."

Heart stood silently by as Key Man chatted with himself, looking for the larger gear.

"Here we go!" He tried to pull out the gear. "Lend me a hand, Heart. It looks like Wonderman Two has sat upon Wonderman One." He laughed jovially at his own joke while Heart helped him disentangle the gear. "Looks good!"

"Ummm ... that's good," she said while a little plan brewed in her mind. "Does anyone ever order parts from you to fix their clockworks or mechanicals?"

"Sure!" Key Man said. "Not too often. We get more damaged devices to repair here at the museum, but every now and then, someone wants to repair something."

Heart followed a cheerful Key Man back inside, cheerful herself in the private contemplation of one day being able to place orders with Key Man to repair and restore beings and creatures on Pink.

As evening drew near, it became apparent to Heart that she would, in fact, be returning with Lady Gervi's new leg, including the bonus of Key Man's specific and carefully drawn plan for the bio-components to make it work as good as new.

The knowledge made Heart deeply happy. Strangely, it made her even happier than Jackson having "neutralized" her father's clone. She knew she ought to be delighted that they so summarily completed their mission. But—she wasn't. Something didn't feel right about the decommissioning of the Clone.

In fact, a lot of things didn't feel right. Yes, the Clone now sat in hunks and pieces in a couple of boxes—somewhere. On the *Gargantua*, maybe. Maybe not.

And now, Jackson was doing something she knew nothing about, which she found troubling. And—she didn't know when she and Equuleus were to return to Pink. Once she had Lady Gervi's leg, she'd be ready to go. But she needed Jackson to tell her where she must to go and when she must leave. She needed Jackson to take her to the *Heart!*

Bringing herself back into the moment, back into Key Man's workspace, she praised him. "Beautiful, beautiful, work," she said, as he put the finishing touches on the limb.

"Thank you, Heart, it's been a pleasure. It really helped being able to get this project completed in a day that this exquisite foot remained perfectly intact." He held the foot that he was just about to attach to the leg up in the light. The impeccable beauty and perfectly meshing gears of brass and steel of the foot caught the light and glinted.

"All these elegant little gears would have taken much longer to reproduce." He looked at the foot as though admiring a rare work of art. "Only the ankle needed some adjustment. Oh! We must ask Martha if she has access to this plastic and fiber black material. I ought to have thought of that before."

"*I* ought to have thought about that," Heart protested. "You don't have to think of everything! No, wait, apparently, you do. Let's see if Martha's free to come look at it."

Martha soon entered Key Man's workroom. She and Key Man began a discussion about the interesting black material.

"I think I can manifest something quite like it," Martha said. "I'll sort out its molecular components on the computer and then print it on the 3-D printer."

"*Oh, my,*" Heart exclaimed. "That will be so ... perfect."

It would be even more perfect, she thought, if she didn't have to process all the alarms beginning to go off. Where could Jackson be? What was his "secret mission?" Why didn't anyone hear from him? Was he all right?

Chapter 19

A short while later, Martha returned with enough of the black plastic and fiber fabric to make a covering for two of the long, graceful, gear limbs.

"Wonderful, Martha, thank you," Heart said, hugging the material to herself, picturing Lady Gervi's delight. "I look forward to being able to tell you both the details of this project. It will make you cry for joy. But for now ...."

"We know Heart, today, we continue with silent discretion. I had the printer print out enough of the plastic fabric for two, as there's a slight difference between the sheen of the fabric fragment and what the printer produced."

Heart nodded. "So thoughtful, Martha."

Key Man carefully placed the fabulous leg in its box, then Heart lovingly put the fabric in with it. "One horrible leg event resolved," she whispered.

"I'll resolve the other one too, if necessary, Heart, don't you worry," Key Man affirmed.

"I know you will. I know you will ...." Heart agreed. But she could not disguise her worry.

"What's wrong?" Martha mirrored Heart's frown.

"I think, maybe, many things. At this moment, I'm worrying about Jackson. Where is he? What is he doing? What am I to do now? We left the details of my return to Pink open-ended, depending on the events as they unfolded. Since what has happened, actually decommissioning my father's clone—and I'm still rather much in shock over it—was never a contingency we came up with, I'm at a loss how to move forward. We have the Clone, tidily in two large pieces, in two large boxes. All right. But ...."

"But what?" Martha asked.

"Too tidy. All too tidy."

"Hmmm ...." Martha hummed. "Looking gift horses in the mouth?"

"In a word, yes!"

"Why?"

"*Too tidy*. Plus, where's Loruza, that evil, and obviously insane turncoat. Off she ran, free to continue her dark madness. What about Keeper A?

Did she simply return upstairs to her office when the sun arose, to look down upon her garden and see the gigantic hole I made in it and say, 'Oh, my, I guess I'll have to get the gardeners to fill that up'— and what about the children at The Darling Undesirables Residence of Long Prairie? With all this madness swirling about, are they the least bit safe?"

"I have questions. But right now, my biggest concern is, *where is Jackson*, is he all right?"

"Heart," Jackson's voice came through her necklace. Heart jumped.

Martha and Key Man couldn't resist a quiet guffaw.

She pushed the little star necklace's receiver button. "Jackson! Where are you? What are you doing? What am I to do?"

"She has questions, Jackson," Martha laughed.

"Are you all right?" Heart finally asked.

"I'm all right. Still a bit bloody from tangling with the Clone and that crazy Keeper with the infinity weapon."

"Loruza and that figure eight thing? I disabled it."

"Seriously? Excellent. But, yeah, it left its mark. I'll be there shortly and we'll sort out the next step. Out."

Heart sighed deeply. "Much better."

"Yes, much better," Martha agreed. "To answer your question about the children at The Darling Undesirables Residence of Long Prairie, I hope you'll be relieved to learn that they have all—every single one of them—been evacuated to an 'undisclosed location,' according to the news."

"Oh! Why didn't you tell me this before?"

"I wasn't sure how you'd take it."

"It's better than them staying there, at The Darling Undesirables Residence of Long Prairie. How did the news express it?"

"That given a strange and inexplicable shifting of Earth, the authorities felt it best to remove all residents to a safe, undisclosed, location."

"Does anyone in *The Cause of All Beings* know where that undisclosed location is?"

"Very likely," Key Man answered, sealing the large box. "Equuleus, do you mind carrying this with me out back?"

Equuleus, who had been sitting quietly in the corner all afternoon rose and neighed, anxious to be of use.

"You'll have to fly solo back into The Periphery, Equuleus," Heart said. "Jackson will have to wrap me up in my precious paisley blanket. Thank you so much for keeping it, for me, Martha."

"Of course, Heart. I knew you would need it." She stepped through Peter's doorway. "Now I must close up the museum." Martha headed toward the front doors, while Key Man and Equuleus made their way to the back door.

Heart stood in the middle of Key Man's workspace for a few moments, putting the two and the two that were right in front of her together.

"*OH!*" she exclaimed. "*Oh, oh, oh!*" She hurried after Key Man and Equuleus to the back door. Just as they reached it, Jackson came barreling through, all blood and storm.

"Was your 'secret mission,'" Heart fired at him without preamble, "getting The Darling Undesirables at Long Prairie to an 'undisclosed location?'"

"Could be," he answered, clearly taken aback by Heart's abrupt question.

"Good. Very good!" Heart said, truly, deeply, happy and relieved.

Jackson took in the big box on Equuleus. "What's that?"

"A surprise," Heart answered.

" For ...."

"Not you."

"That's not a surprise."

"Ah, no. It's not."

"What's it doing here?"

"I'm taking it to Pink."

"Right."

Heart couldn't help but smile at two characteristics of Jackson. He hated being in the dark about anything. He hated having to ask questions in order to get out of the dark.

"What's our plan?" Heart finally asked.

"I need to sit and think it out."

"All right. Let's put this box in your vehicle then come back and plan our plan."

Jackson nodded, and they all trooped out.

"Problem," Jackson said.

"What?" Heart asked.

This 'surprise' will not fit in the front. It'll only fit in the back. We had you trussed up in the back when crossing The Wall. I'm not sure we can get you entirely wrapped up in the paisley blanket if you're sitting in the front seat."

"We'll make it work," Heart said, not about to be thwarted at the last minute in getting her gift to Lady Gervi.

"All right. I'll do my best, but making the point beforehand."

"Thank you for thinking it through, Jackson. Especially when you've had a day where you've had more than enough to think about already. But, if you fly high and fast, I don't think there'll be a problem. That's not like being dragged under The Wall by a dog—even if an exceptional dog! That's a different sort of experience."

Jackson nodded. He put the long, rectangular box on the back seat, strapped it down, closed up the vehicle and they all went back into the museum.

"Let's go into my room," Heart suggested.

"Your room?" Jackson asked.

Ahm ... assuming it's still there as my room. We were so busy all day, I didn't even think to take a peek at it. Is it still there, Key Man?"

"It is, and always will be, as long as I have anything to say about it."

"Perfect!! Let's go, Jackson."

Jackson didn't move. "Why do you want to be in your room?"

"I just want to spend some time in my sweet, little room. Do you really have a problem with that, Jackson?"

"Equuleus won't fit."

"He can sit outside the door." She turned to Equuleus. "You don't mind sitting outside the door, do you?"

Equuleus shook his head while studying Jackson.

"Yeah, I know," Heart said.

"Know what?" Jackson asked.

"Just a bit of conversation between Equuleus and myself." Heart could tell Key Man was listening to the whole exchange. But he said nothing.

They all stepped into Key Man's workroom. Key Man handed Heart the little key to her room. She went to the back wall, ran her hand over it until she found the nearly invisible keyhole, then inserted the slender key, pushed on the door, and stepped into her diminutive room.

Oh! It was even sweeter than she remembered it. All the pale pastel pink and yellow. All the frills and lace. The charming bedside table with the antique light, made of a doll figure in layer upon layer of pink and yellow gathered lace and satin and ribbon.

She remembered the impression the room had made on her the first time she'd been in it. She remembered wondering if Key Man thought she was really so feminine, though her hair had been quite short and she knew that she moved like a boy.

She had changed considerably since those days. Living in her father's castle, with opulence and refined feminine touches everywhere, she'd become accustomed to pastels and fine fabrics.

She seated herself in the little rocking chair. "Isn't it sweet?" she asked Jackson.

Jackson stood awkwardly in the middle of the room. "Sweet. Right."

"Perhaps *Equuleus* ought to come in here, and leave *you* out," Heart suggested.

"Not an altogether bad idea," Jackson agreed, much to Heart's disappointment.

"Will you just … *sit!*" Heart finally ordered.

"Where?"

"On the bed. On the floor. Bring a chair from Key Man's room. I don't care, just roost. You're making me crazy."

Jackson looked around the frilly room, then stepped out and returned with a no-nonsense, straight-backed chair. Incongruous in the frilly room. He seated himself at some distance from Heart.

She exchanged a look with Equuleus who had settled in the doorway, once Jackson stopped prowling around.

"*What a princess,*" Equuleus said in her head.

Heart could not resist a guffaw.

"What's funny?" Jackson asked.

"*Sorry!* Equuleus made a joke." She wagged her finger at Equuleus. "That'll be enough from you," she advised, mockingly. "All right, let's get down to business. When am I to return to Pink?"

"Right. Here's what must be done before then. We have to get to the *Heart!*, which means crossing The Wall, with you trussed up in the paisley blanket, and Equuleus flying solo. We'll have to wait for him to join us. In the meantime, I'll be going over the details I have to attend to with Peter. By the way, I'll be returning to Pink with you."

"You will? I thought the main reason we brought both vehicles was for you to stay here."

"It was. Along with not wanting to fly the *Heart!* around while you were here, as its occupant may have been surmised by The Purists."

"You mean me."

"Of course."

"But ... why are *you* returning to Pink?"

"Because I'm taking the Clone to Father Inventor."

"Oh. Yes. Father inventor will want those components. Sure. But I can take a couple more boxes on the *Heart!*"

"*Hmmm ....*" Jackson intoned.

"It's sounding like you don't want Jackson to return with you," Key Man suggested from the adjoining room.

"No. *Oh, no!*" Heart said, aghast. "That's not what I mean."

Are you sure, Heart asked herself, discovering she experienced two, opposing, states of mind. On the one hand, she looked forward to a real, true, solo piloting experience, all on her own.

On another hand, it was kinda scary.

On one hand, it would be a relief not to feel like she was constantly dancing on broken glass to make Jackson happy, or not raise his ire.

On another hand, she would miss him.

What!?

What kind of self-abuse did *that* thought reflect, and who might she talk to about becoming healthier?

Her extended pause hung heavily in the delicate yellow and pink room.

"Well then, what *do* you mean?" Jackson finally asked.

"My meaning is obvious. You have many things to do here. If you're only going to Pink to deliver a couple of boxes, I can do that. You don't have to use your precious time to be a delivery service."

Jackson nodded. Heart could tell he had something to say that he didn't want to say. "The thing is, Heart ...."

"Yes?"

"The thing is, the *THING*, the Clone, is not entirely out of commission."

"Oh! What ... how so?"

"He's, well, still alive. He ... he talks incessantly. He's fairly crazy-making."

"Tape his mouth."

"Peter tried that. He simply talks from somewhere else."

"Well ... disturbing, but I can handle it," Heart said, somewhat dubious, even as she spoke. Being alone on a spacecraft with her father's voice attempting to compel her to ... who knew what. Yeah, seemed pretty scary.

"We don't know what other tricks he might have. He might be able to mobilize. We could put him in a strong crate and he might still get out. He does have Father Inventor's ... ability to invent. There are too many unknowns. We need to fly in close tandem, so he realizes he's not going to get away with anything. Even if he could."

"Do we *want* him on Pink? I mean, Pink right now ...."

"I know. Pink has plenty to deal with. But, we're convinced ...."

"Who is 'we'?" Heart asked.

"Peter, me, The Mystic, a few others. Anyway, we're convinced that Father Inventor is probably the only one, anywhere, who might get through to the Clone. You know the first sentence of the mission statement of *The Cause for all Beings*—to not cause the total demise of any sentient being, if it can be prevented."

"Yes, I know," Heart said. She wanted to say, "I wrote it." Which would not be true, but it might as well be true, it being her core belief. She even had compassion for the awful grub-men, and hoped they might live a life that held meaning for them. If such a reality was an option.

"Well, all right then! We're going back to Pink, in tandem."

Jackson looked at her directly, and dared her to look away. "What was your hesitation?"

"I ... ah ... I know, it doesn't sound particularly grown up, but I was looking forward to actually flying alone. To prove to myself that I could pilot by myself."

Equuleus gave a series of soft snorts.

"Yes, my friend, with you as co-pilot. Goodness! A lot of princesses here." Heart shook her head. "So ... will we leave directly?"

Jackson shook his head. "At the risk of being called a princess. *AGAIN!*" he emphasized, looking from Heart to Equuleus to Heart, while in the other room it was Key Man's turn to chortle, "I must point out that I am entirely bio, and I need to recoup. I need some down time, or I'll start to be a danger to myself and everyone."

Jackson raised his shirt, showing a bloody, ugly wound. "I think I need the Wondermen to take a look at this, this thing that that wicked, crazy Keeper did to me with her Infinity weapon."

Heart leapt up, shocked at the sight of Jackson's ragged, open bios. *"OH! Jackson! Oh, no! Key Man, come here, look. No, first, summon the Wondermen."*

She ran around the bed and stood over Jackson, helpless. She heard Key Man move toward her room, at the same time calling the Wondermen. He came through the little door.

"Look, Key Man. Why didn't he say anything? Why didn't you say anything?" Heart felt herself grow dizzy.

Key Man took in Jackson's condition, then Heart's. "Sit down, Heart. You're about to faint."

Heart sat on the edge of the bed, while the Wondermen could be heard running down the hall. "They can't fit in here," Heart whispered.

"Right," Jackson said, standing, who also looked about to topple.

"Good lord," Key Man exclaimed in exasperation, "My workroom has become an infirmary. Lean on me, Jackson. You stay here, Heart."

Jackson obeyed Key Man, leaning on him, and they exited into the hall, while Equuleus moved out of the way. Heart did *not* obey Key Man, following quickly after them. In the hall, the Wondermen assessed the situation and had Jackson lie on the marble floor.

"Too cold," Heart protested, running back into her room, pulling the blankets off the bed, then scurrying back into the hall with them. Wonderman One picked Jackson up gently, while Heart laid out the blankets. Then Wonderman One placed Jackson down on them.

"How did I not notice the blood?" Heart wondered aloud, seeing, now, the unmistakable bloody hole in his clothing.

"From ... *uhhh*," Jackson moaned as Wonderman Two adjusted his position, "from all the dirt? *I* couldn't even see it. I did feel it, though."

"Don't hurt him!" Heart admonished Wonderman Two.

"Sorry. Don't mean to, Heart. Don't mean to."

"No, I know, WondermanTwo, dearest. I know." She patted him then stepped back, remembering all too vividly when, not so long ago, the Wondermen had saved her life.

She, Key Man, and Equuleus stood by watching as the Wondermen pulled out their mystical healing vials from their chests, one blue, one red. They leaned over Jackson's wound, apparently, studying the extent of the damage.

"Jackson is all bio."

"We know!" Heart wondered why they felt they needed to say something everyone knew.

"Just making the record."

"Oh, yes. Of course." They had done the same with her, putting huge emphasis on the phrase, "Heart is also composed of *dark energy.*"

They each put a small needle-like receptor in the two ends of the long wound.

"Not life," Wonderman One said.

"Threatening," Wonderman Two concluded.

"Excellent!" Heart breathed.

"Small tingling, Jackson," The Wondermen said together.

"Right." Jackson breathed deeply and slowly breathed out. "Uhhh ....right," he repeated as Heart watched his back arch, the treatment obviously more than a small tingling. "Just like getting hit with the Infinity weapon in the first place." He struggled to not move.

"Oh, Wondermen, please, it's hurting him badly."

"Sorry, sorry Jackson, Heart, sorry," they babbled together, but continued their procedure.

"Bios have a very low threshold," Wonderman Two began.

"To pain," Wonderman One continued. "Necessary for survival."

"So brave," Heart whispered, wondering how Jackson kept moving toward occasions that had a high probability of causing this degree of pain.

"Not brave. Just doing what I must," Jackson protested.

"I wasn't talking about you, I was referring to my self, standing here watching this."

Jackson chuckled then moaned. "Adding to my pain there, girl."

"Sorry." Heart felt a weird little grin grow on her face. He called her 'girl.' Somehow that landed in a place in her much like how she felt when someone winked at her. Sweet. Familiar. Even … *affectionate*.

As they watched, the wound began to heal. Heart could see the deeper layers of bios come together, then the healing worked its way up to the dermis, and then the epidermis. It stopped there, though.

"Must allow the last bit to heal slowly, naturally," Wonderman One said.

"Less scarring and infections clear out," Wonderman Two concluded.

"Good as new," they said together. "But Jackson is all bio, and bio being must rest. Stay lying down for several hours."

"*Several hours!*" Jackson muttered.

"*Right!*" everyone, including the Wondermen and Equuleus, said, imitating Jackson.

The laughter and moaning brought Martha from the front of the museum. "Oh, my, oh, dear, what's happening?"

"Healing Jackson," the Wondermen answered.

"Oh, no!" she cried in distress, seeing his nearly-healed, but still terrible-looking, wound.

"He'll be all right," Heart reassured.

"Easy for you to say," Jackson muttered.

"Let's get him in the bed," Heart ordered. "Martha and Key Man, grab those two corners of the blankets, and I'll get these two corners. Lifting. Gently."

"*Uhhhh*," Jackson moaned. "Just like being in a baby's cradle-*uhhh*."

"Hush," Heart advised. "Or I'll shake the blankets."

"You're mean when you have power."

"I am never mean."

"This is true," Jackson agreed softly.

They got him situated in the bed, and Heart turned down the lights. "Sleep now, and recoup. Sleep until you're done. Call us if you need anything." She gently placed her hand on his forehead for a few moments. "Sleep."

They all tiptoed out of her room and, leaving both her room door open a crack and Key Man's door open a crack, they went into the foyer of the Museum of Scientific Improbabilities and Unpredictable Oddities.

The museum was tightly closed up for the night, and everyone sat where they found themselves, silently reflecting for a few moments.

"Thank you, Wondermen. Again, and again, I have the privilege of thanking you."

"Again," Wonderman Two nodded.

"And Again," Wonderman One nodded in synch with his twin.

"We have the privilege of saying you're welcome," they chorused.

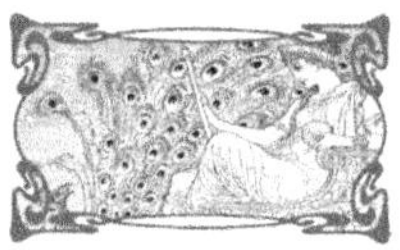

Chapter 20

"I was headed down to Key Man's rooms," Martha said after they all caught their breath for a few moments, "to tell you I got a communication from Peter, regarding Swen."

"What?" Key Man jumped up.

"He's all right. He's fine. But, apparently The Mystic has suggested that, as both you, Heart, and Jackson are going to Pink, it might be a good idea to take Swen with you. She said Father Inventor is likely to be able to contribute the necessary bios for Swen's leg.

"Reading between the lines," Martha continued, "I think what's being said is there's probably little hope for his severed leg. Peter said that The Mystic said Key Man is an artist among artists in repairing and fabricating clockworks and mechanicals. But it would be a great advantage for Swen to be under Father Inventor's care."

"Oh!" Key Man murmured, taking it all in. "Well, yes, of course. It's obvious, and a huge advantage for Swen. If he wants to go, that's wonderful. Jackson will be returning, so Swen can come back with him. It works out very neatly. I wouldn't have it any other way."

"I knew you'd come to that conclusion," Martha smiled at him with tenderness.

"How wonderful," Heart exclaimed. "And, once again, I wonder why I didn't think of it myself!"

"Quite a lot going on in that fertile brain of yours already, dear Heart," Martha tittered, her round, charming face breaking into all its round-smile shapes. "Well, what shall we do while Jackson sleeps and recovers? The night is young, and we have our Heart ... our Hearts! Both Heart and Equuleus."

"I know what Heart would like," Key Man said slyly.

"Do you now?" Heart asked. "And what would that be?"

"A certain clockworks moon in a starry dome, with a tiny piano player at a tiny piano, playing magical music, joined by the most beautiful, tall, elegant pair of dancing clockworks beings anywhere!"

"*Ohhhhh! Key Man! You remember!*"

"Of course I remember. I never forget anything."

"I would *so very much love* to see them this wonderful night. This night, when I know that all the Darling Undesirables of Long Prairie are safe, somewhere, where *The Cause of All Beings* knows where my darlings are, and The Purists have no clue. This night when the wounds of hate are being healed by the power of *LOVE*.

"This night that I share with you, my family by choice ... let us have music, conceived by my father years and years ...."

"And years," Martha added ....

"And years," Key Man pitched in ....

"Ago!" they all chorused.

With a show of flourish and ritual, Key Man rose and strutted to the wall, sliding open the door to the bank of keyholes. Extracting a key from the myriad of keys about his person—and how *did* he know which to choose? Heart wondered again, as she had before—he put the key in its keyhole, and a clicking and clanking soon came down the dark phalanx of showcases, home of antique and fantastic clockworks.

The bone-colored full moon, smiling serenely, began its slow and patient climb to the dome's sky, while little starry lights twinkled.

Key Man inserted the second key into its lock, and the tiny piano's music preceded it, the little wheels squeaking quietly, almost in rhythm. As soon as the piano and the tiny woman who tickled the keys came into the subdued light of the synthetic moon and its stars—for Martha had turned off the museum lights—she began to sing new songs that Heart had never heard.

Heart thrilled with the music and with what she'd learned from her relationship with HelperFriend, that the tiny piano player created her songs to suit the occasion, just for them, for this moment.

When her piano had rolled to its spot at the far end of the rotunda, Key Man then inserted the dual-headed key into the dual keyholes. Glide-step, glide-step Heart heard with a superlative thrill.

This moment! Time stopped. All of being held its breath while the glorious couple swirled into the space, their sweet embrace, their intricate, perfect steps, their love of one another, the music, the dance and the moment reflecting in their eyes. Equuleus sat on the floor beside Heart, Martha came and joined them.

Key Man pulled out his little stool from the little door in the wall and they all nodded their heads in rhythm to the music, utterly submerged in the moment.

After several songs, Heart noticed an exchange between the dancing couple and the tiny piano player. The music paused. The dancing couple swept toward Heart. She saw Key Man stand, curiosity on his face. He took a step toward them, but waited. The gorgeous, jet black-haired clockworks man kissed his partner on the cheek, and released his embrace. Smiling, she stepped into the shadow of the hall.

Then the dancer extended his hand to Heart. Stunned, ensorcelled, she stood and put her hand in his. The glorious and sweet music began again. Heart, who had no idea she could ballroom dance, danced to perfection, the clockworks man seeming to know how to make her move as she'd never moved in her life.

She looked into his eyes, and there, deep inside, beneath the ceramic or glass or whatever substance the artist had appended to the clockworks, there deep inside, she saw his clockworks, whirring and swirling and sending a message of love – from the clockworks, from the gear heart of this amazing being. She returned his gaze of love, knowing love was the one and only universal language.

He didn't love her more or less than his partner. He just loved her *different*. His partner was a part of himself through all time. While Heart... *HEART!* Moving about the Universe, spreading the universal message of love, was loved, universally.

This was a thank you from the clockworks. Who, Heart now realized, communicated without devices of any sort, like a flock of birds. She saw in his look a pure awareness of her life and work on Pink.

All the clockworks in The Museum of Scientific Improbabilities and Unpredictable Oddities loved her with their clockworks and mechanical hearts filled with gratitude.

*   *

After the amazing dance, after all the clockworks had taken themselves back to their showcases, the dancing couple, reunited, the tiny piano player and her piano, the clanking moon that had reached the far wall of the rotunda—after the rotunda became silent, Martha turned the lights on dimly, and they continued to sit in quiet companionship for a while, until Heart, loath to say it, but knew she must, broke the silence.

"My dears, you too must get some rest. Tomorrow is another day. No doubt we'll be leaving very early in the morning, so off to bed with you now. In case there's much roaring about by Jackson in the morning, let me say I know that you know I love you to the depths of my heart, right here, in Equuleus ...."

He whinnied softly and nodded, clearly sad to be leaving Key Man and Martha who had been his companions for many, many years while he was trapped in the large, *and still empty!* showcase that stood near them.

"As you wish, Heart," Martha agreed. "You know we would sit here with you all night ...."

"Until the end of time," Key Man amended.

"Even until then," Martha nodded. "But we will leave you now until the early rays of dawn."

Heart gave her a hug, then turned and hugged Key Man. The two little people rambled down the middle hall to Key Man's rooms, and Martha, out the back door to her home.

"*Hmmmm* ... I wonder where Martha lives," Heart said. "Do you know, Equuleus?"

"Not exactly. I know she lives nearby. Whenever something happens, she's here almost immediately."

"Strange that I've never thought about it before ...."

"Even more strange that I haven't," Equuleus muttered, sounding just a bit confused.

"Ah, my friend, and my heart, you were in stasis. Don't be hard on yourself. How else could you have endured the years and years inside that?" She pointed at the showcase.

"Valid point. Thank you."

A peculiar sensation overtook Heart. She couldn't understand it. She could only respond. "Equuleus, dear, would you mind if I went for a little walk by myself for just a few minutes? I have something that needs contemplating."

"All right." He sounded hesitant and slightly bewildered, but Heart knew he would be all right.

"Be back in a few."

*　　*

Heart walked down the dark marble-floored hall that the clockworks had all gone down. Their showcases now stood in total darkness, total silence, the hall nearly completely dark. She walked as stealthily as she could, trying not to activate the floor lights, though every now and then one started to glow faintly.

She went to the end of the hall, completely bemused by her own sense of compulsion. It felt like a strange dream. Like one of her strange dreams. She almost wondered if she was awake. Eventually, she came to the back door, rarely used and always locked. She hesitated, and yet was compelled to try the door. It opened to her touch. She knew she'd better not step through because once it shut, she would not be able to get back in.

But she stepped out anyway. Right before her was a large, open, flat space. This was where *The Tent* had been erected by the Wondermen. This was where she learned how to ride upon Equuleus and *stay* on Equuleus. The Tent—so huge, it scared her at first sight.

Of course, it shrank in comparison to *Gargantua*. All things were relative.

"All things are relative," she said aloud, not knowing why. A huge thing one day was the next day small—including events. One day getting to Earth was huge. Another day getting to Pink became paramount. One day she found someone very challenging. The next day, he became her hero. One day she had a clear sequence of events that comprised her mission, the next day she was obsessed with a pile of gears in a small shed.

Everything was relative. The only thing that stayed constant was the energy of love.

Even love changed. Well, *it* didn't change, but how she felt about it and thought about it changed. She'd heard a woman talk about a verse from her holy book. She'd said there was a verse that said, 'Perfect love conquers all.'

"But what if," she'd said, "you put the emphasis on the second syllable, to per*fect* love—that we each ought to work on per*fecting* our love."

That woman had it right, Heart thought. The per*fecting* action, per*fecting* love—that's where real change, real love, started to have the opportunity to do its work.

Why am I standing outside of The Museum of Scientific Improbabilities and Unpredictable Oddities, thinking these abstract thoughts about love? Heart asked herself.

As she had this thought, her attention was drawn to the sky. She realized it had been a long time since she'd thought about her favorite constellation, Leo, and within Leo, her favorite star, Caffau's star, one of the oldest known stars in the Universe, in the heart of Leo.

She studied the night sky, and there, faint Caffau's star seemed as though it was coming toward her. No. *Yes*. It was. It was more than an illusion, it was ... it was that fantastic dream she had now and then, she told herself. That fantastic dream where this being, stunningly beautiful, no, that was not accurate, she never saw a particular being. But it was a beautiful light.

It was the heart of Leo. The heart of Leo coming to visit her, to teach her something to tell others. And, she thought wryly, to make her sound as if she was crazy.

Perhaps she was—but it was a good crazy. It was a crazy where, when she'd done something larger than life, she received a visitation and was told she'd done well. The star would tell her he was proud of her.

That he loved her.

That he always *had* loved her ....

That he always *would* love her.

Down the star came, closer and larger, larger and closer. The light of the star so bright, Heart thought, she must lose herself. She might dissipate or evaporate in the star's light.

"I will never harm you," she heard the star say in a voice of tinkling chimes, as it continued to approach her. *There!* There was Pink, and the star zipped by it.

Standing her ground, Heart braced herself. She expected to be hit by a star!

Instead, it stopped before her, hovering, a brilliant, iridescent light of shifting colors. "Heart, my Heart," a voice rang out her name, a voice of many small bells, slightly tuned together, a few of them slightly de-tuned. An altogether pleasing and hypnotic sound.

"Am I awake?"

"As awake as any sentient being on Earth is or can be. All of Earth, everyone and everything is a little asleep, a little hypnotized. All the time, sleeping ... sleeping and dreaming, dreaming and drifting."

"Drifting and dreaming," Heart said.

"Drifting and dreaming. Dreaming of happiness. When it's just ... right there!"

"Dreaming of love ...." Heart said, feeling herself slip into another form of consciousness.

"Dreaming of love ... when it's just ...."

"Right here ...."

"Right here." The Heart of Leo wove his light around Heart, and she felt the light, the shadows, the weaving, the plaid of maps, the paisley of life forms all, all in her and through her.

She understood everything. Everything. Everything became supremely lucid.

"It's ... it's ...." She could not put it into words.

"It cannot be put into words, dear Heart, my love."

"But if I can't express it, how will I share it?"

"You *are* the essence of what you attempt to describe. You have accomplished wonderful, wonderful service here on this little planet, Heart. So far from me and yet so close.

"You chose well to live this peculiar life on this planet, where the evolution of spirit falls behind. You are a brave star, my beloved. *Ah!* Here comes your beautiful nemeses and powerful friend. The one who makes you grow! Until we meet again. Continue as you have and you will change this world. You have already done so, and there is ... there is ....

The star began to recede. A great cavern of sadness and emptiness filled the galaxies of Heart's interior. "Don't leave me! ... Don't leave me alone!"

"*You* ...." the bells chimed,
　"*Are never* ...." the bells jingled
　　"*Alone,*" the bells whispered ....
Or was it the wind in the fir trees, high above, the breeze like a song of chimes, of small bells?

The Heart of Leo completely gone, swallowed whole by the baby-fresh, pale, long rays of the peeking morning sun.

"*Wait* ...." Heart whispered.

The door behind her opened, and there stood a grouchy-yet-beautiful Jackson, hair askew, shirt torn, dirty and bloody. Still looking tired and, as always, impatient with her.

"Been looking high and damn low for you! What are you doing out here?"

"Conversing with my destiny, if you don't mind!" Heart brushed past Jackson, back into the marble hall.

He turned, let the door slam and grabbed Heart by the shoulders. *"Would! You! Please! Not! Cause! Me! So! Much! Worry!"*

She looked at him and grinned. "It's cute the way you get angry."

"*Arg!*" Jackson raged.

"I know. I vex you. You are quite articulate on the matter. *Arg, arg, arg,* right back at you, too, if you bother to think about anything. Where were you yesterday? All day, I'm wondering and worrying. Oh, just saving all the Darling Undesirables of Long Prairie, that's all. You couldn't tell me?

"I mean—You couldn't tell me!?! Don't you '*arg*' me! You have caused me enough *args* to last two lifetimes."

Heart stormed down the hall, toward the rotunda, to join Equuleus. But he was not sitting in the pattern of light and shadow coming through the grating of the front doors where she'd left him. She turned the corner and stormed down the next hall to Key Man's room, where Equuleus would have gone when she left him for a few minutes, which, apparently, had become a few hours.

Key Man's door was slightly ajar, and as she came to it, she heard Key Man and Equuleus softly talking to one another. Not meaning to spy, she couldn't resist tiptoeing up to the door.

"The battle won, the war thus pending," Key Man intoned.

"All that flies, all that walks, all that swims, all that crawls will welcome the day!" Equuleus said.

"We are patient, we are true, we are vigilant, waiting to be called. We hear the call, we know its voice because we are made first and before all, of love," Key Man whispered.

"Love fashioned itself into form, into a myriad forms, out of itself, out of Love. Love imagines ever and always, new ways to express itself," Equuleus recited.

"Because the essence of Spirit, the truth of Divinity is the manifesting of form-and-not-form by Love. The Immortal is created of the unstoppable force of Love, which first, '*IS*' and then, '*BECOMES.*'" Equuleus recited.

"Which first '*IS*'" Key Man repeated, "from which all forms '*BECOME.*'"

"I love that verse," Equuleus said softly, with an intensity of emotion Heart had rarely–*if ever!*— heard from him.

They were reading, together, from *Ourbook!*, Heart realized. They were doing it surreptitiously, without her knowledge. Because they knew if she knew, she would disapprove. Vehemently.

They were reciting *Ourbook* together, acquiring strength and succor from it, bonding with one another. Knowing that they had in common these words, this wisdom.

Further, Heart thought, everything she'd just heard was precisely as she believed! Where and why had it come upon her to be inflexibly judgmental about *Ourbook*? Might it not serve her to give it some of her attention, rather than toss the entire book away from her awareness?

WHY, she now asked herself a burning question, had she been so resistant to this book?

Well, she answered simply, because that's what she'd been taught at The Darling Undesirables Residence of Long Prairie. Of all things to take in and accept whole—to reject a book of wisdom teachings!

She didn't have to accept the entire thing if she didn't want to, but why alienate herself from her possible growth? Why alienate herself from her own people—who or whatever those "people" may be. Humans, clockworks, mechanicals, bios, those with dark matter implants, people or creatures— any thinking, feeling being, those who took into themselves these wisdom teachings—were they not her "people?"

She resisted the entire prophecy components of the book because everyone who believed in it seemed to believe she was "The Being" it referred to as the one who would bring about "spiritual evo-lution" as they called it.

She didn't want to think about being that *BEING*. She simply had work to do, things to take care of, beings to love, to heal, to nurture. She wanted to love and care for her father. Yes, this world needed healing. But she was only a small, small cog in the greatest of clockworks, the clock-works of time.

She heard Jackson coming down the hall. He must have paused there at the far back door, look-ing after her, wondering what that conversation was all about.

So did she. She went up to him as he came to her, not wanting it to appear to Equuleus and Key Man she'd been eavesdropping at the door. Even if she had been.

"You are extremely strange," Jackson said. A puzzled expression on his features.

"You're a curiosity yourself," she replied, with-out the heightened emotion that had been in her voice just a few moments before. She had much to contemplate, and the sooner she could be by herself to do so, the better.

"You're probably right." They continued to Key Man's rooms.

"Are we leaving directly?" Heart asked.

"Yes. Immediately, if not sooner. No one's going to pay attention to my vehicle, indistinguishable from the million others in the sky, but I really didn't want Equuleus up there getting attention."

"Oh, no! You're right. Oh, that's worrisome. Is there anything we can do about it?"

"Well, we're at the wall. All he really needs to do is cross over, and there's pretty good tree cover here. Once he's on the other side, he can fly low. The residents in the periphery are not a problem. They know Equuleus exists. They know Heart may come to Earth on occasion, unbeknownst to the world at large.

"But, yes, let's get going. Many, many things to do."

"True, true, true!" Heart laughed.

Jackson unceremoniously opened Key Man's slightly ajar door without knocking.

"So like you!" Heart exclaimed.

"What?"

"Just—opening someone's door without knocking,"

"*It was open!*" Jackson protested.

Heart nodded. "Like I say, so like you."

"Okay, kids, no sparring! Let's start out this day on strong footing," Key Man said, studying their interaction from where he stood by Equuleus.

"Not to worry, Key Man, dear, we're just playing." Heart went up to him and gave him a big hug.

"We are?" Jackson asked, mystified.

"We are. And, we are on our way, too. We must get Equuleus across The Wall before all of civilization awakens, and he's seen by millions rather than a few sleepy thousands."

She went to her little room where Jackson had spent the night. But for the rumpled bedding, the room had its sweet, childhood dream about it, all the pink and yellow ruffles and lace packed away for another time. She picked up the key from the bedside table, turned out the light, closed the door and locked it.

"Should we not wash the bedding?" Jackson asked. "I was pretty rough with it, I fear."

"That's the record I'd like the little room to keep. One other day, I may need to step in there and be reminded of this *amazing night.*

"Let's be gone," Heart continued, handing her key to Key Man. "I'll return your precious Swen to you before long, my friend. I can't tell you how dear it is to me to know I'll have the privilege of sharing my life on Pink with him. I would have had it transpire many other ways than that he is in pain, but I am thrilled to have him for a bit. You don't mind too terribly, do you, my own Key Man, my borrowing your dear friend?"

All of Key Man's hundreds of keys jangled together lightly, creating a delicate quivering chime, as tears sprung to his eyes. "No, darling Heart. I, too, am delighted to imagine the two of you together, talking for hours, laughing and bonding. I'm quite excited to imagine what he'll see and learn and know, being there with you and Father Inventor. To get to know what your life is like.

"I realize he probably won't be able to share it with me when he returns, but I'll feel the wonder of it in him when we sit quietly together. That's more than enough." Key Man put his arms around Equuleus's neck, holding him close. "My precious Equuleus, how wonderful to have spent this time with you. There are no accidents!"

"There are no accidents," Equuleus repeated wrapping his head around the little Key Man.

So touched by the sight and the emotion coming from them, Heart had to step out through the door and take a deep breath. Some expressions of love were overwhelming.

At that moment the back door opened. Martha, all smiles and breathless came hurrying up to Heart, round body, round smiles, round face, round cheeks, round open 'O' smile. "I was afraid I was too late! I didn't want to miss your departure. Oh, I'm so happy you're still here."

She hugged Heart warmly, which Heart returned with equal warmth. "Yes, but we must get aloft. We don't want too many people observing Equuleus. We ought to have left earlier."

"True," Martha exclaimed. "Well, back outside then."

Jackson, Equuleus and Key Man came through the door, but Heart turned to take one last mental picture of the room, and then, remembering the little 3-D album in her pocket, pulled it out and snapped an image of the room. Then she stepped through the door and took a 3-D of the group as they stood in the hall filling with morning light, in a moment between one time ....

And another.

Chapter 21

Outside, they were met with a glorious morning of birds chirping and a pink-gold-blue sky.

"It's wonderful!" Heart breathed. "There is no place like Earth, anywhere!"

Everyone mumbled quiet agreement, when Heart remembered her question of the night before. "I had this question come to mind last night, Martha, that I found strange I'd never wondered before."

"What is that, my precious Heart?"

"Where do you live? Peter and Key Man have rooms in the Museum of Scientific Improbabilities and Unpredictable Oddities, but every night, you go on your little roller-like feet, all smiles and cheer, and out the back door you go! Then, the next morning, in the back door you come. It's as if you dematerialize just outside the door in the evening, and re-materialize the next morning."

Martha chuckled at Heart's image. "Why, Heart, it's never been any secret. I live right there." Martha pointed to a tiny, itty-bitty house directly across the street, that had more gingerbread on it than it appeared its square footage would allow. Painted in an improbable variety of mostly yellow and lavender, with touches of orange and a pale, sweet green, it couldn't have been more "Martha" if it had a large sign across the front saying, *"Martha's House."*

Heart's eyes opened wide. This little house—that no one would ever miss if they had sight—right in front of her. She must have seen it again and again. But she had never "seen" it. "Where did that come from?"

"It's always been there."

"I've never seen it."

"We see what we're looking for," Martha said. "But, occasionally, it's all right to ask for help in gaining sight."

"Another lesson to ponder," Heart replied. "May I take a 3-D of your adorable little castle, to remind me that I must ponder this lesson some more?"

"Please do! I'm flattered."

Heart impressed on her 3-D album a couple images of Martha's home, then had Martha stand in front of it from where they were, making the house look half as tall as Martha, already not very tall her-self. Heart knew she would look and look at this image. She knew it would give her great pleasure and comfort, in her life on Pink, so far from her true home.

Oh! To stay in that tiny gingerbread house *one* night! A dream she knew she would often dream.

"Does it have a guest room?" Heart asked in a small, little girl voice.

"But of course!" Martha affirmed. "Waiting for you, any time."

Heart nodded, taking the invitation into herself deeply. "All right. I will collect on your invitation one day. Now, let's truss me into this vehicle."

Jackson retrieved the paisley blanket from under Lady Gervi's leg. Heart gave Key Man and Martha one last round of hugs, then got into the seat and giggled with glee while they all fussed and fretted over getting the paisley blanket completely around her, and strapped in with the safety harness.

So sweet to be so sweetly loved!

The door closed, then Jackson came around and tolerated a round of hugs. "I'll be back soon, you know!"

"So what?" Martha retorted. "You can't have too many hugs!"

Wordlessly, Jackson climbed into his vehicle. "All right Equuleus, get yourself over The Wall, we'll meet you on the other side." He shut the door, fired the engines, and lifted off.

Heart saw in her mind's eye Martha and Key Man, her two tiny beloved friends, getting smaller and smaller as they stood at the back door of The Museum of Scientific Improbabilities and Unpredictable Oddities, waving at them until they were out of sight. She pictured Equuleus in the sky before them, the sun glinting gorgeously off his gear-driven wings.

Oh, yes, if anyone happened to look up, if anyone happened to catch sight of him, they would not believe it. It would be very much like, Heart thought, not seeing Martha's house, which had always been there. She didn't see it until it was pointed out to her. And it wasn't pointed out until she asked to be shown.

No one would see Equuleus, unless he was pointed out to them. That was the nature of belief. She relaxed, knowing he was all right. Knowing that if anyone saw him, they were believers, even if they didn't know it.

She felt a darkness upon her for but a few moments while the Dark Energy of The Wall prodded at the Dark Energy in her own life force.

"*Uhhh ....*" she couldn't help uttering, as she felt, but just for a moment! as if she'd be pulled right through the bottom of Jackson's vehicle.

Then it passed.

"You all right?" Jackson asked, worry in his voice.

"It's over, I'm fine. Can I come out now?"

"Let's give it a few more moments."

"All right. How's Equuleus doing?"

"He's behind us now. I can only go so slow. I have him on 3-D reception. He's flying low and making good time, as are we. We'll be at the *Heart!* in a few minutes." Jackson paused. "I think you might come out now, I believe you'd like to see the terrain."

Heart burst out of the paisley covering. "I'd *love* to see the terrain!" She peered below at the passing trees and valleys. "Oh, Jackson, look!"

"What?" He asked, alarmed.

"Just ... *look!* Look at all the wonders below!"

Jackson relaxed. "Right. The wonders below. I'm familiar with them, Heart. You don't have to startle me."

Heart grinned to herself, continuing her engagement with the natural flow of the land underneath their flight. *Earth!* She suddenly felt maternal toward the sweet planet. It grew all these wonders, and sometimes it must seem to her, the planet, completely unappreciated. But, still, she grew so much beauty.

Heart tore her eyes off the scenery to see where Equuleus was on the hovering 3-D, but all she saw was lines and dots. One appeared to be moving at a fairly good pace, so she assumed it was Equuleus, but .... "Could you show the actual images, Jackson?"

"I can, but it's distracting."

"Just for a few moments, so I can see the real Equuleus."

"Right." Jackson waved his hand over the transparent image that hung between them, and Equuleus instantly appeared.

"Oh, he's loving it, just as much as I am!" She thought to him, "Is it not beautiful beyond all imagining?"

"*Oh, Heart!*" Equuleus exclaimed in return, unable to imagine another single actual word.

"*Yes!*" she replied. The two of them now in conscious synch, Heart returned her gaze to the wonders below, occasionally sighing and softly exclaiming, filled to the brim and overflowing, delighted that Jackson left her to her own private reverie.

"Straight ahead," Jackson said.

"*Oh!*" Heart all but yelped. Suddenly the beautiful, sylvan sight below gave way to a gigantic swath of near-black.

"*Gargantua.*"

"Don't be alarmed, Equuleus. *Gargantua* straight ahead."

"I had my share of alarm at the sight of it," Equuleus returned, "when it appeared over The Darling Undesirables Residence of Long Prairie."

"I don't know which is more disconcerting—seeing it take up the night sky, or seeing it take up the beautiful forest in broad daylight," Heart said to Jackson and Equuleus.

"To me, it's reassuring, not disconcerting," Jackson replied.

"I suppose I ought to take on that attitude, as well." Heart nodded. The mission of this stunning, breath-taking five-sided craft was the same as hers—to protect the rights of all sentient beings.

"It would be nice if *The Cause of All Beings* could be supported by means other than scaring the bejeebers out of folks."

"No argument there, Heart. But the *Gargantua* is not about instilling frightened respect for it and what it stands for—although it performs that function rather neatly. It's a small city, capable of sweeping in and relocating endangered populations to a safe location until the madness in that area sorts out and settles."

"I ... *seeeee* ...." Heart said, realizing that The Darling Undesirables of Long Prairie had been removed, en masse by *Gargantua*, which was why Jackson had immediately taken off, as soon as the Clone and Swen had been floated up to the open door of the *Gargantua*.

At that moment, Heart saw the *Heart!*, absolutely dwarfed by the *Gargantua*, emphasizing its vastness.

"There's the tiny, little *Heart!*" she said.

"Ummm, right ...." Jackson began to maneuver the descent to land near the *Heart!* They touched down smoothly, and Heart applauded.

"Well done, dear wounded soldier! And, oh dear, how could I not have asked first thing this morning how your wound is?"

"Well, now, there's a good question. Instead of the entirely weird diatribe I *did* receive, about *args* and such. *That's* a weirdness."

"True. I don't take it back, but you're right on both counts. It was strange, and why didn't I ask about your wound?"

"It's good, I have to say. Miraculously so." He unlatched himself and got out.

"Excellent!" Heart struggled with getting untangled from the paisley blanket, in which she was good and well wrapped, and then unlatched the safety harness.

"Coming?"

Jackson, already some distance away, turned to see her struggling. "Oh for ...." He came back and, just as he opened the door, Heart succeeded in freeing herself.

"I've got it ...." she said.

He reached in, picked her up from the seat and set her on the ground. "There now!"

"What's up?" Peter asked, coming from the direction of the *Gargantua*. "You all right, Heart?"

"I'm fine. Just some entanglement with the paisley blanket and safety harness." She turned back to retrieve her paisley blanket and folded it lovingly.

Equuleus flew in a circle overhead, then came in to touch down perfectly beside them.

"I've already put Swen in the *Heart!* He can't wait to get to Pink. He's all very doggie about it, barking and tail wagging."

"Tail wagging?" Heart exclaimed. "I've never seen Swen do what I would call 'tail wagging' even though he has a tail."

"Well, he's a newshound, it's in his ... something blood or mechanical implants or whatever. Anyway, it's the hottest story ever, as he'll be the only newshound to have gone to any of the moons."

"Sure, of course!" Heart said. "He *is* a news-hound, and this would be the breaking story. Except, of course, he must keep his silence."

"He knows that. Just to have it in his data banks, he said, made the injury almost worth it."

"Oh no, there are better ways. But he *is* a hero for his valiant fight for *The Cause of All Beings*. If this feels like an award, then I'm happy."

Peter opened the back door of Jackson's vehicle. "What's this?"

"Something of Heart's, that's a secret," Jackson answered.

"Well, it can't stay here. One of the Clone boxes needs to be back here, and the other in the front seat. It's going to be tight, even at that."

"No problem, Peter. I have a shelf specifically constructed for it in the *Heart!*" Heart began to untie the safety harness.

Peter moved around to the other side and helped her. "What is it?"

"It's a surprise."

"I see. I wondered about that shelf in the *Heart!*" He pulled out the box and took it to the *Heart!* where the back hatch stood open. Peter and Heart went in. There Swen sat curled up in Equuleus's place, looking like a happy puppy.

"Heart!" he said and barked. Then cleared his throat, "Sorry! Heart!" he said again in his modulated, classy newshound voice. "Too much time with my cousin, who, as you know, is pure bio dog."

Heart rushed up to him and gave him a gentle hug. "How are you feeling my friend?"

"I'm good. Don't mind sympathy and hugs, of course, but I'm doing very well, considering."

Peter had placed Lady Gervi's leg on the shelf and tied the strap. "That doesn't seem like enough to hold onto it."

"I've got magnetics. And, also, under this shelf, Equuleus must specifically be here, and Swen ... how to hold Swen?"

"Oh no, am I problem?"

'No, you're not a problem, but we do need to make sure you're safe."

"How strong are the magnetics?" Peter asked.

"For Equuleus, Father Inventor figured it out precisely so as to hold him, but no more."

Peter did a few calculations on his wrist calculator. "It looks like, if we tie Swen to Equuleus, we can boost his magnetics 12.4 percent and they should both be perfect."

"Swen is significantly bio, Peter."

"Oh, right. Let's see. Good call, Heart. I don't think it would have hurt either of them, but, taking Swen's preponderance of bio into consideration, we'll need to boost the magnetics only seven percent. But there'll be more responsibility for Equuleus to make sure he holds onto Swen—and gently!—if you do any thrill riding."

"Not intending to do any thrill riding. Straight to Pink and my father, as fast and safely as we can go!"

Peter augmented the magnetics for Equuleus and Swen while Heart watched. He turned and surveyed the interior of the *Heart!* "There now, every-thing seems ship-shape!"

He turned, smiling, to Heart, the little frown Heart had noticed since she first came to The Mystic's cottage slightly less pronounced.

"Who *are* you?" Heart asked.

Peter grinned a warm and intimate grin, but, still, held something back. "I'm your doorman, Heart. The doorman to The Museum of Scientific Improbabilities and Unpredictable Oddities. I'm the overseer of that, and well, a bit more."

"Yes, Peter. That, and *quite a bit more*, I believe."

"Well, my dearest," he replied, putting his arm around her shoulders and walking her back to the hatch, "that's a conversation for another time." He waved Equuleus into the *Heart!*

"I thought you were going to talk the day away," Equuleus said.

"Not this day," Heart said. "All right, we've made some modifications."

Peter unstrapped Swen.

"You'll be in your place, Equuleus." She strapped him in. "Then Swen tied in front of you. The magnetics have been bumped a little to hold you both. All nice and neat, and off we go to Pink."

As Peter strapped Swen to Equuleus, he gave Heart an are-we-sure-about-this? look.

"Perfect!" Heart nodded, glancing down at Swen's wrapped shoulder and back to Equuleus. "Take good care of our Swen," she admonished Equuleus.

"I'll do what I can. Which isn't much, but we're good to go."

"Excellent." She patted both creatures then went with Peter to the back hatch.

He stepped out onto the beautiful *terra firma* of Earth. "Get yourself strapped into your seat, young pilot. It's time for take off!" He gave her a little salute, which, much to her surprise, she returned. Then she did as he said, strapping her safety harness about her, giving a glance over her shoulder at the two creatures all cuddled together.

She looked out the window to watch Peter help Jackson get the two boxes of the Clone into his vehicle. They were large boxes and had no protection other than some sheets of fibrous material that Heart hoped was strong as steel. It took them a while to get everything fitted and tied down.

Finally, Peter shut the doors while Jackson climbed into the pilot's seat and fastened his safety harness.

"Let's fly!" Jackson exclaimed. "Engage engines. Follow me Heart. We'll make a pass over The Mystic's cottage, give a little wave, then sharp ascent up and away from The Wall."

"Right!" Heart replied, firing the engines, she and the *Heart!* were ready to take to the skies.

Chapter 22

Once they were aloft, with Earth behind and Pink in front, Heart relaxed, feeling pretty sure of herself, and, basically, pretending she was, in fact, piloting the skies on her own, just as she'd fantasized. Even better than her fantasies, her two precious friends were with her.

Swen! Swen would share her life! For a short while, granted, but, they would have done it, and they would then both know it could be done. They could each picture the other's life when apart, to bring them together in their thoughts.

"Ah my dear canine newshound, here we are together, and here you are, on your way to Pink."

"I'm on my way to Pink, Heart. I'm crazy excited."

"Me too, me too. Though under the circumstances ...."

"A newshound gives his all."

"Oh, Swen, you gave your all, and more than all. *Oh-oh!*" Heart just recalled that Swen's bios, could not withstand open exposure to Pink's environment.

"What, Heart? What?"

Heart exchanged a look with Equuleus. "His bios."

Equuleus whinnied. "Everything going too fast. We haven't had time to prepare. We'll have to ask Father when we get a bit closer to Pink."

"Right. Too close to Earth and possible pick up by the Purists."

"Is this about me?" Swen asked.

"Well, yes. The outdoors of Pink is a hostile environment for bio beings. And you're largely bio. So, we'll have to see what solution Father comes up with." Heart thought hard. "Wait!"

She locked the *Heart!* into its current heading, unlatched herself from her safety harness and went to storage receptacles in the back of the *Heart!* She'd never gone through them.

Maybe there would be ... "*Aha!*" she cried triumphantly, pulling out a protective suit.

"Ah ...." Swen groaned with great reserve, "hate to break it to you, Heart, but I guess you missed the fact that I'm a dog, and thus am *dog*-shaped. That suit is for a human, and thus is *human*-shaped."

Equuleus snorted. "He's got you there, Heart."

"Oh, stop it you two!" Heart tried to sound serious, but she utterly adored the teasing. "Maybe Father Inventor will make you human-shaped now, give you arms ... Oh, Swen, seriously, maybe he really can give you an opposable thumb, a real one that you can use."

"Ah ... hmmm ...." Swen was completely speechless.

"Horrible idea? Good idea? Swen, did I insult you? You know I think you're more than perfect. But you yourself have said ...."

"No, I'm not insulted, Heart. I'm just ... not sure yet. I think I'm a bit precious about whatever is left of me that is dog-like."

"Of course, my lovely dog, we only want you to be the dog you've ever been. But, seriously, back to this suit." She brought it over to Swen and held it up to him. "I think I might be able to pull it over you enough so you can be brought from the hatch of the *Heart!* through father's door—a short distance."

"Excellent!" Swen bark-spoke. "Sorry, still over-dog excited."

"*Auuuuugh!*" Came from Jackson's vehicle.

Heart rushed to the front and looked over at him. He appeared to be struggling. She locked herself into her safety harness, took the *Heart!* off auto-pilot and moved close to him. "What's happening?"

"The Clone—as we feared, he's becoming active."

"What's he doing?"

"He's making a hole through this protective fiber. It's supposed to be indestructible, but he's making headway through it."

"Which box is it?"

"The one beside me. And, I think the one in back is responding. I hear sounds."

"What contingency did you and Peter put in place, in case this happened?"

"What we put in place was this metal fabric. It's not doing its job."

"Well, if he has any intelligence, he knows that to do you damage will for sure be the end of him."

"I don't know if what remains is capable of having that understanding."

Heart thought frantically. What could she do? "Well, talk to him, and use that logic. Tell him to relax until you land or he will damage himself."

"I doubt I'll sound convincing, talking to a dismembered machine hand."

"All you have to do is believe what you're saying. The rest will follow naturally."

"All right. Clone, you must relax. You must not harm the pilot or you'll not survive."

Jackson paused.

"Well?" Heart prompted. Jackson could be so exasperating.

"Ahhh, he's started up again. Don't know what to do, Heart. Close quarters here. Oh! Right, it's his hand. Seems to have its own intelligence. Shape of hand in the metal fabric. He's scrabbling about to get hold of me. I'm slammed up against the frame as much as I can get. He'll ...." Jackson's vehicle suddenly veered completely off course.

Sounds of struggle from Jackson's audio.

"Jackson! Jackson!" Heart cried as his spacecraft flew wildly away. Heart zipped after it, thinking frantically.

"Okay kids, I'm going to do something pretty dramatic, you'll have to let me know immediately if it's not working for you."

"What's that, Heart?" Equuleus asked, alarmed.

"I'm going to try to get right alongside Jackson, then slam on the magnetics going the opposite direction from the two of you, to the outside of the *Heart!"*

"Why, Heart?" Swen asked.

"Ah!" Equuleus said, understanding. "To try to immobilize the Clone with magnetics. If she can magnetically hold him to the outside of Jackson's vehicle, just as we're magnetized to the wall, it can't harm Jackson."

"I heard that," Jackson whispered. "Give it what you've got, Heart. If it doesn't work, I'm gone anyway. This hand is at my windpipe and I'm not ... conscious much longer ...."

Frantic, Heart slid up to the passenger side of Jackson's vehicle. "Hang on, you two," she called to Equuleus and Swen. "Give me strength," she prayed. She could see Jackson, she could see that he was trying to get his craft under control. She could see he was barely conscious. "Here we go!"

She slammed the magnetics on, full blast to the exterior of the *Heart!* and bumped into Jackson's spacecraft, resulting in a horrible scraping sound, but the two spacecraft became locked together.

"You okay?" she called back to Equuleus and Swen.

"Ah ... we're still here, if that counts," Swen said. "I think this is harder on the horse than me."

Heart looked back. Fear ran through her like an arrow when she saw Equuleus's head lolling.

"Jackson, Jackson, you with me?"

"Right," he said faintly. "Right," he said more strongly.

"Let's get back on our trajectory. This is taking a dangerous toll on Equuleus. Look, Pink, straight ahead."

"I'm on it Heart. Back off the magnetics."

Heart readily complied.

"Oh!" Jackson gasped. "He's tenacious. If I could open the window, I'd boot him out."

"I'm contacting Father. We're far enough from Earth. He might have the perfect ...." Then a solution hit Heart. "I think if the Clone heard a directive from my father, it would obey."

"Maybe Heart."

She opened connection with Pink. "Father, emergency here. Clone strangling Jackson. Give it a command."

Immediately she heard her father's voice—which, of course, sounded just like the Clone's voice.

"Stand down," her father commanded. "Wait for further orders."

"Yes!" Jackson whispered. "That's working. Release magnetics, Heart."

"Gladly!" she shut off the external magnetics, checking to make sure the internal flow was where it needed to be, then looked over her shoulder. Equuleus shook his mighty head as if recovering from a fall. "You all right?"

"Not sure."

"We'll be on Pink before long."

"I love the sound of that," Equuleus replied.

* *

Heart's father continued to give occasional commands in response to Jackson's comments of movement from the two big boxes. Adding to the drama was Jackson's lack of foresight that he'd have to get into his protective suit in tight quarters. At least he'd put the garment under his seat. With almost no room to move, and the two boxes taking up every bit of space not occupied by Jackson, it would be tricky.

"You'll have to wait until you land before you try to get into your protective suiting," Heart advised.

"Kinda figured that out, Heart."

"And I have to, very gently, get this human-shaped suit on Swen, who, as he reminds me, is dog-shaped."

Heart heard her father chuckle, and, in the background, she heard HelperFriend laugh out loud, accompanied by shrieks of laughter from Violet—"dog-shaped dog," she squealed, "*soooo* funny!"

Heart grinned. It was good to be back at this home, too.

"Who's that?" Swen asked, somewhat skeptically.

"That's our comical little friend, Violet. Oh, Swen, you're in for a lot of surprises. And a lot of treats."

Still sounding a bit skeptical, Swen added, droll, "What any dog likes ... a lot of treats."

The two spacecraft soon came in to land on Pink, Jackson first, then the *Heart!*

A mighty cheer rose up from many voices.

"Oh, Jackson!" Heart had to practically shout about the noise, "Look at the dome!"

"Yeah. Incredible. They've gotten it completely back together in the short time we were away. Just for you, Heart. Just for you."

"Well, I doubt that," she said modestly, knowing Jackson was absolutely correct.

Swen, who could see nothing from the floor, raised his voice above the din, "What am I hearing?"

You're hearing the residents of Pink, Swen. Oh, lookie, Jackson, look at the signs ... 'We love you Swen!' 'Welcome to Pink, Swen!' Look, Jackson, look down there in front, at Yippee! he has his own sign 'Yippee loves Swen!'" Lady Gervi stood beside him on her one leg and wheel.

"Oh, oh, oh, I'm going to cry, I really am. They love my Swen like I do."

"You don't need to cry, Heart," Jackson said. "Look at HelperFriend, he's crying enough for both of you. He's already got a little metal puddle."

Heart giggled at HelperFriend's, grinning, gear-spinning face, sparkling metal tears falling like rain. Violet was hopping from his shoulder to shoulder and onto his head, waving a sign, that made even Jackson guffaw ....

"Marry me, Swen!"

"She always has to top everyone!" Heart observed.

The Folks had been told to stay clear until Jackson got suited up and Heart got Swen in his human suit, but it was clear it took all their reserve to keep their distance.

Heart flipped off the magnetics, then her safety harness, and jumped from the seat, grabbing the protective suit from where she'd flung it during the crises with the Clone. She released the straps that held Swen and Equuleus, and moved Swen gently to the middle of the space, holding him while she watched Equuleus struggle to stand.

"Oh, Equuleus, I can't bear it. I can't ...."

With a mighty effort, he rose to his four feet, stomping each in turn, and shaking his head again.

"All right now!" he whinnied. "Where's the party?" He stretched his wings to the ceiling, which was not much of a stretch. "Let's get out of this bucket of bolts!"

"Equuleus!"

"Beautiful bolts, but, yeah, let me out!"

"Hold. Your. Horses." Heart laughed, while she pulled the suit over Swen. It worked fairly well. She was able to pull the visor of the headgear so he could see. She zipped him up, then opened the hatch.

"Can't wait to see what's out there," Swen said as she picked him up.

Equuleus stepped from the hatch, then spread his wings their full extent, grandstanding for all he was worth.

The crowd loved it and, if possible, roared even louder.

Then Heart stepped out with Swen. Even swathed and wrapped up in the protective suit, practically unseeable, The Folks chanted as one, *"Swen! Swen! Swen! We Love You Swen!"*

Speechless, Swen gaped at the crowd. Finally, he said in a small voice, imitating Heart, "I think I'm going to cry!"

By then, Jackson had managed to struggle into his protective suit. He stepped out of his spacecraft and joined Heart, Swen, and Equuleus.

The crowd yelled and hollered and, yes, even cried.

Heart looked over to her father, who beamed at them from within his own protective suit.

"Love you!" she mouthed.

"Love you more!" he returned.

Carrying Swen, she headed for her father's room, followed by everyone. Then she went in through the double baffles, followed by her father, Jackson, HelperFriend, and Violet.

"Let's get him out of that suit," her father said, gesturing to his cot. Heart put him down carefully and slipped him out of the suit.

"It's wonderful to meet you, Swen," Father Inventor said. "I've heard so much about you, and I want to thank you for taking care of my Heart."

Oh ... goodness ...." Swen said, seemingly at a loss for words.

"My-oh-my, I think that's the first time I've ever seen Swen at a loss for words," Heart said, laughing.

"I have words now," Swen said. "It has been not only a great privilege and honor to do whatever I've been able to do to protect Heart and to help her with her destiny. But even more, it's been most entertaining to be with her. She's not only brilliant, she's fun."

"Ahhh, now *I'm* at a loss for words," Heart said shyly. "Thank you, Swen. And now let's get at the business at hand ...."

"I just love you, Swen," Violet hopped down onto the cot from HelperFriend's shoulder. I do, just love you. You're *ammmmmmazing!*"

Jackson picked her up without ceremony. "Right. Hush now, rabbit."

"I beg yo ...."

Jackson put a hand over Violet's mouth. She mumbled a bit, then became almost still, with only her ears twitching.

Father Inventor had ignored the distraction, contemplating the wound. "Do we have the limb?"

Heart opened Swen's backpack and brought out the leg, carefully wrapped in an herbal material of The Mystic's making.

Heart's father unwrapped it, handling the material with curiosity. "Interesting! Well, I must say, this limb is in a promising condition. The material is quite preservative. Very effective. Your clockworks and mechanicals are in fine shape, except for right here at the shoulder, but all the components are there, and our artisans can have that shaped up, 1-2-3.

"The bios are a bit compromised. But not from the moment you were put in The Mystic's hands. She immediately put this protection on it, and, for what it has gone through, it's in fantastic condition. However, I will have to contrive a bit of a bio-component."

"So, Father, while you're at contriving bio-components ...." Heart turned to go to the *Heart!* "I'll be right back ...."

"I'll get it," Jackson said. He stepped out the door and the crowd roared anew. He made his way to the *Heart!* then returned with the big mystery box.

Heart opened one end and took out the diagram for the bio part Key Man had designed. "Could you also manifest one of these?"

Her father studied the diagram for a moment, awareness suddenly coming upon him. "Oh, Heart! You did this too, along with everything else?"

"Well, we had a bit of time on our hands, Key Man and I."

"What?" HelperFriend and Violet, herself somewhat subdued, asked. "What is it?"

First Heart slipped out the fabric. Everyone knew what it looked like.

"Oh, Heart," HelperFriend, Whispered in a dozen voices, "Oh, Heart ... did you ... is it possible?"

She triumphantly slid out the stunning new leg for Lady Gervi, grinning about as big as she was capable of grinning.

"Oh, Heart, oh, Heart, oh Heart," HelperFriend, awash with emotion, gears stuck, metal tears squirted from his eyes and projected around the room.

"HelperFriend," Father said, "you must contain yourself, or we'll have to send you outside."

Heart reached over and patted her own HelperFriend. "I'm glad this makes you happy. I hope it does the same for Lady Gervi!"

"It will Heart, of course. How can you even say such a thing? Oh, Heart, Oh Heart ...."

"Don't be stuck," she advised.

"No. It's just, you know, I've felt so guilty, what I did to her."

"You did a wonderful thing for her, making her mobile while all this amazing reconstruction has gone on. You must be kind to yourself."

"Still learning that part, dear Heart."

"Can you do that, Father? Can you contrive that bio for Lady Gervi's leg?"

"Indeed I can. Curious mystery, the two bio parts that need to be made are quite similar. Two for one. Perhaps I ought to make a couple extra."

A banging sound from Jackson's vehicle came over the sound system.

"Oh, goodness, Father, that bothersome Clone. What do you want us to do with it? Next thing you know, all its parts will be running around crazily, scaring everyone."

"We won't have that!" Her father connected his audio with the interior of Jackson's spacecraft. "Rest now. It's a good time to rest. Go into stasis. There is much work to do in the future. You must conserve your energy."

The terrible sounds from Jackson's spacecraft stopped.

Heart's father turned to her, "Though, as you can imagine, I'm most curious to start poking around at the Clone, we must attend to first things first. First, begin the healing work, next, party. The Folks have been planning it since you left!

"The Clone I'll save for another time. HelperFriend, if you wouldn't mind getting the two boxes from Jackson's spacecraft and taking them to the cryonic storage."

HelperFriend left the room, moving one box at a time through the door baffles. A hand-shaped chunk of fibrous metal stuck out the side of one box, while the other box had many dents in it.

Heart shuddered when she saw that, glancing at Jackson. He shook his head. She could just hear him saying in his mind, "Right."

"This is such beautiful work," Heart's father said, studying Lady Gervi's leg. "Even if we had no bios, she could completely make this useful after some practice. Not with quite the same well-oiled grace of the added bios, but still utterly functional. The fabric Heart, is a measure of thought that simply stuns me. I am so, so proud of you."

"Well, Father, it was Martha who produced the fabric with her 3-D printer."

"Yes, and job well done. So! I say, it's possible to attach both of these legs right away, though bios will take some time. I have to grow stem cells and then fabricate the parts. But both legs are better than no leg, and Swen and Lady Gervi can practice getting around on their limbs until the bios are ready.

"What say you, Swen?"

"Bark, bark, *barkbarkbarkbark* ...." Oh-goodness-me, was that me?"

Heart laughed. "I don't see any other dog in the room."

"I'm all ... whatever it is that I am. Grateful. Stunned. Delighted. Happy. Grateful. Yes, and again, grateful. Yes, please, reattach my limb."

"One down, and one to go. Let's replace the leg in its gift box and go outside to present Lady Gervi with her great gift," Heart's father suggested.

HelperFriend had returned to the room and began crying again, with gigantic tears of joy. "Can't wait to see, can't wait to see!" he blubbered.

Heart's father put his protective suit back on, Jackson had not taken his off, and Swen would stay inside on the cot, listening to the crowd's reaction.

First Heart, followed by Jackson carrying the box, followed by Father Inventor, then Helper-Friend and Violet stepped through the baffle out to greet The Folks.

"I know we're all in a party mood," Father Inventor addressed the crowd, "but first, Heart has returned to Pink with a gift that she would like to now present. Lady Gervi, if you would kindly come forward."

Everyone became silent, and the crowd parted to let Lady Gervi and Yippee through.

"It is so wonderful to see you back on Pink, Heart," Lady Gervi said graciously. "But I'm sure I don't need any gifts. You are the gift to us all."

"Thank you, dearest," Heart said to Lady Gervi, giving her a warm hug. "However, I did feel there was something you could use, and ... well, I hope you agree." She took the box from Jackson and handed it to Lady Gervi.

"Oh," she said barely audible. Its size utterly telling its probable contents. She handed Heart Yippee's leash, and opened the box, then slipped the beautiful, sparkling leg out.

"Oh ... oh, Heart! How? How? Oh, Heart!"

"How? By the amazing talents of my dear friend, Key Man."

The crowd, hushed with awe at sight of the precious gift, broke into wild accolades and cheers, then rushed Heart, hugging and kissing and patting her, giving her love, love, love.

In each and every face, whether bio or gear or mechanical or hybrid, she saw the passion of empathy. She saw the sharing of joy of one of their own, about to be made whole. They each felt it personally. No one was jealous, no one was apathetic, no one was angry that it wasn't them, even if they had injuries.

"Father Inventor says he can attach your leg right now if you would like. No rush, but if you would like ...."

"Yes, Heart I would very much like."

"There is a bio-component Father has to make, but you'll be able to walk around on this one, a bit stiff. Do you still want to do that now?"

"Yes, Heart."

"Oh, and there's another part." Heart reached into the box and pulled out the plastic fabric.

"Oh, no, this is so, so ... how did you even think of it?"

"We girls gotta stick together, my friend!" Heart smiled.

*   *

It did, indeed, only take a short while for Father Inventor, assisted by Heart and HelperFriend, to attach the two limbs.

Then the party began in earnest, indoors and out. Heart went from one spot to the other, trying to keep up with all the happiness everywhere.

All of Pink was in fine form. The dome was up, the Clone was on ice, Lady Gervi, striking figure in any crowd, was nearly returned to all her glory, and Swen was in dog heaven, being loved all to bits by everyone on Pink, and even, much to Heart's cha-grin, seemed to immediately understand Yippee's funny, strange, language.

But, for a few moments, Heart needed to chat with her flowers, so much more beautiful to her mind than all the exotic roses in Keeper A's treach-erous garden.

Leaving everyone to party and dance to Help-erFriend's mystical music, she stole around to the front of the castle, and into the kingdom of flowers in their modest greenhouses. "Thank you, my little, happy friends," she said to her flowers. "I know you send me clarity and direction, when I wonder which thread of the plaid, which road on my life's map I ought to follow, there are my flowers, guiding the way."

She then wandered out behind the castle, looking up at Pink's moon, where Xavier, ever patient ever true, smiled down upon her.

"Oh, you! You know what's going on, don't you? Well, then, I needn't tell you. I'll just say, thank you, my sweet moon boy, for all you have taught me. And all that you continue to teach me." She closed her eyes for a few moments, listening to the secret he had to share in this moment.

With that, she turned, and in the midst and flow of the wild party, Jackson stood at the dining room window, a vignette of light about him from all the dark matter and dark energy lights.

Such an indescribable light around him!

He looked away. But then, he turned back to her. She walked up to the window, and put her hand upon it. He put his hand to hers. She smiled, then she went around the castle and entered through the front baffles. Equuleus stood in the foyer.

"Talking to Xavier again?"

"Yes. Seems like the right thing to do, on this night of all nights!"

"Agreed."

She heard the slightly asymmetrical click of dog feet coming down the hall. Swen, accompanied by Jackson, came to join her.

She put her arm around Swen, "How does that leg feel?"

"Just fine, Heart. A bit stiff and, well, mechanical, but surprisingly good. Even my fur isn't a mess. I have this lovely scar."

"It is a lovely scar."

"Yes, I ought to have at least a scar as one of the three who took out of commission the Inventor's Clone."

"I agree, Swen. Jackson, too, has a lovely scar."

She reached for his shirt, but he grabbed her hand, and looked deep into her eyes. "Will you always be in love with Xavier?" He asked, sounding angry.

"Ah, no, Jackson. I will always love Xavier, but I am not *in* love with him. He has become a ... a guide. Everyone can use a guide."

"That's all right then." He released her hand and showed Swen his scar, which was healing beautifully.

"I have no scar. Oh!" She suddenly remembered. "Instead, I have these wonderful 3-D images to share—they are like healing after the scars of long ago." She moved to the stairs. Jackson sat on her right and Swen on her left, with Equuleus at her feet, she turned down the lights and projected her entire childhood into the space before them.

"The question I have for you, my dearest Swen, is why you never told me you were everywhere I was?"

"Ah ... hem ... I'm not in *every* image."

"No, you *took* some of them."

"Busted," Jackson chortled.

"*It is good to have guides, it is good to have watchers,*" Swen quoted.

"*Ourbook,*" Heart said simply.

Equuleus looked at her sharply.

"Not to worry. Not to worry. Wisdom finds its own centering."

"Hear that, Equuleus," Jackson said, surprised. "She quotes!"

Heart smiled. Swen put his chin in her lap, Jackson put an arm around her.

She relaxed into them and felt the deepening calm of the four of them, together—the home, the secure and peaceful—home of her heart.

Boook 4 of *The Darling Undesirables* is *Heart's Quest,* Here's Chapter One – a preview of coming attractions!

Chapter 1

Heart sat cross-legged on her cot with Violet, the little lavender rabbit, curled up in her lap, her rabbity ears twitching contentedly, while Swen stretched out on the bed, with his long-doggie snout on Heart's knee. Equuleus, the winged gear horse, stood by the window, seeming to contemplate going for a flight.

Suddenly, someone pounded on the door like he'd break it in.

All four of them jumped practically out of their skin.

"Must be Jackson," Heart observed.

"Right," Swen said, in an uncanny imitation of Jackson. "No one else around here ...."

The banging ensued at the door again.

"... needs to pummel a door to get attention. At least he doesn't ...."

The door slammed open in its frame.

".... fling the door open before you invite him in," Swen finished, sarcastically.

Violet hopped up to stand beside Heart, putting her furry fists on her fuzzy hips, giving Jackson a disapproving look.

"Nice of you to let me invite you in," Heart added her disapproving look to Violet's. Swen didn't even bother to raise his head.

"I knocked!" Jackson barked.

"We heard," Heart retorted.

"You needn't," Violet sputtered, indignant, *"hammer, pummel, batter, bludgeon, whack, bash and clobber the door, sir. Heart is sitting right here!"*

Heart patted the little lavender rabbit soothingly. "Violet makes a valid point, Jackson. Could you not wait for me to answer the door? Or at least, wait until I invite you in?"

"No, I could not. I *knocked*. Enough chatter. I have to get back to Earth. *Now*. I've been told to collect the dog, if he's coming."

"I *beg* your ..." Swen began, while Heart cried out, *"Now?! Right now?"*

"Right now. Or sooner."

"No!" Heart protested. "Is there never any peace for us?"

"Apparently not," Jackson stomped up and down the room, clearly agitated to nearly his limits, the muscles in his jaw clenched. In fact, Heart noticed, the muscles in his entire body, wound up, ready to spring.

Indeed, something quite serious had developed. She stood and pulled a chair in front of her. "Sit."

"I can't."

"It's not a request, Jackson. Sit."

He took in her expression, then sat.

Heart returned to her position on her little bed, holding Jackson's gaze. "*What is going on?*"

"I am not to tell you."

"I don't care what my father says, you *must* tell me. I'll find out soon enough. *What is going on?*"

"Apparently …" Jackson hesitated, then sighed and continued. "Apparently Father Inventor's clone made clones."

"*Oh!*" Heart, Swen, and Equuleus exclaimed in unison.

"This is not good, not good at all, it will never do," Violet rattled, quivering. "Say it isn't so! How will we ever cope? What are we to do? I'm extremely dismayed, distraught, disconcerted, disturbed, discombobulated, unsettled, so on and so forth…and furthermore…."

"*Will! You! Shut! Up!*" Jackson commanded.

Violet clamped her little **rabbit** mouth shut, and put a paw over it for added security. "*Sorry!*" she squeaked.

"Well, I'm dismayed too," Heart added. "But … they're a further cloned generation, they'll be weak. And how many can there possibly be, two or three weak clones? Can't *The Cause of All Beings* control them without you immediately flying off?"

"There are *not* 'two or three weak clones.' There are in the neighborhood of *one thousand* clones of your father."

Equuleus whinnied, and Violet silently hopped back onto Heart's lap, curling up into a little, tight, quivering, lavender ball. Swen jumped off the bed and took over Jackson's occupation of pacing up and down the room.

"*A thousand?*" he muttered. "A thousand Father Inventor clones, working for the bad guys? *We're doomed.*"

Heart said nothing in the midst of the commotion. Finally she shook her head and said, "I don't believe it. I don't believe it, Jackson, that's a press release made up by the Purists to frighten *The Cause of All Beings*. Plain and simple. I refuse to accept it. Nor should you."

"You're wrong, Heart. It has been as shocking to your father and me as it is to you. But it comes to us via an impeccable source. In fact, there's nothing about Father Inventor's clone or clones anywhere in the news. Nothing at all."

"But, Jackson, *a thousand clones?* Really? How could it be? Wouldn't the number one clone, which we have here on Pink, which my father and HelperFriend are reconditioning—wouldn't he have told us? With all his babble about how awesome he is, he'd not miss the opportunity to brag about this wondrous feat. Even if it was the next generation turning out clones, he'd tell us.

"Unless your 'reliable source' is an eye witness, I wouldn't believe them. And if they *are* an eye witness, *I wouldn't trust them.* Whoever they are."

"Our source," Jackson insisted, "has been eye witness to enough of the clones to know this estimate is correct. Furthermore, our source is impeccably trust-worthy."

"Strange," Violet said in her muffled voice.

"Quite strange," Heart agreed. "Where are these clones supposedly hanging out?"

"It seems they're in the underground crystal matrix. Which, you'll be surprised to learn, is extremely far-reaching."

"Oh!" Heart exclaimed simply. "Horrible."

"Yes. Horrible," Jackson agreed.

Heart was suddenly awash with a deep fear for Jackson. "What can you do, Jackson, alone?"

"I can only do my best."

"But …" Heart tried to contrive an argument, "you simply cannot fight them all, all alone!"

"And I won't. There's everyone in *The Cause of All Beings*, there's everyone in The Periphery …."

"That's redundant. Everyone in The Periphery is in *The Cause of All Beings*," Heart pointed out.

"True."

"And how are the people behind The Wall in The Periphery supposed to help you? They're not free to move about."

"True again, Heart." Jackson nodded. "Are you seriously trying to tell me to stay here and ignore all that's happening on Earth?"

"Ahm … sort of sounds like it." Heart said quietly. "But I know you won't."

"Right." Jackson jumped up and looked at Swen. "Coming?" Without waiting for an answer, he bolted from Heart's room.

Swen and Heart exchanged a look. "You must go back to Key Man," Heart acknowledged. "Your leg is completely healed, including the bio-component my father implanted."

Swen nodded. "Yes. I hardly even have a scar. Which, I must say, is rather a disappointment."

Heart chuckled. "Key Man misses you."

"And I miss him, Heart. But it's hard to leave like this. Without any warning, without a proper good-bye."

"Such seems to be the nature of our relationship, dear friend." Heart kneeled down and hugged the big hound close. "We will meet again."

"Yes," Swen agreed, neither of them sure of their words.

If what Jackson had told them was even partially true, Heart thought, the future of The Darling Undesirables, and those living in The Periphery, as well as many other innocent beings, was in grave danger. How far were the Purists willing to go for their twisted, intolerant beliefs?

"I'd better …." Swen moved toward the door.

"Yes. Let's go." Heart nodded.

Equuleus went out on the landing.

"I'm not going!" Violet turned her back on them.

"Why, Violet?" Heart asked. "That's not very nice."

"*I'm very nice!* If I don't go down, Swen won't leave. He won't leave without saying good-bye to me!"

"Oh, Violet!" Heart tried to laugh, but her voice came out almost a sob. "Your ego knows no bounds! You must realize that Swen will most certainly leave. And you'll feel terrible if you don't wave good-bye."

Violet's floppy ears trailed across the floor as she hopped down from the bed and dragged her feet to Heart and Swen. "I have nothing further to say beyond my protesting your departure."

Swen snuggled Violet. "Protest duly noted, my fuzzy friend." He turned and ran down the castle's winding stairway, while Heart picked Violet up and jumped onto Equuleus. They flew down and around, meeting Swen on the castle's marble rotunda floor below.

"Ah! I'm going to miss that sight!" Swen exclaimed.

Heart nodded, but said nothing. They filed down the hall to Father Inventor's room in silent sadness.

About the Author

I live in a forest in the Pacific Northwest with a few domestic and numerous wild creatures, where I create an ever-growing inventory of books and stories.

When you support my work you help support ten acres of natural forest, and all its resident fauna. *All the creatures and I thank you!*

If you would like to receive my newsletter, ***Home of the Heart***, send a note to: Blythe@BlytheAyne. com. You'll receive occaional news of new releases, giveaways, and other goodies.

Or, if you have questions, comments, or observations, I'd love to hear from you!

Blythe@BlytheAyne.com

www.BlytheAyne.com

www.ingramcontent.com/pod-product-compliance
Lightning Source LLC
Chambersburg PA
CBHW070827190726
48292CB00006B/2136